Praise for THE WHISKEY BARON

———

"A stunner of a first novel with roots that run deep in the countryside and textile culture of the Carolinas Piedmont... Insightful and beautifully crafted."

—Raleigh *News & Observer*

"*The Whiskey Baron* is an exciting page-turner of a story, but it's also far more. Sealy's voice is precise throughout, as are his insights of human nature. The history of this unique time period in South Carolina's mill history is explored with a keen eye and ear."

—*Pank*

"The search for a murderer in a small South Carolina town ignites this strong debut novel, but *The Whiskey Baron* is more than a literary thriller. There's plenty of action as well as well-drawn characters."

—*Foreword Reviews*

"Sealy's gritty, superbly crafted novel, *The Whiskey Baron*, hooked me from the opening paragraph... I hated like hell for it to end."

—Donald Ray Pollock

"*The Whiskey Baron* evokes Cormac McCarthy and Ron Rash, but Sealy's cast of small town dreamers and schemers in Prohibition-era South Carolina is uniquely riveting. An atmospheric and unbearably suspenseful debut novel."

—Holly Goddard Jones

"This book transcends the notion of its being a Southern novel. It's an American novel, and Mr. Sealy a grand new talent we'll hear much from, I am certain."

—Bret Lott

"A simmering powerhouse of a novel."

—Wiley Cash

"Sealy's familiarity with the landscape and mastery of Southern tradition shine in his depiction of 1930s small-town South Carolina."

—*Charleston* magazine

"*The Whiskey Baron* is a novel ... the pleasures of both mystery novel and literary fiction. This impres... ...es Jon Sealy as a significant new voice in Southern fiction ...

—Ron Rash

"Jon Sealy has written a lyrical page-turner. *The Whiskey Baron* is a captivating, beautifully-written novel. Who can resist a man named Mary Jane involved in illicit liquor sales? I foresee the beginning of a long, successful career."

—George Singleton

"*The Whiskey Baron* finds Sealy renewing some of Southern Literature's finest traditions while conceiving a unique and well-researched story of an era and place not much covered in the ranks of the genre he so rightfully has joined."

—*Necessary Fiction*

"Sealy considers one the great unknowables—the mystery of how the human heart finds hope in the most unlikely circumstances and nurtures ambitions that burn bright enough to consume their possessor."

—*Chapter 16*

"By bravely getting certain factual questions out of the way, Sealy gives himself space to delve into the psychology of his characters as well as to give a rich historical view of Appalachia."

—*The Provo Canyon Review*

"Whiskey and murder are the dominant play shapers, but…the beauty of Sealy's writing carries the day, or in this case, carries the book."

—*The James Dickey Review*

the whiskey baron

JON SEALY

HUB CITY PRESS
SPARTANBURG, SC

Cover and book design: Emily Louise Smith
Proofreader: Megan DeMoss
Cover photograph © Alex L. Fradkin / Getty

First hardcover edition: May 2014
First paperback edition: May 2015

Library of Congress
Cataloging-in-Publication Data

Sealy, Jon, 1982–
The whiskey baron / Jon Sealy.
pages cm
ISBN 978-1-891885-74-7 (cloth : alk. paper) —
ISBN 978-1-891885-79-2 (ebook)
1. Sheriffs—Fiction.
2. Murder—Investigation—Fiction.
3. Distilling, Illicit—Fiction.
4. North Carolina—Fiction.
5. South Carolina—Fiction.
I. Title.
PS3619.E2551W55 2014
813'.6—dc23
2013032664

HUB CITY
PRESS

186 West Main St.
Spartanburg, SC 29306
1.864.577.9349
www.hubcity.org | twitter/hubcitypress

for Emily

Certain unexpected problems are involved in the rat problem [...]. The rat serves one useful function—he consumes the corpses on No Man's Land, a job which the rat alone is willing to undertake. For this reason it has been found desirable to control rather than eliminate the rat population.

—MAJOR GEORGE CRILE, draft report, 1916

PART ONE

The end of August. A Saturday. Dog Days. The blush of the evening sun and the spatter of starlight and even still the summer heat weighed down on the piedmont like a furnace stoked by some night watchman. Sheriff Furman Chambers dreamt of horses:

He was young again, and brushing Whiskey, his prize horse, the same copper Arabian who reared up on him in his sixteenth year and shattered his arm. He brushed her while flies flickered nearby in the barndark, and farther off he could hear the gallop of horse hooves. A shaft of light from the half-open door caught motes of dust in the air, the line between light and no-light scored in the dirt by his feet. Through a pasture four men approached on horseback, each wearing dark overcoats and hats, too much for this heat. Furman himself, eyeing them while he continued to brush Whiskey, was shirtless and felt the scorch of the afternoon sun on his back. The barn door creaked as he stepped out to meet these strangers. The three hung back and stared at their leader, a Swedish blond who raised a gloved hand to Furman. "Hep you?" Furman asked, and the man grinned but did not speak. He lowered his hands to the reins, and with that the sun began to darken and a surge of shadow washed across the land of living fire. The man on the horse snapped his fingers and the other three lunged for Furman and a ringing filled the air. A shriek that surely belonged in Hell. The horsemen carried him to their leader, who for his part grinned the grin of a madman as the shriek pulsed once again.

No siren call from Hades, no horsemen and no eclipse, nothing but a telephone thirty-two years into the next century.

Sheriff Furman Chambers, now sixty-seven and far off that farm, rose to answer it on the fourth ring. As he got out of bed, Alma rolled away from him and tucked her head under the covers. She'd slept through plenty of these late-night calls and likely wouldn't even remember being woken. Such is the rest of a soul at peace with the world.

"Hello?" he rasped, his mouth dry and clotted.

"Furman, this is Depot Murphy. I'm sorry to wake you, but there's a situation down here on Highway 9."

Chambers leaned against the wall and the weary bones in his left arm crunched. He grunted.

"You all right?"

"Yeah, just my arm. What kind of situation?" He pumped his fist and tried to clear his head of the spiderwebs. Sleep had been a long time coming, and rousing up like this, mid-dream, he could feel it in his chest, something wasn't right with himself.

"Two boys have been murdered out in the street in front of the Hillside Inn."

"God almighty. What happened?"

"I don't know for sure. I was behind the bar when I heard the gunshots. I walked outside and saw two boys laid out in the road. Folks is starting to crowd around now. I don't know what exactly happened," Depot said again, "but I think you best get down here."

"I should say so," Chambers said. He was still half asleep. Depot was quiet on the other end, so he said, "Ah hell, what time is it? Never mind. Listen, go on out and tell the crowd to keep away. I'm going to wake up my deputy, and we'll be out there directly. Is Larthan there?"

Depot paused, and Chambers thought he heard him take in a breath before he said, "I don't see him right now, but I think he's still here. You know he likes to keep a close eye on his business."

"Well if you see him, tell him I'd like a word."

"This is a real mess, Furman."

"I know it. I'm on my way."

Chambers returned to the bedroom and got dressed. Tucked his shirt into his trousers, scratched at an ingrown hair on his lower back. Moonlight slanted through the corners of the shade and gleamed on his belt buckle as he fastened his holster, checked his pistol.

Alma stirred under the covers, mumbled, "What was that about?"

He told her he had to go.

"It can't wait until morning?"

"Not this time. Depot Murphy says there's two boys got shot out on Highway 9."

"Them's all drunks and gamblers," she said. "You're too old to be messing with all of that."

"I got to get on." He leaned in to kiss her on the forehead. "I don't know when I'll be back."

She didn't reply.

On his way out, he saw the clock read two, and for a moment wondered whether to read it as early or late before stepping into the night. The summer had been hot, and dry, and the heat shimmered over the land even now in the darkest hour. The landscape was a spooky shade of blue, God's dark uninterrupted by the constant glow of lights in town. He hated to break the night's stillness with the rumble of his car, and he flinched when the engine caught. As a younger man, he might have been inclined to speed with lights flashing and squeal to a halt at the scene of the crime, but if nothing else, time had at least given him the blessing of patience. Whatever was waiting for him would be there.

ooooo

The Hillside Inn was west of town, a wooden shack down in a gulch off Highway 9. Once a boardinghouse for folks passing through, everyone knew it was now just a front for Larthan Tull's whiskey operation. Chambers parked in some loose gravel a ways from the tavern and killed the engine. Ahead of him, a small crowd stood in the road, huddled like beggars, the fires of kerosene lanterns burning at their sides. The Hillside itself was down from the road, far enough where passersby would miss it. Dim lights in the windows cut through the dark enough to reveal loose boards dangling at odd angles from the building. Shingles half-cocked, planks of wood strewn about by the front door. Leaning against an old water oak, hunched in the gloom, was Larthan Tull himself, solemnly sipping from a jar.

As Chambers approached, the men in the road parted around the two bodies that lay at their feet. Boys really, their flesh chewed by shotgun pellets. The men had been murmuring among themselves, but as Tull rose from the water oak and swayed over, they quieted and lowered their eyes.

Chambers could see Tull was drunk, but not out of control. He figured a man with as many responsibilities as Tull had would have to stay in control, especially in a business where the casualty rate was higher than average. A dapper slick businessman, Tull was big and lean, not much younger than Chambers, though he could pass for anywhere between thirty-five and sixty. He had Scots-Irish blood, a ruddy face with clean skin and a square jaw, cold eyes recessed in shadow.

"Furman," he said.

"Jesus, Larthan. These boys employees or customers?"

"They work for me." Tull took a sip from the jar and waited. His firm posture gave his body the appearance of being carved from the trunk of an old hickory. Even though he wasn't as stout as Chambers, he had an almost military stableness about him, not a man to ever wind up in a brawl with, no matter how much he'd had to drink.

Chambers walked over to where the boys lay in the road and knelt by the first, who couldn't be more than eighteen. The boy wore a plain white buttondown and slacks over a brand of cowboy boots he could only have gotten in Texas. His body was cold and stiff, twisted so that his left arm was beneath him, the inside muscle torn and ragged. A hole carved through half his chest, ringed by pocks of shot. A puddle of drying black blood gelled around him and oozed along toward his leg before petering out.

Chambers stretched his own aching arm out to his side, pumped his fist a few times. Tull stood beside him with one hand on his hip, jar in hand, and said, "That one's Harry Evans's boy, Lee. Lived up on the mill hill with his pop."

"I know his father."

"A worthless man," Tull said.

"Maybe not interested in your business, but that don't make him worthless."

"He wasn't interested in his son, either. I took Lee out one night, and the boy was gone from home three days before his father started inquiring about him. Wasn't for me, this boy would be scrounging around for enough bread to get him through another day at the mill, and his father eating meat and living large and not at all wondering about his son's health."

"Wasn't for you," Chambers said, "this boy wouldn't be dead in the road."

He turned to examine the other body. Someone had clearly unloaded on both of them at close range, and had taken off half of this other boy's jaw. Where his cheeks and jaw should have been, rotten teeth, loose in their sockets, hung like fenceposts at the base of his skull.

"That one's Ernest Jones," Tull said.

"The boy the widow took in a few years back?"

"The same. His daddy used to come in here until he lost a lot of money in a card game and took off for out of state. When his momma died he went to live with the widow, but he was always hanging around here until I finally gave him a job."

Chambers rose and looked down the road. Tire tracks bit into the loose chert by the roadside, and two spent shells still rested on the macadam. The blood on the road was sticky and drying fast, the holes in the bodies already clotted with flies. They would begin to smell fast in this heat. He said, "You here when it happened?"

"I was at home," Tull said. "But my man Depot was here."

"I talked to Depot. I thought he said you were here when it happened."

Tull shook his head. "I got here quick, though. Depot called me before he called you, wondering what he should do. I told him, hell, son, call the sheriff."

"That a fact."

"Yeah, he was here, counting the deposit like he always does this time of night. Slow business day. These two sitting in the back, and in walks Mary Jane Hopewell, mad as a hornet and waving a shotgun around. Depot told him to get out, but he wouldn't leave until these two boys came with him. Then, I shit you not, he promptly marched them up the hill here and fired twice, one round after another, and killed two of my best workers."

"Where's Depot now?"

"He's over on the porch. Poor man never saw someone get killed before."

Chambers picked up one of the shells. Twelve gauge. A small crowd still gathered in the streets, and he needed to speak with them before they went home. He'd seen all he needed here. "Mary Jane Hopewell, you say?"

"I do say."

"I've known his people for years. He's a wild one, but I wouldn't have pegged him for murder."

"Me neither. He was a pretty good customer himself, you want to know the truth."

When Tull grinned, his eyes did not move, as though he were studying you even as you spoke. His steadiness unnerved Chambers. Usually after a crime, folks got a little nervous and would shift from foot to foot. But not Tull. Sinewy, still, calm. Like he knew what the future held and was just waiting idly for them to get on with it. Reminded Chambers of his grandmother, who died when he was very young. She would sit on the porch with that same kind of quietude, a patience acquired partly through old age but also because she had a second sight. His great-grandmother, she said, told the future and knew everything that would happen before it did, and his grandmother said that by the time it reached her, the gift had been watered down. She had to be near a person to know what his future held. But Chambers always thought the ability had been a comfort to her, took away her worry so she could sit in her rocker and watch the world pass.

And here was Larthan Tull, bemused as though he had a second sight as well. Chambers had met all manner of human beings, and although he didn't have his grandmother's gift, he could look at a man and know his quirks and fetishes. His secrets. And he could tell by looking into Tull's shadowed eyes that this was a man with secrets that stretched back as far as his childhood, so long repressed that he might not even know what they were. Whatever happened to Tull, he'd respond like a dog that gets mean after too many beatings. It wasn't evil Chambers saw in Tull's eyes, it was the amoral indifference of a godless universe. Evil at least meant there was something larger than ourselves out there, but Tull seemed to confirm that maybe there was nothing. Nothing at all.

Chambers said, "Any ideas about why Mary Jane would come in and shoot these boys?"

Tull shook his head.

"Any arguments? A bad card game?"

"You never know what kind of violence the human beast is capable of, Furman, once he sees through the illusion of free will."

"Free will."

"We're all locked on a stage here. You've got a job to do. I've got a job to do. Mary Jane's job was to get drunk. As long as we play our parts, everything runs along smoothly. The show goes on. It's only when the curtain is pulled back and we see the scaffolding and the strings that we realize something is amiss. And then, who knows?"

"You're saying Mary Jane killed those boys over scaffolding."

"Who knows, Furman? Maybe Mary Jane saw the scaffolding all along, and that's why he was a drunk. Maybe after a while being a drunk wasn't enough. You could tell me a thing or two about that, why a man drinks."

"Didn't Depot keep a shotgun behind the bar?"

"He said he didn't have time to reach for it when Mary Jane came in, waving his own gun around."

"Sure, sure. A man pointing a gun at you makes it hard to know what to do. Why don't we go take a look at that gun, though. You mind?"

"Come on in." Tull led Chambers into the dim tavern. Before Tull, the Hillside had been a boardinghouse for folks passing through, back when more folks passed through Castle County. Tull had boarded up the stairway and ripped out the downstairs wall to open the whole room. A pool table was over in what was once the dining hall, and a few wooden booths lined the back wall. The bar itself was to the right, solid oak with stools pulled up to it. There was a light by the bar and a light by the pool table, and shadows hovered over the rest of the room like spirits.

Tull went behind the bar and pulled out an old Remington Model 10. Chambers inspected it and saw it hadn't been fired in quite some time. Dust coated the barrel, the metal itself ungreased and looking to rust.

"You ought to oil this," he said. "Would it even fire?"

"Depot just keeps it for show, in case someone gets rowdy. We're not in the business of shooting people here."

"I should hope not. Well. Walter ought to be here any minute, and we'll get those boys cleared up. I'm a go speak to those folks and will probably stop by later to talk more."

"I'll be around," Tull said.

Outside, across the street, Roger Howe and Jim Weber and the Vanderford boys and a few neighbors lingered, spitting tobacco and waiting on the sheriff to walk over and give them the word. Chambers said, "Folks, there's not much going to happen tonight. Walter'll be here to take away them bodies soon, but for now if any of y'all saw what went down I'd appreciate a word. Otherwise I'll be making the rounds to collect official statements from everyone later in the day." The neighbors all shook their heads and wandered a ways off, yet they didn't leave. Chambers pursed his lips. These country folk would all be getting up for work in a few hours, but they never would turn away from some juicy gossip.

He knew many of them sold some of their extra crops to Tull's soda plant, but he didn't know if any of them were into anything else. Spenser Watkins, a childless man, had founded that plant twenty years ago. When Tull had come to town, he'd passed many evenings on Watkins's front porch, smoking cigars and watching the world go by, and in less than a year he'd worked his way up to co-managing the business. In 1920, the two men had once again sat on Watkins's porch for a few months, and not long afterward Castle County had a flourishing bootleg trade and Tull was overseeing the Hillside Inn. Since Watkins's death, Tull had moved back to the plant and left Depot Murphy to cover the Hillside. What all went on in the soda plant, only a few men actually knew, but the entire town had made its collective judgment.

The country had been dry twelve years now, but even in times when money was too tight to drink a sweet water, people still seemed to find the money to buy liquor. Half the town's residents—good churchgoing folks—were irate about its mere existence and wanted Chambers to shut Tull's business down. But the other half of town, even if they didn't go in for all the debauchery, bought whiskey off Tull, including Chambers himself, and to shut down the Hillside meant to shut whiskey out of Castle County. Even some of the good churchgoing folks didn't want that. Of course, the system of turning a blind eye was over now that there had been a double murder.

Folks who farmed out here still knew the value of hard work, no matter who bought their crops. All they seemed to want was to be left alone, more and more now that the railroad was coming through and the population was growing. Chambers didn't have much sense for how the economy worked, but he figured if the country ever made it out of this downturn it wouldn't take long before no one would be able to just own a farm and live off it. They'd either have to deal in tobacco or find work in the mill for as long as that lasted. Everyone was secure in the mills now, but Chambers was old enough to know the world moved in cycles, and that some new thing was coming, maybe not in this generation, but the next or the next, that would limit what their sons could do if all they knew how to do was work a loom.

Chambers nodded to the neighbors, walked back down the slope to the Hillside porch. In the darkness Depot sat on a rail with his foot propped up. A bowling pin head, razor-close hair and a ruddy Irish face. A lazy eye that made him look dumb, which might help if you had to control a bunch of drunks by yourself night after night. He didn't speak when the sheriff approached, and Chambers leaned against the opposite rail.

"Furman."

"Long night."

"Aye."

"I heard it was a slow day. Anyone else here other than you and Ernest and Lee?"

"No, just us."

"Well what happened?" Chambers asked. To the man's continued silence, he said, "Depot, I know what goes on in there, and I'm not aiming to stop it tonight. You don't have to tell me what you was doing, just what happened to them boys lying in the road. How'd they get there?"

"They were in the back telling stories—"

"And no one else was here? Larthan?"

"Just us," Depot said again. "Anyway, we was killing time. I was joking with them from the bar, when Mary Jane Hopewell walks in carrying his 12 gauge. 'God almight,' I says to him, and the boys just stared.

"'This don't concern you, Depot,' Mary Jane says to me, and I says, 'Like hell it don't.'

"'I won't be long,' he says.

"I thought about grabbing my own gun, but he raised the 12 gauge and says, 'I won't mess up your place. I just need a moment with these two boys,' and he points to Ernest and Lee. They were just drinking, not causing anybody any harm, but I imagine they were pretty drunk because they stood up and didn't seem to mind at all someone waving a shotgun around and looking for them. 'Let's go boys,' Mary Jane says to them.

"'We ain't going nowhere,' Ernest says.

"'Yeah, what do you think you're doing?' Lee says.

"'I know what I'm doing and why,' Mary Jane says.

"'Hellfire,' Ernest says and slams his whiskey. 'We were leaving anyway.'

"The three of them walked out of the bar, and a few moments later Mary Jane shot them here in the street."

When Depot finished his tale, Chambers brushed his hair with his hand. Depot's story was straightforward enough, and Larthan was right. The man did sound shaken up—he had a quiver in his voice, like a young buck approaching a gal at a dance for the first time—but instinct told Chambers he was being lied to. Mary Jane Hopewell was a troublesome good old boy, nicknamed so on account of wearing Mary Jane dresses for too long when he was a child. He'd come off the farm twenty years ago and into the mill like the rest of them. His brother Joe and his family had soon followed, and they lived a respectable life in the Bell. Went to church twice a week, had two boys who worked in the mill, a pretty wife who came into town once in a while wearing a blue and white gingham dress and a bonnet and catching eyes all along Main Street. Mary Jane himself wasn't as successful as his brother. Married as a young man for about six weeks, his betrothed had taken off with a traveling salesman, a real fast talker with nothing real to say, and Mary Jane had been in and out of work ever since. Lived in a hovel by the dump and knew every lowlife who set foot in Castle County, though he himself was a nice boy. He drank plenty, he lost borrowed money in card games, and he sometimes woke in a gutter on a Sunday, but he was honest and forthright and gentle. He may run with those cast into the outer darkness, but he wasn't one of them, Chambers believed, or at least he'd never given anyone reason to think him dangerous. Some folks thought he was a little simpleminded, because if he was sober you might find him playing baseball with some kids, or you might find him sitting by the river with a stray dog for hours on end. Lately he'd been seen in the company of Widow Coleman. His old running mate, Shorty Bagwell, was in the jailhouse for driving drunk through Miss Meacham's flowerbeds. Chambers made a note to check in with the widow and with Shorty to see what they knew.

To Depot, he said, "You saw Mary Jane shoot them?"

"No, but hell, Sheriff, who would have done it otherwise?"

"I'm just trying to get the record straight, and not rule anything out."

Depot didn't reply.

"Like I was telling Larthan, I've known the Hopewell people for years. Not well, but the ones out in the Bell work hard and go to church and walk a straight line. Mary Jane is a bit of a hellraiser, as

I'm sure you know, but he doesn't strike me as the killing type. Can you think of a reason why Mary Jane might have done this? Did you hear any arguments, anything out of the ordinary?"

Depot spat over the rail. "Not that I know of. All I know is what I just told you."

The ambulance drove up and parked on the street with its lights on, so Chambers said, "I know it's late here, and I'm sure you want to get some sleep, but tell me something."

"Yeah?"

"Why they call you Depot? I never did understand it."

"I don't know. I've always been Depot," he said. "I think it's cause I liked to play around trains when I was a youngun."

"That'll do it," Chambers said. He turned and walked toward the ambulance.

The widow Abigail Coleman lived by the river. Forty years old now, a lifetime of bad news and about to get some more. Her husband was a casualty of the war, and Chambers had shot her teenage son in 1926. A few years ago, she'd taken in Ernest Jones, who helped her farm corn. She sold much of her crop to Larthan Tull, but she had a still herself set up on the creek down in her property bottoms. She made premium whiskey and buried it along the river, mostly for herself although she was known to sell a jar to the occasional hellraiser who'd gotten too wild for the Hillside Inn. Not having spoken with her since he'd shot her son, Chambers dreaded the news he had to bring her today.

When he arrived at her farm, east dawn was finally peeking through, the sky a blue wall with a streak of pink like a curtain rising for the day's drama. The farm was a good plot of rolling land by the river. A rutted logging road cut through the fields and disappeared into a distant line of trees, down toward the water. The broom sedge was near waist high, overdue for baling, and blushed wine-red in the eastern light. Heads of blackjack popped up over the sedge. Behind the house was a good garden of corn and beans and tomatoes and squash, the leaves of the squash wilted like tobacco in the heat.

Chambers parked in front of the farmhouse, approached the front door, knocked.

The widow came to the door, a phantom-pale figure with straight brown hair dusted gray, a high forehead and a flat, narrow face, the bulbs of her eyes behind vein-blush lids.

"He ain't here," she said.

"Ma'am?"

"I don't know who you're looking for, but he ain't here."

"How you know I'm looking for someone?"

"Sheriff, you haven't come by in years, and both of us know why. There's only one reason you'd come here, and that's because you're looking for some troublemaker. Lord knows enough of them hang around here. Ernest and Mary Jane and the rest of them. I don't know which one you're aiming to find, but you won't find any of them here. I haven't seen a one of them since sometime yesterday."

Chambers took off his hat. "Ma'am, you're partly right," he said. "I am looking for Mary Jane. I've also got some bad news. Ernest and Lee Evans were shot in front of the Hillside a few hours ago. Depot Murphy tells me it was Mary Jane who shot em."

The widow's eyes didn't waver. She leaned against the doorjamb and stared at the sheriff for long enough to make him uneasy.

"I'm sorry to bring you the news about Ernest."

"Where's he at now?"

"My deputy drove him to the funeral home."

She stared off beyond him at the rising sun. She pressed her tongue into her upper lip, ran it along her teeth. Finally, she looked him right in the eye and, without flinching, said, "It's funny. When the army told me about my husband, I was sad, but mostly I was relieved that I still had my boy, and that he was too young for the army to take him. When I heard what happened to Jimmy, it was like the world shifted into black and white, and it's been that way ever since."

Chambers kneaded the brim of his hat with both hands and shifted from one foot to the other until he said, "Any idea where I might find Mary Jane?"

She looked away from him, off to the sunrise again, and shook her head.

"Or any idea why he might have shot Ernest and Lee?"

"Sheriff, you know as well as I do what all goes on in this town. Half the farmers around here sell Tull their corn. He sells some of it back to us, but a lot of it goes up to Charlotte. Aunt Lou, you know her?"

Chambers had heard of her, but he kept out of that business. He had his beat, and the boys up in Charlotte had theirs.

"Any violence that happens here, your best bet is to look at the liquor. Larthan Tull, Aunt Lou. I don't know what Mary Jane might be mixed up in, but as long as there's a liquor trade, there's bound to be trouble."

"I know about Tull," Chambers said, "but I also know what goes on along the river here."

"I didn't say I was innocent."

"Well, what are you saying?"

"I don't know, Furman. You just told me my friend Mary Jane shot that youngun I took in. I don't know what to make of anything right now."

Her eyes welled up, and he wanted to reach over and comfort her, but he held back. She blinked her eyes clear and squared her jaw. After a pause for her to recover he said, "I'll leave you be. You call if there's anything I can do."

"Thank you," she said.

"Would you mind if I have a look around out here? I'm not here to bust up a still, but I do want to find Mary Jane."

"Help yourself."

She closed the door in his face, left him on the porch with his hat in his hand.

As he stepped off the porch, he slipped and grabbed hold of the railing, and a fire shot up his left arm like a charley horse stretching back fifty-one years. He couldn't grasp anything with that hand anymore, but no matter how much he told himself that, his reflexes worked in some other part of his mind. He caught his breath and waited for the pain to subside. Then he kicked at the pavement, smelled the air once more.

Though not a cloud was left in the sky, rain was coming. He could feel it in the bones of his busted arm, the way his collarbone ached so that he felt the pain behind his shoulder and on down his back. Yesterday's heat had not burned away in the night, so it was ninety already and only looking to get hotter. The humidity was oppressive yet, but he trusted his body more than the clear skies, because who knew what kind of weather lay over the horizon, what invisible matter hung in the very air he breathed? He had a half-century of accurate soothsaying that would be enough to convert even the most skeptical. His body hadn't lied to him since the horse smashed his arm, his internal barometer the only benefit of that long-ago accident.

They had been breaking the horses, he and his older brother James. Chambers sixteen at the time, the horse a copper Arabian that hadn't been properly broken as a colt. She reared up on him, and he lacked the maturity or patience to break a horse as it should be done. He did everything wide open, and for it Whiskey toppled over on him that spring afternoon, crushed his arm from the shoulder down. Grace of God it wasn't his legs or skull, folks said. Lot of men broke their hips with a horse. He just broke his arm, and not his writing arm, either. Kept him out of work, but he could get around enough to do light chores and develop a lifelong habit of reading. Novels, mostly, history. Although his arm healed nicely, he would feel a tightness in inclement weather for the rest of his life.

And late at night, tossing and turning in bed, he couldn't lie in some positions. He was a stomach sleeper, and liked to keep his arm under the pillow, but it would cramp up on him and he'd have to shift onto his back, where he could never settle into a deep sleep. This was especially noticeable after he crept into his thirties, married to Alma and sharing a bed every night. After he turned sixty, it seemed like the bone dried up altogether so that the motion of his shoulder rotating around the clavicle felt like filing wood down to shavings of dust. He could no longer reach above his head, so at Alma's urging, he went to the doctor, who told him there wasn't anything anyone could do. A pain he would carry for the rest of his days. Unknown to most of the county, he was prone to buy a bottle of Larthan's whiskey once every few months, and he would take a nip some evenings when the pain was bad enough.

When he thought of that spring afternoon with James, he remembered the way the cut hay smelled like dust. The jimsonweed by the barn choked him. The short fur of the horses, their meaty flanks. His brother now lived way out in the country. Chambers couldn't see anything but the old man he'd become—the old men they'd all become—but the smell of a farm today was the same as in his youth. He recognized it on the widow's land as he neared the barn. The door open, a horse in its stable. Morning light ribbed the dusty floor, the smell of ripe plants and dirt and old leather, the way a barn was supposed to smell. Tools hung from the wall to the left, all sharp angles like some contraption for torture. Chambers inspected them, the shovel and the rake and the hoe, and they were all rusted and dry and in fine order.

He patted the horse and walked out to stare at the field, the woods in the distance. He squinted at the trees, saw the family plot at the forest's edge, and began walking. As he crossed the field he broke a deep sweat. Six stones, spread out over four generations of Colemans, the husband and his parents and a grandfather, an uncle, and at the very end the widow's son, Jimmy Boy, the only man Chambers had ever killed. Back in 1926, the sixteen-year-old had gotten liquored up one night and caused a commotion in a card game out on the mill hill. By the time Chambers arrived, Jimmy Boy was waving a Luger around, firing random shots at the room. All the other card players had cleared out, leaving him alone in the house. An oil lamp had exploded, blowing bits of glass across the room, an oil slick across the floor, darkness. Jimmy Boy a silhouette against light from the kitchen.

"Hey, Shurf," Jimmy Boy said.

"Hey, Jimmy Boy, how you?"

"I had four queens here."

"That's quite a hand."

"I had four queens and they took my granddaddy's saber with a straight flush."

"Some bad luck there, Jimmy Boy."

"Cheating, is what it was. They took my granddaddy's saber. He carried that with him to Cold Harbor and back. I had four queens."

"Let's talk about this. I'm sure no one out there wants to take your granddaddy's saber."

As Chambers took a step into the room, Jimmy Boy yelled "No!" and opened fire. A window burst behind him, and Chambers dropped to one knee, drew his gun and shot the boy in the leg. He'd only been aiming to wound him, but he'd hit the femoral artery. The boy bled to death before they could even rouse a doctor out of bed.

A senseless death. Jimmy Boy had been drunk and bet his prized possession because he'd believed with four queens he couldn't lose. He'd lost. Sounded like he'd lost fair and square in a run of bad luck. It happened sometimes. Odds were against it, but sometimes you ran out of luck and had to live with the consequences. No sure thing in this world, a lesson the boy had never had the chance to learn. Bad luck against Jimmy Boy and his four queens, bad luck against Chambers when he hit that artery. The extinguishing of that boy's soul had left an indelible mark on the sheriff's own soul. Even now, at Jimmy Boy's gravestone six years later, he couldn't help but remember that first sleepless night, when he'd come home and told Alma he'd killed a man. The only darker night of his soul had been when he received word of his first son's death in France. News of the second son had followed so quickly that he was still numb from the first and felt nothing, as when a shock victim feels not the surgeon's scalpel until the day after, when the pain is twice as great.

The sun had fully risen when he got back to the car. He cranked the engine and thought about the long week he had ahead of him. He wanted to go home to Alma and get some sleep, but instead he rolled back into town as the sun climbed and the day warmed.

Castle, named for medieval legends, designed to be a piedmont fortress. Out of town there was the Bell village on one side and farther out was Eureka. The county itself was divided into parishes—Wilkesburg and Leeds and Bullock Creek—with a few towns and hamlets strewn along the railroad tracks—Lockhart and Union and Blackstock. The nearest city was Rock Hill and then Charlotte to the north, though a lot of folks hadn't ever been that far. Other folks, like Mary Jane's family, had come east out of the mountains, trickled through Spartanburg or Gastonia until they found what they were looking for, steady work or someone they knew, or maybe they just stopped when they got tired of traveling.

He parked the car on the north end of Main, walked around and entered the sheriff's office, the first one there.

Today was Sunday, a day of rest. While churchbells tolled mid-morning, he lay on a couch in the office, lit a cigarette. Listened, then slept.

When the sheriff left the farm, Mary Jane came downstairs and stood behind her without a word. He had blond hair, blond eyebrows, ice-blue eyes rimmed by almost invisible eyelashes. His hair and skin dusty brown so that his blue eyes were the only part of him that seemed unaffected by the night's events. He wore the same bloody shirt he'd worn into the house last night. His overalls were undone around the injured shoulder where the shot had laid into him, and the shirt was torn and stiff with dried black blood. Abigail had bandaged his shoulder last night to stanch the wound, but even now he was afraid to move too quickly lest the bleeding begin again. He rested his chin on her shoulder and stared out the window with her, at the empty hills and far-off woods.

"What are you doing out of bed?" she finally asked.

"I heard the sheriff."

"I took care of it. He's gone back to town."

He nodded, and continued to stare out the window.

"That won't be the last visitor we get, will it?" she asked.

"I reckon not."

She turned and met his gaze with eyes that had known more hurt than most, even in these hard times. Pregnant at eighteen, a war widow at twenty-six, childless at thirty-four, she'd learned to keep her own counsel, which Mary Jane found more endearing than anything a rosy-cheeked twenty-year-old could offer. Let the country folks say what they may about the sins of the widow and the drunk, he and Abigail made a fine couple. She put her head to his chest and said, "We'll just have to send them away, same as we've done all along."

The burn in his shoulder told him otherwise. The wound smelled like iron and something else. Rot, maybe. Pellets were still lodged inside the flesh, and he knew he wouldn't begin to heal until they cleaned the wound. They'd need to change the bandage regularly and pour whiskey over him to stave off infection. He needed to lay low for a while. Abigail would continue to abet him, but Larthan Tull would soon come knocking, and Larthan Tull would insist on more than a few friendly words at the front door.

As if reading his thoughts, she pulled away from him and fingered the ragged edges of his shirt, stared at his shoulder and refused to look him in the eye. "I should run you a bath," she said.

He thanked her, grateful for what she hadn't asked. There was nothing to say about what had happened. He'd shown up at her door last night at two in the morning, woozy from loss of blood and disoriented by how quickly his world had gone south. She'd taken him in without a word.

"Ernest is dead," he'd told her, and she'd pursed her lips.

"I figured him to be with you if he weren't," she'd said.

He'd drunk whiskey until he could sleep and then he crawled into bed with her with only a vague plan for the morrow. With the fateful knock from Sheriff Chambers today, he knew he owed it to Abigail to make a decision, yet the truth he couldn't reconcile to himself was that she was stronger than he was. She'd endured the worst life had to offer, and would fight against Chambers, Tull, the entire world, without a thought to her own safety or comfort. But he believed he still had a chance to get through this, to build a life for them beyond the law-breaking world of liquor distribution, if only he could cut a deal with Aunt Lou in Charlotte before Tull came knocking—or sent that bullet-faced associate of his out with his shotgun.

While she went out to pump some water from the well, he returned upstairs and took the jar of whiskey she'd brought out to help clean his shoulder last night and he drank from it. The white liquor was their own, not from Tull. It warmed his throat and he could already feel his mind cool. There were some things a body could get wrapped up in. It starts small, a still set up on the creek to save some money. Brew your own whiskey rather than paying dues to Larthan Tull. Pretty soon you've got a good recipe together and start to sell a little, a jar here or a jar there. Pure corn liquor, no additives, no problem. You come up with a plan for yourself, bring in a couple of partners, and soon you've got a business going. Wasn't planned. Just happened. And it just happened that someone didn't like your business, accused you of a plan, and took a shotgun to you all.

Luck ran in Mary Jane's family. He believed that. When the farm failed, they'd been able to find work together, and Joe and Susannah were living a good life out in the Bell. Had two good boys, a steady paycheck. No problems. Some of that luck had spilled over to Mary Jane, but sometimes the luck ran out and you found yourself scrambling through the woods, shotgun blasts at your back. Briars hooked your shirt and brambles cut into your pants, and you tripped on a root and got a mouthful of dirt. There you lay, dark all around and your business partners dead, and you knew you shouldn't have made it out of there alive. What did you do next?

His father had been a sharecropper. He'd worked other folks' land, but at least he was off his own family's dole, each man in every generation somehow carving out his own self as different from his father. Mary Jane had been named Wesley Jr. after his father, but, being a younger sibling, he was the sensitive type growing up and his mother kept him in dresses all the way to grammar school, long after the rest of the boys had quit. The first time someone called him Mary Jane, the name stuck so firm it might as well have been etched in his birth certificate. Lately, he hoped people might start calling him Slim on account of how tall and lanky he was, and that his best friend since high school was so short and stocky. He liked that name: Slim Hopewell had a tough ring to it, Slim Hopewell could go into business against Larthan Tull, but the fact that he had a bullet hole in his shoulder and was about to go on the lam probably meant he was still Mary Jane at heart.

He'd been raised on Wes Ancrum's farm, over in Union County. He'd gone to school in town with kids from all backgrounds, kids whose fathers owned farms, kids whose fathers worked in the mills, kids whose fathers owned businesses. And kids judged each other, the farm kids hanging out with farm kids, the mill kids hanging out with mill kids, the town kids with town kids. Mary Jane and his siblings were muscular, developed quickly. Farm-fed and farm-raised, almost like livestock, they were all expected to work the farm after school, and, though it was a struggle, their father wouldn't let them drop out of high school. He seemed to know, even before his body wore out, that this was no life for their generation, that the world was heading toward some great change like a locomotive bringing in progress.

When the war began, Mary Jane was a wasted drunk, same as now only younger, and after one too many fights out on Main Street, the local judge gently suggested he might want to serve his country in battle. In Europe, he'd been prepared for the conditions. The mud and the smoke, the endless march and march and march, followed by all the sitting around. Then came the offensive, which began in the spring of 1918. British and American troops held the lines against the German onslaught. They dug into trenches and aimed their carbine rifles out across No Man's Land at a line of Germans in olive green uniforms, who in turn fired back at the Americans and the British. The pop-pop-pop of the carbines created a steady drone, but it was the roar of the Howitzers spattering shells across the plain that Mary Jane would remember. They left a hollow ring in his ear, tinnitus that would forever haunt him, as if even his eardrums were cursed with the aftershock memories of that battle. Then the advance, where men charged from both sides, out of their trenches and into the plain, where bullets whizzed and sucked into meat, and men fell over and lay bleeding and calling for Christ to kill them. A shell burst nearby, dislodged something in his brain so that he lost time and woke back in the trench alongside the other wounded. Still the patter of riflefire and the guttural moans of men in agony. As dusk settled in, the lines retreated back to their fronts, the plain between them once again No Man's Land, a land solely for dead or dying.

He lost consciousness again and when he awoke rain had begun. It rained through the night and by morning he'd picked up a cough, hacked up wet chunks of dust he'd inhaled in the battle. The trench had become mud, mud, and more mud, mixed together with blood. At dawn he and a man from California, a twenty-year-old sergeant named Burris, followed a scrawny kid from Nebraska over the top into No Man's Land, where the wounded lay among the dead on both sides, English and Americans and Germans all asking for help as one people. That morning was one secret he would never tell, not even to his brother Joe, a secret he would not even allow himself to remember in his consistent, routine days after the war. Mary Jane and Burris were not good Samaritans, there to help the dying into the next life. Rather, they ignored the dying and rummaged through the dead's pockets.

"You can't help them," Burris had said. "There's nothing we can do."

True, there was nothing they could have done, but that rationalization didn't make anything better. This world was rotten, Mary Jane knew, and those who survived the war would not be the ones elected for heaven after. Burris would lose an arm in the next battle, and Mary Jane visited him once before he was discharged. Burris's face swelled up, a bandage over his forehead, a nub wrapped in gauze where his left arm should have been.

"None of it matters," Burris said.

He took another swig of the whiskey and heard the door slam shut downstairs. He lay back on the bed, leaned his head against the wall. Slats of light filtered through the blind, and motes of dust swirled in the air, moved toward the floor where the light cast its shine, as though the dust were actually particles of light that moved laterally through the air between the blind and the floor, so that the floor seemed bombarded with light-dust from the window.

"Mary Jane?" Abigail called. "I've got water on the stove if you want to come down."

When he came down, she unfastened the other strap of his overalls and cut away his shirt with a bowie knife. The cloth fell apart in her hands. She bit her lip as she worked, and hovered over him as she unfastened the bandage she'd put on last night. The meat of his shoulder was bruised blue and red, the skin cool to the touch. She took a sponge to it, gently wiped clean the dried blood that edged the holes themselves. "You're lucky he didn't hit you head on," she said. She'd said this to him last night as well.

"He wasn't aiming at me," he said, remembering how Ernest stood in front of him, the shotgun blast that hit his jaw and sent blood and bone matter careening off into the night. Stray shot hit Mary Jane's shoulder as he turned to run, hunkered low like a simian scurrying through a plain. Another blast kicked up dirt nearby, but he kept running, crashed into the woods and never slowed.

"You're lucky all the same," she said.

"I can't stay here. Furman isn't the only one who's going to be out here."

She continued to wipe his shoulder. The wound had reopened, and she dabbed it with a towel.

He said, "I don't want to drag you in any further. I've got the money to get us out of this, but I have to go up to Charlotte."

She opened a quart of moonshine, dipped the towel in, and said, "This'll sting." He never flinched as she rubbed his shoulder with the whiskey-wet towel and rivulets of alcohol slid down his arm. "There's shot still in there."

"It'll work itself out."

As she patted his shoulder dry, blood seeped into the towel, a flesh-burn, a muscle-ache, a bone-sore.

He said, "I've got a plan where I can take care of us, but I can't do it hunkered down in your bedroom, waiting for Larthan to figure out where I'm at and come knocking."

"I know you're in a spot."

"I am, and I'm sorry for bringing you into this. You and Ernest and Lee."

"Those boys would've gotten into mischief with or without you."

"But I was old enough to know better. I got greedy and thought we could get away with something."

She packed another bandage on his shoulder, a little too roughly for someone who'd forgiven him. He knew it was possible she might never fully forgive him, just as it was possible she felt she had nothing to forgive. She was so tough to read on matters of the soul. For himself, he knew his responsibility for Ernest and Lee, knew he'd brought them into a whiskey operation that went directly against their employer. He also knew he should feel worse than he did. Guilt, remorse, regret. Something. But something had died in him during the war, maybe out on No Man's Land with Burris. Death became an abstraction, a thing to reconcile with and move beyond, a thing to forget. Thus, his mind had filed last night away, into the lost thoughts with which he might one day stand in judgment, and he thought of tomorrow, of building a life for Abigail and himself. For that, he must act.

He said, "I can leave tonight. It should only take a few days to get to Charlotte, and by this time next week everything will be fine. Would you stop?" He pulled her hands away from his shoulder.

"Do you even know what you've gotten into?" she asked.

He held her gaze until she looked away, and when she did, he saw completely the truth about the two of them. No matter what happened to him, she would endure, so the weight was on him, his own private reckoning. As she'd said, he was in a spot, and his solution was not to run away and hide, but rather to run through it, deeper into the fire.

"I think it's a bad idea for me to be hanging around here today," he said. "I don't want to leave until tonight, so I'll head down to the river. Just act normal if anyone comes by."

"Normal."

"For the circumstances. I promise in another two weeks neither of us will have a thing to worry about."

The cotton mill was closed on Sundays. This morning everyone from the mill hill suffered in the heat at the base of the hill, listening to the Baptist preacher quote scripture in his sermon about longing for the heavenly city. *And I saw a new heaven and a new earth: for the first heaven and the first earth were passed away; and there was no more sea. And I John saw the holy city, New Jerusalem, coming down from God out of heaven, prepared as a bride adorned for her husband. And I heard a great voice out of heaven saying, Behold, the tabernacle of God is with men, and he will dwell with them, and they shall be his people, and God himself shall be with them, and be their God.*

"I'm thinking of faith," said the preacher. "Maintaining our faith in the face of the world is a trial, for the temptations to disbelieve are many. We have tired hearts, and in times such as these we wonder, 'Can it be real? Will we see the New Jerusalem one day?' But remember Paul's words to the Corinthians: *For we know that if our earthly house of this tabernacle were dissolved, we have a building of God, a house not made with hands, eternal in the heavens.*"

While the preacher analyzed the passages he quoted, on and on through his sermon, Willie and Quinn Hopewell—Joe and Susannah's boys—squirmed by their parents and grandfather on the fourth pew from the back. At twelve, Willie was gangly thin and seemed always to have a loose limb folded in an awkward position. His skin was freckled and lightly tanned so that he looked perpetually dusty, which was often the case because thus far in his life he'd spent more time playing in the dirt than contained indoors. When he was very young, he'd taken seriously his mother's command that he wash all of the dirt off when he bathed, and had vigorously scrubbed at his suntan, trying to make his arms as white as his thighs. He'd confessed to his brother that he couldn't get clean, and Quinn had played along, told him their mother would switch him good if she saw him, so he'd spent the next two days walking around with his arms crossed behind him.

Four years older than Willie, Quinn worked in the mill full time. His body was grown, his arms thick and muscular from operating the machines. This morning, he sat rigid on the end, and kept trying to make eyes at Evelyn Tull, who sat alone in a pew two rows up and one family over. The inside of the church was painted yellow and smelled closed up and musty, hot and unpleasant in the late summer heat. Everyone sweated. Many stank. No one commented. Willie crossed and recrossed his ankles and noticed every time Quinn's head turned to look at Evelyn. He agreed she was pretty, and part of him stirred at the sight of the smooth white skin on her neck, below the tufts of black hair, and although he'd never kissed a girl he thought about kissing her. Her lower teeth were slightly crooked and her lower lip pouted out, glazed this morning in gloss. Her black hair was pinned up to reveal a neck long and white as a swan's, and she sat with her back erect so that she looked like a proper lady from town.

She and her father, Larthan Tull, lived in a big house near York and Main, but ever since Larthan had walked into Castle fourteen years ago with his baby daughter, they'd attended the Calvary Baptist

Church out in the country between Castle and the Bell, on account, Larthan said, of he went to a church of the same name up in the mountains before. He rarely came anymore—a real sinner, a lot of folks said—but Evelyn never missed a Sunday. Today she looked so serious, so devout, bowing her head at all the right times, never a squirm or a look of agitation on her face. It was as if the spirit of the Lord really were within her as she listened to the preacher.

He that overcometh shall inherit all things; and I will be his God, and he shall be my son. But the fearful, and unbelieving, and the abominable, and murderers, and whoremongers, and sorcerers, and idolaters, and all liars, shall have their part in the lake which burneth with fire and brimstone: which is the second death.

An elbow to his ribs drew Willie's eyes away from Evelyn, his mind away from the line where the skin of her neck met the folds of her cotton dress. Quinn hissed into his ear, "I'm making my move whenever he finishes the sermon."

Willie turned to their parents, caught his mother's eye. She pursed her lips and looked back up to the preacher.

"Distract them when everyone's letting out."

Willie shifted, but his brother took his arm and nodded, his eyes searching Willie's for a sign that he was in it with him, on his side, brothers for life. Would he really do it? Quinn had flirted with girls before, Willie knew, but Evelyn was in a different class altogether, and Willie thought his brother might be trying something new. The preacher'd talked about sin enough that Willie knew his brother's guilt would be his own. Over Quinn's shoulder, Evelyn shifted her head, just enough to glance at the brothers out of the corner of her eye, and once again Willie saw the glaze of her peachwhite lip and imagined her mouth against his.

Quinn eyed him still, waiting for a nod, and Willie gave it as the preacher finished his sermon.

"I make the same appeal to you today," said the preacher, "as Paul to the Romans: *Therefore, brethren, we are debtors, not to the flesh, to live after the flesh. For if ye live after the flesh, ye shall die: but if ye through the Spirit do mortify the deeds of the body, ye shall live. For as many as are led by the Spirit of God, they are the sons of God.* The word of the Lord, amen."

More words for the millhands. When the preacher finally gave the benediction and the organist began the notes that meant it was time to go home, Willie shot off the pew as his family slowly rose beside him. While the congregation shuffled into the aisle, his brother nudged him again before hanging back. Willie waited for his parents and grandfather to get into the aisle and led them out toward the door before him. They didn't notice as Quinn slipped to the side corner with Evelyn.

Outside, the sun blasted against them so that only his mother's face beneath her bonnet was protected. They stood by the door like an uncertain herd of cattle. Willie led them off the walk into the grass, and to distract his mother from searching for his brother, he said, "Momma, Mr. Jefferson said he might have some work for me. Chopping wood this fall."

"That's good, Willie. Where's Quinn?"

"I saw him making eyes at that Tull girl," Joe said. "He's probably off trying to catch her away from her father."

Willie imagined his brother sweet-talking Evelyn, and for a moment a shot of jealousy rose up in him at the thought of Quinn with the girl, but he fought the feeling away. He could go up to a girl if he wanted, but he didn't know what he would do if he did. He wasn't big like Quinn, as sure and as headstrong. He said, "Daddy, with the money I get chopping wood and the money I'm getting for sweeping, I'll be helping out."

Joe looked at him. "Son, you're not staying on at the mill once school starts."

"Why not?"

"Because we can afford for you not to."

"But Daddy—"

"You know," his grandfather said. "I'm surprised with the preacher talking sin and the lake of fire, he didn't bring up Larthan's business."

Joe scoffed. "What's he going to say about it?"

Willie's grandfather was a lean old man with big ears and a big nose and a permanent droop to his face, like a basset hound. The mill workers called him Happy, though his real name was Abel Washington, and he'd come off the farm in the spring to live and work in the mill with the rest of them. He scowled and looked up the hill, where the twin smokestacks of the Bell mill loomed over the village. Standing there, you could tell he was silently cursing Larthan Tull's iniquity. Ruining half the town with his bootlegging and his gambling den, he wasn't good Christian folk, and the preacher ought to say something. There they were, waiting on the New Jerusalem, and Tull had turned the county into a veritable Sodom and Gomorrah. Signs and wonders, indeed.

"Someone go find Quinn," Susannah said.

"I'm here," he said from behind them.

"You get lost?"

Joe sucked his teeth. "Let's go."

A light breeze carried the thick air across their skin, and Willie wanted to hang back and ask Quinn what had happened with Evelyn, but his brother swayed close to their parents. Their grandfather, their mother's father, limped in the rear. Nearing seventy years old, he still worked full time in weave room #6, a welcome addition to the family's pooled finances but perhaps an unwelcome strain on their already cramped living situation. Willie's job this summer had been to go through the weave rooms and sweep up lint and dust that sprinkled onto the ground from the machines. The whir and clack of bobbins and spinners all but drowned out the koosh-koosh of the broom. Dirty rags to wipe down machines, men spitting snuff on the floor, hot lint sticking to his clothes, his hair. He worked half days, thirty hours a week, and when he made it to weave room #6 his grandfather would always give him a wink, appeared happy even though he would come home coughing and sullen and would hack away all night. Everyone worked a half-day Saturday, and the mill gave them Sundays off, so by this time every week his grandfather had coughed all the lint out and could talk.

Willie paused to wait for him as the family neared the crest of the hill and turned up Harvey Lane. He said, "Did you hear me telling Daddy about splitting kindling?"

"Yeah, I did. That's good, boy. My daddy had me chopping wood when I was your age."

"Really?"

"Back on the farm, I started work when I was five years old. It was my job to get up and start milking the cows. In the afternoons all summer, Daddy paid me an allowance to pick up sweetgum balls out of the yard. He always liked to walk around the yard barefoot at dusk, and didn't want one of them balls biting his foot. Paid me a penny a bag, starting when I was younger'n than you."

"That's all?" Willie said. A penny a bag was hard to believe. The mill paid him two dollars a week, and he knew that math added up to more than a penny for the trouble it would take to gather a bagful of gumballs.

"Yes sir, when I was your age I was saving up to buy me a rifle, but ended up spending a few years' worth of allowance on a clean suit and a tin of pomade so I could go to town and start chasing gals around."

"Daddy," Susannah said from in front of them.

"It's true. Boy, wait till you get a few years older. You're going to find some pretty gal that gets you so flustered you won't know whether to thank God or the devil."

"Daddy. That's enough."

Susannah slowed and patted Willie on the back and led him on-ward, shaking her head. But he'd heard it before. Abel had been with them several months now, long enough for Willie to figure out his stories were on a cycle and he repeated himself every few weeks, one endless loop of how times were different way back when, how on the farm money went straight to the bank to pay off loans, and how a bad year for crops meant another loan to pay off the first. By that accounting, life in the Bell village was a dream, for there was always credit at the store, always work to be had. Yet the old man was forever dissatisfied.

Years later, Willie would think that it wasn't a bad life, that al-though they were poor, they didn't know it because everyone was poor. The houses in the village were all the same design—small off-white vernacular bungalows with gabled roofs—and had small, fenced-in backyards with clotheslines and tiny gardens for corn, to-matoes, squash, and bell peppers. As many as three generations of a family crammed into each of these houses, everyone white—blacks were not allowed to work in the upstate mills here—and many of these families had come down from mountain farms after several years of drought and failed crops, living off borrowed money that they could no longer get an extension for. Husks of black snakes on fences, the eyes of glowering barn rats at their backs, these families packed their belongings and left that uncertain, hardscrabble life for a guaranteed weekly paycheck.

Like all their neighbors in the Bell, the Hopewells lived in a single-story Craftsman with a gabled roof that faced the street. The residence had wood siding painted beige and light green shutters, the paint chipped and cracked. A small square yard sat in front, and a two-foot stripe of crabgrass separated their house from the neighbors on either side. From the road, six stairs led up from the street to the yard, where a picket fence marked the front edge of the property, and six more stairs rose from the sidewalk to the porch. The wide porch stretched across the entire front of the house, and was partially hidden by hanging ferns and cypress trees that grew in the yard.

At the corner of Harvey Lane, their neighbor, a man named Mink Skelton, from the Cajun country, waved and caught up with them.

"Y'all hear what went on last night at the Hillside?" he asked.

"Not a thing," Joe said.

"Shoot," Mink said, nearly salivating with the gossip. As they walked up Harvey Lane, he recounted the night's events, emphasized the cold-bloodedness of it all, a note of glee in his voice. "I haven't talked to anyone that was there yet, but it sounds gruesome."

"I'll say," Susannah said. She turned up the walk to the house. "Shoo, Charlie," she said from inside. A mangy collie mix trotted up to Willie, and he knelt to scratch it, listened to the men talk.

"They found out who done it yet?" Abel asked.

Mink grew quiet. "Rumor has it, Mary Jane was the one." Willie eyed Quinn, who hunched over with his hands in his pockets. Joe waved his hand at the neighbor, who went on, "It was Ernest Jones and Lee Evans that got killed. Depot said Mary Jane walked in, dragged them to the street, and shot them."

"Mary Jane's not a killer," Joe said. "Those were his friends." He trailed off as though finally allowing himself to consider the possibility.

"That's just what I heard," Mink said.

"It must have been Larthan."

"You might want to go talk to Sheriff Chambers then. He's hunting Mary Jane right now."

"I'll do that."

Abel grabbed a wooden fence stake in the front yard, wiggled it to see how sturdy it was, and said, "Anyone seen Larthan?"

"Evelyn was in church this morning," Joe looked at Quinn. "She say anything?"

"Not to me."

"You do know who her father is?"

"Yes sir."

"Well. I doubt she knows more than the rest of us do."

Abel said, "Such a shame, a father like that. At least he raised her in church."

"Passed her off, is what he did. Those church ladies did as much to raise Evelyn Tull as Larthan ever did."

"Strange he never brought her into one of those downtown churches," Mink said.

"He knows his clientele. Get to know more farmers and whiskey drinkers out here in the country than he ever would at some town church."

"You think he'll shut down for a while? Lay low?"

Joe spat. "He won't be closing down, long as he's got a line of customers. So you're trying to tell me that the sheriff is honestly considering Mary Jane to do that."

"He's already gone out to see Widow Coleman this morning. Paid his respects and asked for Mary Jane."

"He didn't do it, I'm telling you right now."

"I know Mary Jane," Mink said. "I know it don't sound like him."

"It wasn't him."

From the front porch, Susannah called to them, "Quit your gossiping. Come in and get your dinner."

"All right, fellas," Mink said, and tipped his hat.

The inside of their house was small, two rooms and a kitchen. Willie, Quinn, and Abel slept in the front room, three metal beds, a shelf, and a dresser, and the bedroom to the right belonged to Joe and Susannah. In the kitchen, where Susannah served green bean casserole with biscuits and gravy, the men sat around the table like disciples. The mid-afternoon light slanted in from the window and the door at the back of the room, glared on the counters and floor so that the grime and dust that Susannah could never clear away seemed almost swollen with life, as though nature herself were re-minding them that this house, this life they'd been living since they sold the farm, was somehow rotten, somehow wrong for them. All through the meal, Willie kept trying to make eye contact with his brother, hoping Quinn would be the one to bring up Mary Jane, but he kept his head down, focused on the clank and scrape of his fork on the plate. Maybe he was too busy thinking about Evelyn Tull to wonder about their uncle.

Willie said, "Do you believe Mink?"

His father set his fork on the plate and rubbed his tongue in his cheek to rid his mouth of food. "Your uncle's not that kind of man. He'll get into some mischief, but he ain't a killer."

"What'd Mink say?" Susannah said.

"The sheriff's looking for Mary Jane. Thinks my brother shot those boys."

"They Lord," she said.

"He didn't do it," Joe said. "You know Mary Jane."

"He could have," Willie said, and everyone looked at him. "Couldn't he?"

"Son, there's different kinds of men out there, all of em capable of different things. I know you've heard us arguing about your uncle, how he drinks too much and runs with the wrong crowd. Things I don't want you messed up in. But there's a big difference between causing some trouble and killing someone."

"Didn't you kill men, in the war?"

"Willie," his mother said.

"That was different. We were at war, for one thing, and it took something out of me. You don't go down that road lightly because you'll never come back from raising a gun against another man."

Chambers had just lit a cigar in his office when the county's house representative called up from Columbia to discuss the murder. It had only been twelve hours since the bodies were found, but it being Sunday the gossip mill had spread like news of the second coming. What could Chambers tell him? "Yes sir, we're working on it. I've got men out looking for Mary Jane Hopewell, and I've taken some statements."

"I tell you, Furman, this isn't looking good. I've got constituents calling me up from the other side of York County asking can't the law do something. This is campaign season."

"We're working on it."

"My office is right down the street from federal investigators and they've already come by once to see what I know about it. I don't know who tipped them off, but they smell something big. They're probably going to set up base in Castle and try to bring down a big fish."

"They think they're going to find a big fish in Castle? This ain't Charlotte."

"It's not a small-town murder they're interested in."

"Then what is it?"

"The whiskey trade."

"Whiskey."

"Whiskey. There's a big organization in Charlotte. None of this mountain still business. We're talking big time. Runners coming in from three states, including South Carolina. You know Aunt Lou?"

"I know who she is, but what's she got to do with my county?"

"Take it easy, Furman. They're after Aunt Lou, but to get to her they're nosing around in Castle. Going after one of her distributors."

"They likely already know all there is to know about him. Nothing new here."

"World's changing, Furman. The old rules no longer apply. Mr. Tull should appreciate that as well as you do."

When he hung up the phone, Chambers stepped outside and stood before the main square to relight his cigar. In Castle's downtown square, a Confederate memorial obelisk rose from the pavement and a bronze cannon aimed across Main to the courthouse and the sheriff's station. Chambers stood in the square in front of the sheriff's station and gazed up at the courthouse clock. A slated building with ornate carvings and embellished angles. The hash marks of power lines and poles. A row of blackbirds sinking one with their weight.

Despite the stock market crash and the ensuing Depression, Castle was still a rich town thanks to the textile boom and the railroads that crisscrossed the Carolinas to bring cotton north. Behind the Confederate square along York Street, rows of white Colonials housed the town's aldermen, the mill bosses and lawyers and salesmen. Magnolias sprinkled the sidewalks, sporting their sweet white flowers, and on any given day you'd see men in fedoras and white shirts ambling through town, sweating in the heat while their wives were at home in flower print cotton dresses. West along the railroad tracks from town, Highway 9 passed beyond the filling station and the Hillside Inn and out to the Bell mill village, where the houses lay bumped together like stalks of corn, where the brick wall of the cotton mill bracketed the side of the hill, and where, beyond the mill itself, a pair of rounded smokestacks rose up on either side and coughed black air out into the summer blue sky.

While Chambers puffed his cigar, a long black car cruised by. Two strange men in gray suits gawked as they passed. Sure enough, he thought, sure enough. The congressman must have known they were already here and had called Chambers as a courtesy. They better be careful if they didn't want to attract attention. Folks would notice expensive shoes on Castle sidewalks. Backwoods whiskey stills would be taken down and moved piecemeal into barns, liquor buried in mason jars, hidden in hencoops. The way rumors flew, if these boys were hoping for a quiet investigation and a big time bust, they'd nearly blown their cover already, before they'd even gotten out of the car. That didn't bother Chambers much. Because of the murder, people would be guarding themselves more closely. All he wanted was for his town to run smoothly. His folks wanted to be left alone. No one wanted change, and it was up to him to make sure everything remained steady.

He walked into the jailhouse next door to check on Shorty Bagwell. There were two prisoners right now, both in for getting drunk and causing trouble. A young troublemaker named Boots Miller showed up in town on Friday, skunk drunk and holding his belly and laughing all up and down Saluda Street. Chambers's deputy heard the laughter through an open window, walked out, and clubbed Boots on the back of the head and dragged him to the jailhouse. Today he sat on the floor of the cell, hummed a blues without missing a beat when Chambers walked in. The sheriff moved on to the back cell where Shorty Bagwell slept on a hard cot, one arm draped over his eyes. Beyond the square of barred light at the top of Shorty's cell, a hawk glided across the white sky. Water dripped onto bald concrete in the empty cell across the hall, its unmetered splat the only timekeeper for those inside. On the floor of the cell was an uneaten pimento cheese sandwich slathered in potato gravy, gorged on by flies.

"Shorty," Chambers said, rousing the man from his slumber.

Shorty started and sat up, a chubby tub of a man whose feet barely touched the ground from the cot. "Well hey, Sheriff."

Chambers clanked the keys in the lock and twisted the rusted iron. The cell door groaned from the friction, and he said, "Let's go, Shorty."

The man stared at the pimento cheese sandwich, said, "I was enjoying some of the county's fine hospitality, thanks."

Chambers led him down the concrete hall and out into the sunlight. In the sheriff's office, Chambers sat across from the grimy man and stared at him. "How long you got left in there?"

"Well Sheriff, you ought to know as well as I would."

"I could look up the exact date."

"Unless Miss Meacham's changed her mind and forgiven me for defiling her flowerbeds."

Chambers laughed, said, "I don't think that's ever going to happen."

"I don't believe it is, either," Shorty said.

In the spring, he and Mary Jane had been riding around too fast through town, and they'd plowed into Miss Meacham's flowers and knocked over a fence. Miss Meacham lived in one of the York Street mansions, and her poor lawn had been a blemish much discussed among the women in town ever since. She'd barked at Chambers over the phone to come out and arrest those liquored-up yahoos before she took a notion to take the law into her own hands. He came out to find her—one of the town's oldest residents—out on her lawn raising high hell, shouting about sin and tarnation, so much that Chambers even felt a little sorry for Shorty and Mary Jane, leaning on her car and saying, yes ma'am, yes ma'am, while she carried on. The both of them sober and bleary-eyed, it seemed at first like they would come in peaceably enough, but then Shorty, still drunk no doubt, decided to grab the deputy's billyclub and start an all-out riot on Main Street. Chambers still had a pink scar on his knuckles from where he'd tackled Shorty and smashed his hand into the pavement.

Chambers quit laughing about it and leaned back in his chair. Shorty rolled his eyes and said, "I got another five days."

"And then what are you going to do?" When Shorty didn't answer, he said, "You got to do something. Make money somehow."

"Maybe I'll get on out at the Bell. I've done that before."

"That's good work. Honest. Beats running whiskey, that's for sure."

"Aw, Sheriff, you know I ain't—"

"What? You ain't running whiskey?"

"Wouldn't think of it."

"That's not what I've been hearing. You heard what happened last night, out at the Hillside?"

"Your deputy filled me in at breakfast."

"Your buddy Mary Jane is in some trouble now. From what it sounds like, he's been doing more than carting whiskey for Larthan Tull. From what it sounds like, he's been brewing his own on the side."

"I don't know a thing about that."

"Don't know a thing. Let's start simpler. You know whiskey is against federal law? And you also know that don't stop folks from drinking it."

Shorty scoffed. "I know one person who drinks it."

Chambers ignored this, sat forward, put his elbows on the desk. "And you know where it's at in Castle County. Who makes it and where it's sold. None of that's a big secret. There are larger forces at work in the whiskey trade, and right now those forces are about to come down hard against this town. What I'm wondering is what else you might know about it. You know Aunt Lou up in Charlotte?"

"Aunt Lou? Who's that?"

"I think you know who she is."

"Now how would I know that?" Shorty put his hands behind his head and grinned.

"Larthan's had some people running loads of whiskey to her every week, sometimes twice a week, for years now. Thousands of gallons a year. Rumor has it you were one of his runners, when you didn't have money for a pint, but that's not what I'm wanting to know here."

"Those are some mighty strong accusations."

"Look, Shorty, you pick your battles in law enforcement. If folks want to drink a little whiskey now and then, as far as I'm concerned it's not my position to get in their way. Matter of fact, I think a little whiskey keeps folks on an even keel. Gives em a release that don't involve blowing two boys up with a shotgun right in the middle of the street. What I'm looking for from you is some information about Mary Jane."

Shorty lolled his head, and Chambers couldn't tell if the man was considering what he was saying, or if he was laughing at him. Chambers cracked his knuckles and was about to return Shorty to the cell when he spoke: "I don't have much I can tell you, Sheriff. God's honest truth is, yes, I've occasionally run some whiskey up to Charlotte when I needed some money. I never met any Aunt Lou. It was always some man in a cornfield. And, yes, Mary Jane's gone with me. We run together, we drink together. But you already know that."

"I know it."

"I go over to the Hillside, play cards, and drink with Mary Jane, but, and again this is the God's honest truth, I don't know anything about Mary Jane starting up his own whiskey business. A man'd have to be a damn fool to want to do that in this town."

"How long you and Mary Jane been friends? Y'all been causing trouble in this town together for as long as I've been sheriff. You're going to try to sit there and tell me you don't know a thing?"

"If he's brewing whiskey, he didn't let me in on it. You ought to talk to the widow. The two of them have been conspiring together for months now."

"Left you out of the loop."

"That's right," Shorty said. He held his head high, or as high as a short chubby man can hold it, and Chambers saw he wasn't going to get anything else out of Shorty Bagwell. But he wasn't going to let him off just yet.

He said, "I've already been out and talked with Abigail this morning."

"And did she say Mary Jane and I have been brewing whiskey together?"

"No, she didn't mention you. She said it was Mary Jane and those two boys that got shot out by the Hillside."

"Well there you go."

Midafternoon found him finishing his cigar as he drove west through the countryside to the Bell village. The mill rose out of the red clay and yellowed grass, its tall smokestacks spewing soot even after the whistle blew to mark the day's end, guarding the square brick walls like sentries. Past the mill, he turned up Harvey Lane and slowed, for here children scampered through the streets like rabbits in a garden. You never knew when a child might emerge from between the close-knit houses and scurry into traffic.

In the heart of the village, he felt the eyes of the millhands upon him, peering through curtains, watching from porches. The law rarely had reason to come out here, and when it did it was more than likely on a Saturday night to bust up a brawl. Folks didn't call the sheriff for two young men going at it in the front yard, but they would if a husband and wife came to blows. Houses so tight here you could hear curses and glass shattering from around the block. But that was on a Saturday night, and often a deputy was enough to break up the disturbance. Chambers didn't know how much word had spread about the Hillside murders. Probably everyone knew he was looking for Mary Jane Hopewell, but he felt the suspicious eyes on him nonetheless.

He parked in front of the Hopewell residence, a gabled bungalow with ferns on the front porch. Cigarette butts and cinders from the mill on the pavement in front of the house. The grass spare and burnt the color of autumn corn, mainly crabgrass and clover over rusty soil. He knocked and immediately there was a click as Susannah Hopewell opened the door. Beyond her, the two boys and the old man sat at the dining room table, and Joe leaned against a doorway.

Chambers's eyes flickered back to Susannah, and he took off his hat. "Ma'am," he said.

Despite having two boys nearly grown, she was still pretty. She came to town every once in a while and drew eyes from storefronts. She had soft yellow hair and comely skin and a slender face with soft lines where wrinkles would soon appear. Her hair had thinned some—he could imagine her seventeen, with a full shock of curls and ruddy skin, pretty as a peach and ripe for the picking—but time had its way with everyone out on the mill hill. She'd fared well, but he could see that in a few more years she would look seventy, wrinkled and thin and hunched over. Age hit you like that, a pretty young thing one day and a grandmother the next. He'd seen it with his mother, then with Alma. Same thing happened to men, but they never burned as brightly in their youths, so the transformation wasn't as stark.

Joe shoved off the wall and came to the door. "Sheriff," he said.

"Hey, folks," Chambers said. "May I come in?"

Joe stepped aside. He was dressed in his Sunday shirt, a white button-down with the top button undone, the shirt tucked into cedar-brown pants. He had a lean face with almost gaunt cheekbones and flat, expressionless eyes. Not a happy man, Chambers thought, but he couldn't pinpoint what made him think it.

Chambers followed Joe back to the dinner table. The inside of the house had dark wood floors and white walls with dark wood trim that seemed to swallow the light. It felt tight and dark even though the sun was still close to its peak.

The boys rose and began clearing dinner plates.

"Offer you anything? Coffee?"

"No thank you. I'm sorry to be interrupting your dinner."

"Not at all," Susannah said. "Please, have a seat."

She stacked a few plates in the sink, wiped the counter, and then left for the other room. When they were alone, Joe sat and nodded at the table for Chambers to do the same. Chambers sat next to the old man, the grandfather whose name he could not recall. Chambers said, "I reckon you've heard about what happened at the Hillside?"

"I believe that story has made its way across town and back a few times," Joe said.

"Made it all the way to Columbia, matter of fact."

"I can tell you this," Joe said. "Mary Jane didn't have anything to do with shooting anybody. I know that bartender said he done it, but he's not a killer."

"I'm not saying he is," Chambers said. "All I have to go on is what Depot told me, but before I can clear or accuse anybody, I need to get a hold of Mary Jane. You have any idea where he might be?"

"Naw," Joe said. He crossed his arms as if to dare Chambers to contradict him. The old man sitting next to him lit a cigarette. White-haired farmer: Chambers had met him only one time before. He thought they may have called him Happy, but like his son-in-law, the man looked anything but.

"When was the last time you saw Mary Jane?" Chambers asked.

"I'd say it's been a couple weeks. He's kept right busy, out at Widow Coleman's farm. You been out there yet?"

"I have."

"And?"

"She didn't know where he was at."

"Well hell's bells, Sheriff, my brother's done took off."

"So it seems."

The boys came into the kitchen and the older one said, "We're going down to the creek for a while."

The younger one added, "Tommy and the gang are going swimming at the dock."

"It is hot out there," Joe said.

"I feel like I'm about to fry," the older boy said. Chambers couldn't remember the boys' names either. He'd always been good with names and had done well with all but the youngest generation. He knew just about everyone over twenty years old in the county, but now there were just too many younguns for him.

"You know, I saw you hanging back to chat up the Tull girl after church."

"Daddy, that was nothing."

"Maybe so, but she's not one to go off sparking on a Sunday afternoon."

"I hear you."

"She's not the kind of girl you want to get in trouble with. Especially now."

"I hear you," the older said again, and turned away. The younger looked over at the sheriff, seemed like he wanted to say something more, but he followed his brother out.

"She's not one of us," Joe called. He looked at Chambers and said, "My oldest has taken a liking to Evelyn Tull."

"She is pretty."

"Pretty dangerous."

"That too."

"What are we going to do about Mary Jane?" Joe asked.

Susannah came in and leaned against the wall and waited for Chambers to answer.

"I don't know. I trust y'all haven't seen him, but if you do, call me. I know he's kin, but it'll be safer for everyone if you don't try to harbor him."

"Mary Jane wouldn't come here and ask that of us," Joe said.

"Well, if he does. I'm sure Larthan would love a word with him as well, and he doesn't have what you'd consider a high regard for the law." Chambers took a breath and said, "I've taken enough of your time. You know anyone else he might be staying with?"

Joe shook his head.

"Ma'am," Chambers said, nodding at Susannah. He put on his hat and headed for the door. Joe followed, and the grandfather sat at the table, still not saying a word, nor looking up at the sheriff. Some folks sure were strange.

As the brothers headed down the hill toward the Broad River, waves of heat in the air blurred the roads and the mill and even the village houses. Above them, always, the mill's smokestacks clawed their way above the treeline and towered over the village, red bricks hot as a stovetop, like embers of coal. The Catawba and Broad rivers bracketed Castle County. Lazy, wide, and brown, they flowed south out of North Carolina and became the Tigris and Euphrates of the South Carolina textile boom. Cotton mills lined their banks like the beginnings of civilization, the first weak and stumbling steps of progress. Just outside of town, there was a spot near the trestle, a clearing in the pines on the banks of the Broad River, out of sight from everyone, where kids went to get into trouble, a good place to drink whiskey, a good place to spark.

Out of sight of the house, Quinn said, "Just hang out with us for a while. Then you can tell them you got tired, or that I went off with the gang."

"What'd y'all talk about after church?"

"I told her the riverbank near Coleman's farm was a good place to watch a sunset."

"She's coming?"

"Hell yeah she's coming."

"Even after what happened at the Hillside?"

"That don't have nothing to do with me or her. Or you."

"What about Mary Jane?"

"That don't concern us either. You were right at dinner. Maybe Daddy doesn't want to admit it, but Mary Jane's a schemer. He could have cooked up something. Probably thought he saw a way to get a good supply of free liquor. Maybe things didn't work out, and, well."

"You don't think her father had anything to do with it?"

"That could be too. I don't know. But she's not making a thing of her father, so I'm not either."

"What are you going to do?"

"That ain't for me to tell right now."

The road leveled out near the church and angled into the highway. The railroad tracks sliced through the landscape and arrowed south toward the river and the widow's farm. They neared where the tracks crossed the highway, and Evelyn stood waiting, still in her Sunday dress and holding a blanket.

When the boys approached, she said, "I told Daddy I had some errands to run this afternoon. He's got business all day, so he won't worry as long as I'm home in bed before he gets done, but don't go telling people I was sneaking around with you, troublemaker. Hi, Willie."

"Hello."

"Don't worry," Quinn said. "He's the only one who knows. I told everyone we were meeting Tommy Cope at the river."

"You better tell Tommy to back you up," she said, laughing.

"That boy? He don't know where he is in the present, much less where he's been."

"I didn't realize he did anything but play pool at the Hillside," she said.

They walked down the tracks. Oaks and pines rose up around them. Heat sizzled on the metal rails, and the woods and the rocks drank up the late afternoon sun, warmed their feet through their shoes.

Quinn said, "I think I'd be in more trouble if people found out. Your Daddy'd come after me."

"Oh he would not."

"You know what the rumor is about the Hillside, right?"

"I heard about the men that got shot last night."

"You know why?"

"No one knows."

"Some say our uncle shot them, but some folks think your father might have done it."

Evelyn stopped. "Do you believe that? That my father's a killer?"

"It's possible."

She hung her head, and Quinn put his hand on her arm. "Hey," he said. "Hey, I didn't mean nothing. That's just what some folks is saying."

"Who?"

"I don't know. Folks. In church. Listen, they're all full of it. Let's not talk about this anymore. It's not important."

The two of them walked ahead slowly. Willie moved into the shaded woods, and his feet chopped at the leaves, stirred the rich humus, and evoked the smell of acorns and sap. Orange sunlight fired through the tree limbs and created a mosaic of sun and shade at his feet, lit up brown leaves on the ground, muscadines and ivy and brambles. Lowhanging limbs of a chinaberry tree, a patch of wild irises. Then the ground fell on a slope away from the tracks. He followed Quinn and Evelyn down the hill to the river. The trestle to the right towered across the water, with its patchwork of rusty beams and angles. The other side of the tracks belonged to Widow Coleman, wherever she was. South of the tracks, county land spread downstate toward Columbia, nothing but cow pastures and pine-woods between here and the capital city. In a patch of clear land by the river, the grass was low and soft and protected by shade from nearby oaks. When they reached the clearing they saw a man in the river, bearded and naked and doing a lopsided backstroke with his member bobbing out of the water with each stroke. The three of them stopped and stared. "Well damn," Quinn said. "I didn't think anybody would be out here."

The man caught sight of them and jerked up in a spasm. Water splashed as he flopped over to hide his member in the darkness of the river, and he shook his head and gurgled. "Hey, y'all," he said.

"Mary Jane?"

"Hey, boys."

His shoulder was wounded, Willie saw. A dark purple stain of a bruise covered his arm and chest, and in the meat of his shoulder ragged chunks of flesh appeared to have been cut out.

The three of them approached the river, where their uncle Mary Jane treaded water.

"Ma'am," he said.

Just then Evelyn seemed to realize what an awkward position she was in, and she turned and started to walk back the way they came.

"Let me get my britches on, y'all don't have to go."

Mary Jane splashed out of the river and scrambled up the bank, dripping like a wet dog. He swayed to and fro as he put on a pair of shorts and said, "OK, y'all, I'm dressed."

"Maybe we should come back some other time," Evelyn said.

"Hey, hey," Mary Jane said. "Don't back up on my account. I was just taking a dip. Stick around."

Quinn took the blanket from Evelyn, whispered to her, "It's OK." He unrolled the blanket in the clearing, and Mary Jane came up with his shirt thrown over his wounded shoulder.

"Whew, uncle, what you been drinking?"

Mary Jane stopped a few feet away.

"What'd you do, raid the widow's liquor stash?"

As Quinn and Willie laughed, their uncle grinned and looked at Evelyn, and when he caught her eye he quit grinning and looked back toward the riverbank. Everyone seemed to notice at once the two square gallon cans resting in some tall grasses on the riverbank. Bootleggers carted moonshine in those cans, and while everyone knew Widow Coleman kept a low supply of homebrew on her land, she wasn't a bootlegger.

Mary Jane coughed, said, "I had a few nips this afternoon, you know how it is."

"Yeah I do," Quinn said.

"The widow sent me down here. She wanted me to pour out all her liquor. Said she didn't want anymore to do with it."

"You got any left?"

"Naw, it's all gone."

He grinned again, and Quinn and Evelyn stared at him. Since no one else was going to ask, Willie said, "What happened to your shoulder?"

They all kind of laughed nervously, and Mary Jane said, "You might have heard something bad happened at the Hillside last night."

"Folks said you killed two men."

Mary Jane scowled. "You don't believe that, do you?"

Willie shrugged. Quinn and Evelyn didn't move.

"Jesus, boys, you know your uncle Mary Jane. You know I might have a few bad habits here and there, but damn. No, me and those two fellas were in a bit of trouble, and someone decided the trouble was deep enough that we were better off dead. Took a hunk out of me, and I'm lucky to have gotten away with just that." Mary Jane ran his tongue back and forth across his lower lip a few times. Willie's eyes flickered from his brother to his uncle and back. It seemed like there was some communication going on below the surface that Willie wasn't aware of, and he couldn't figure out what was actually going on. Then his uncle said, "Were y'all here to swim? Why don't you and me go get in the water and leave these lovebirds alone for a while?"

Willie followed Mary Jane to the river, removed his shirt and shoes and waded in. The water was cool and clear and speckled with sunlight that passed through the trees. Brown sand at his feet stirred and clouded the water as he waded further, until he tumbled over and the whir of the water and the rustle of the trees in the wind fell silent, the world vanished. When he came up, he shook his head. Mary Jane, now in his britches, couldn't do much but wade through the water, but he played along as Willie splashed around in the water. On the riverbank, Quinn and Evelyn lay on the blanket. She seemed to be crying, and Quinn had his hand on her shoulder. Willie knew her father had a reputation, that he made liquor and ran an illegal business, and he knew Quinn here with Evelyn was more dangerous than just going against their father's word. But there was so much he didn't understand. Who shot the men last night, and why? What was Mary Jane going to do now? His uncle tossed him around in the water for a while, and eventually he said, "All right, boy, it's time for me to move on. Don't listen to any rumors you hear about me."

"I won't."

Mary Jane looked at Quinn and Evelyn on the riverbank, said, "That boy's getting into some trouble there."

"That's what Daddy says."

"You need to steer clear of her father. He's going to be looking for me, too. I've got to go away for a while to take care of some business, so while I'm gone you just stay away from him."

Mary Jane wiped water out of his hair and waded onto the riverbank. He put on his shirt and shoes and waved to Quinn. Then he picked up the canisters and shuffled away. As his uncle left, Willie thought he could hear liquid sloshing in the tin.

L arthan Tull wanted to find Mary Jane Hopewell. The man had crossed a line with his liquor project out on the Coleman farm, and it was a line Tull was surprised to see him cross. What did he think he was going to accomplish out there, run Tull out of business and make easy money and hole up with Abigail Coleman and live a happy family life? That's not how this worked. This was business, cutthroat and violent. If you didn't go into it with clear eyes, a stone heart, and a thick roll of cash, you should go back to sweeping up cinders in the cotton mill and leave the real work to the men.

Out beyond the Hillside, toward the Bell village, the widow owned a good tract of land south of Highway 9. Riverfront property, but her house was inland to where you couldn't see the Broad. A tributary or two ran like veins through her land, and it was those tributaries that caused the problem. For years, Tull had been buying leftover corn from area farmers, who for their part knew what for, even if Tull offered them the pretense of needing it for corn syrup for his soda factory. Back before the husband had died, the Colemans had produced more corn than most farmers out here, and lately, ever since she'd taken Ernest Jones into her house and Mary Jane into her bed, the widow had been growing more corn than husband and wife ever had. But Tull guessed old Mary Jane thought he could do better on his own, cut out the middleman, and sell some shine directly. Tull had known about it longer than Mary Jane knew he'd known, but he'd let it go on because the bulk of Tull's income came from Aunt Lou, then from the Hillside. Mary Jane couldn't compete with either of those, and if he wanted to have some boys down from the mill hill for a few drinks on the farm, well, it made folks happy and gave them the illusion of choice in the market. Little fish, big fish.

But with a double murder happening outside his tavern, that was more serious than brewing a little whiskey on the side. From what Depot had told him, the good old boys out drinking on the widow's farm had come up with the idea that Mary Jane could give Aunt Lou a better product for less. Let's go to the distributor! That's easy money! Like that was all there was to it. Tull wasn't about to let some no-count bootleggers cut in on his business, and he'd indicated to Depot that the boys would have to be dealt with, swiftly and harshly. Still, he'd thought his right-hand man more competent than to rouse half the county with gunshots and a puddle of blood on Highway 9. One drunken squabble, it seemed, and now two were dead and Mary Jane was on the run. The least Depot could've done was take out all three in a single swoop.

"It was the damnedest thing," Depot had said before the sheriff had arrived. "Mary Jane just up and shot those boys in the street. I never did see a man so out of control."

"Business will do that to you," Tull had said, his mind already churning ahead to deal with Mary Jane. "You take on too much too fast and you get wrung out."

"Most businessmen I know don't wind up shooting no one."

"Everybody's different."

"What you aim to do?"

Tull aimed to put a stop to any nonsense between Mary Jane and Aunt Lou, and he aimed to charge Mary Jane a tax for the inconvenience of it all. The way Tull figured it, the man owed him about five thousand dollars. Call it a whiskey tax. He'd earned more over the years, and maybe Tull shouldn't have let it go on so long, but there you go. The five thousand was a rough number Tull calculated after looking into Mary Jane's expenses and spending. Helped to be in good with the town banker. Based on the numbers the banker and Tull came up with, Mary Jane had at least that much sitting around in a mattress somewhere, and Tull intended to collect it. Didn't really care about Mary Jane's life. Mary Jane had watched Ernest and Lee die for their part in the transgression, and he'd run off scared. He could keep running, far as Tull cared, but that five thousand, that was a chunk of change.

He parked the Studebaker and stood smoking beside it and took in the scene: the slope of the garden down toward the woods, the logging trail to the bottoms, the crest of trees across the way where the land rose again from its trough. Though it was only the end of August, the tulip poplars had already yellowed from the heat and the late-summer thirst. In the garden by the house, beans and squash had browned on the vine, the peppers had been scorched red, and the tomato vines were bent over so that the fruit wasted away in the dirt. And they thought they could run a whiskey empire.

She stepped onto the porch, shouted, "What you want?"

"Mary Jane around?"

"Hell no he ain't. What you want?"

"I want to find Mary Jane."

"He ain't here, so go on away."

"Maybe you can help me," he said. He walked up to the porch where she stood, still holding the screen open. "I believe he had some money for me. I just came to get it, and then I'll leave you be."

"We don't have no money."

She shaded her eyes against the afternoon sun and squinted at him. Tull could see she might have once been pretty. Didn't have the weary, worn-out look most of these farm wives had. Lord knew her life had been hard enough, especially now that she was in an affair with a bumbling entrepreneur like Mary Jane Hopewell, but Tull had come to believe there was a strength to some people, and you either had it or you didn't. Something you were born with, like integrity, the ability to endure. In rough times, some folks picked themselves up while others wallowed in their failures until the day they died. He'd known plenty of both, couldn't say where it came from, only that if you were one of the latter, you couldn't just up and decide to endure one day, as much as some philosophers liked to believe. People didn't change, and there was nothing you could do for them except take their money in exchange for a drink.

There was also the question of how much she knew of Mary Jane's actions. Hell, she lived here, she had to know what was going on. Tull smiled at her and said, "My name's Larthan Tull. You wouldn't happen to have any coffee on, would you?"

"I know who you are."

He waited. Then he stepped onto the porch, and she retreated to the house.

"If he comes by, I'll tell him you were looking for him," she said.

Tull reached for the screen. When she tried to slam the door in his face, he kicked it open and followed her inside. She cowered against a wall, eyed him with trepidation but not quite fear. The outside of the house hadn't looked like much—needed paint, some shutters were loose—but the inside was downright homey. Warm wood paneling, daguerreotype portraits along one wall, each room clean if not spacious.

The widow backed into the kitchen. "You and the sheriff both come by looking for him, but I've not seen him since last night. He left and didn't come home."

"You heard what he did?"

She looked away and nodded.

"If he's smart, he's somewhere in Alabama by now." He watched her with a careful manner. She pressed herself against the wall, slid through the doorway and back into the kitchen. He followed, said, "I'm sorry for all your losses, Mrs. Coleman. Believe me, if I'd known what Mary Jane was up to before he got into it, none of this would have gotten so far. Him and the boy Ernest might both still be here.

But as it is he's in some serious trouble. I'm not sure he'll ever be able to come back to Castle. The law wants justice for that murder, whether it was justified or not."

"Did you kill those boys?"

"No ma'am."

"But you do feel like those boys cheated you?"

"They took it upon themselves to come up with a business scheme. Way I hear it, it involved selling some of your special liquor to Aunt Lou. Of course I'd cut their throats for that, but it seems I'm late to the party."

"They weren't after Aunt Lou," she said. "They never thought twice about Aunt Lou. There was no call for them to be killed."

Tull squinted, flexed his jaw. "I'm a businessman, Mrs. Coleman, not a killer. I was never looking to take anyone's son from them. Lord knows this country's lost enough for a generation."

He moved forward, into the kitchen, and she cowered against the counter. On the shelf behind her were rows of glass mason jars full of fruit already canned for winter.

"Mr. Tull," she said, "there's nothing I can do for you. I've lost everything, my husband, my son. They left me with nothing. No money, nothing but the house you're standing in, and I aim to stay here till the end. Mary Jane does come back, whatever was between you and him will get settled before he sets foot back in this house."

"As far as I'm concerned, everything's already settled. There's just a matter of some money, and then I'll never see either of you again."

He reached for a knife by the sink, and she whimpered. "Please," she said. "You have a daughter. What would you do if she were left to fend for herself?"

He stopped.

"I have nothing," she said.

Without answering, he carried the knife out of the kitchen. "You stay there," he said. He studied the living room, knife in hand, and finally he walked to the couch and stabbed at the cushions. He pulled out cotton stuffing, and he stabbed into the back of the couch, searching, searching. Then he moved to the wall and pulled down the portraits, one at a time, but behind each was the bare untouched wall. There was a grandfather clock in a corner, and he knocked it to the floor. Bells clanged. Glass shattered. He kicked at the wood on the back of the clock until it splintered and his foot went through. Nothing. No trap door, no box of money.

"Save yourself a mess, Mrs. Coleman," he yelled. "Tell me where it's at."

"I don't know," she screamed. "You leave me alone."

He moved to the bedroom and took the knife to the mattress.

"I have nothing! Nothing!"

He ignored her as he methodically set to the house. He'd burn it down if he thought that would get him his money faster. But nothing. No hoard, no cache, not in this house. Mary Jane could have brought the money with him. Could have scrambled from the Hillside, come here, packed a bag, and hit the trail. Hounds at his back, the police, Larthan Tull. What would he do, show up on Aunt Lou's doorstep and expect to be welcomed in with open arms? He couldn't go there. He couldn't go home. As long as Tull was alive, Mary Jane Hopewell couldn't keep his liquor business, and it seemed a foolhardy plan indeed to take his money and run with it. Then where would he go? What would he do?

When Tull finally gave up and left, the sun was sinking fast out of the sky like a meteor caught in gravity's grasp. He turned onto Highway 9 and chased the sun back toward the Hillside. He passed a dirty boy walking along the roadside. When the boy turned to stare at him, his eyes seemed to widen, but Tull passed him by.

After leaving the mill hill, Chambers gave up on his day and drove down Main, past the courthouse and the Hendricks brothers' filling station. He lived at the base of a hill south of town, in a single-story bungalow with pillars on the porch and a gabled roof. His children were gone—both of them buried in Europe—and he and Alma had lived here upward of twenty years, had the lot paid for in full, and could probably afford to live elsewhere. Perhaps in one of the Queen Anne or Colonial Revival homes on York Street, with their ornate columns and porticoes. Sometimes he did think it would be nice to sell all of this, move out there, and spend his weekends playing the banjo in a swing underneath a willow tree, but he wouldn't do it until he'd finished his stint as sheriff. Although he'd lived in the county all his life, some of those old farmers off in the country—Wilkesburg or Jonesville or out toward Union—wouldn't trust a man who lived in a house bigger than his family needed. Sometimes it was bad enough connecting to them when you didn't have societal airs. No good could come from moving up to York Street. Old Confederate money bought the world in town, but all it meant to a farmer was that the owner hadn't ever woken up at four to go spend a hot August day milking cows or out picking cotton.

His wife sat on the porch as he pulled up, rocking. He sat on the rocker next to her, and together they rocked in silence for a few moments. Finally she said, "How was it?"

"It's bad this time." He told her about the murder, but left out the more gruesome details. "The county rep called and said some federal agents are coming to shut down the liquor trade."

"Good. Nothing good ever comes out of that part of town."

"Most of them aren't bad people. Most of those mill folks just want to support their families. Some just need a release every once in a while."

"I'm talking about the Hillside, not the Bell."

"I know what you're talking about," he said.

She quit rocking. "You going to be here for dinner?"

He nodded. "I'm home for the day."

"I'll get it started then," she said, rising.

"It's early yet."

"I got to soak some beans."

He reached for her hand, and she put her other hand on his shoulder and squeezed it softly. After a moment, she went inside and left him out there rocking alone. Even after nearly forty years of marriage, he found it tough to discuss his job with her. They'd married when he was twenty-eight. He'd worked on the railroads in Texas and Arkansas, and as a young man he came home to marry a local debutante. In her youth she'd been rebellious, attracted to this mysterious older man with plenty of brawn and no pedigree. To her he seemed wild and free, and she wanted to be with him, or thought she did for long enough to upset her parents and get married. But, in the ways of nineteen-year-old women, she up and grew more conservative on Furman before he was ready for it. She seemed content to stay on the family farm and live out their days growing corn and milking cows. They'd bickered when he'd gotten a job in town as a deputy, and when he ran for sheriff, he thought he'd pushed their marriage to its breaking point.

If she'd ever considered leaving him, it would have been in those months of campaign where he'd had to sell himself to every roller in the county. Why was he a better choice than the previous sheriff, who was then as old as Chambers was now, a man who barnstormed and campaigned like a pugilist all the way through election day? And why had Chambers decided to make that move? What was it all for? Alma had asked him this on more than one occasion. He was a loner, and not one for self-promotion, unsuited completely for life as a politician. Yet he'd had a fire in him in his forties, a competitive soul that knew no bounds and, he'd thought, would only be satisfied by reaching the top of the local law enforcement food chain.

All he could say to his wife was, "It needs to be done."

"What does that even mean?" she'd asked.

Looking back now, he thought that if the opportunity had come up, she might have run off on him. She was nearing forty then yet still had the vestiges of her former beauty. Nothing more formidable than a woman in her thirties. But they had two teenage sons, and a war was starting. She didn't work, didn't have an income, and had her standing with society to think of. Alma Ayers came from good Methodist folk, and she participated in church functions regularly. Where would she go? He never believed she had a sense of what the world was really like—had never seen a man killed, had never been hustled or hustled anybody, had never been out of the region. But she knew she was right, and more than once she refused to leave the house when he had a stump speech to make. They'd argue and slam doors and not speak. Then she'd crawl into bed and keep her back to the middle, her body as far to the edge as she could get, and she always seemed to sleep soundly, more soundly than he ever could on those nights, not that he was afraid she'd actually run off but just out of the unease for the situation. So many chambers of the human heart.

Now in his sixties, he had to admit she'd been right all along. She knew him better than he knew himself, and at times he thought himself a buffoon for ever giving up farming. His real complaint was that the world had moved on so that a man couldn't carry on like he once could. You had to have ambition and a cold heart to stay ahead of the bill collectors, the revenuers, the machines, the dust, the labor of life, even death itself. In this way his marriage to Alma was such a comfort to him, all the more so as he grew older and the world shifted around him. The physicality of their younger years had given way, first to stagnation and then to a tense, frustrating bleed after their sons died. But now that frustration had born something new. She was separate from his work, knew almost nothing of what it was like for him to go out there day after day, the weight of his responsibility, such as it was. And what must that have been like for her? To be in the home, tending to their domestic lives, while he left her every morning? She'd been right about him when he ran for sheriff, yet she kept silent when he was up for reelection, just let him meet and greet and speak, and she congratulated him on another year of winning unopposed. In the past twenty years, she'd never said a word to make him feel like he'd wasted his life, for which he was unspeakably grateful. When he came home to her, he rekindled a sense of himself and something that would otherwise have been lost.

This afternoon, while she soaked beans and chopped vegetables in the kitchen, he went in and treaded lightly, his shoes plodding on the wood floor, and he took off his hat, kicked off his boots, and rolled up his sleeves. He eased out the squeaking back door and stood barefoot in the yard, the grass brittle and brown, a few hanks of green all that was left in the yard. Dust stuck to his feet, the ground cool beneath him. By the house, he sat on a makeshift bench he'd made last year out of two slabs of granite and some scrap wood he had lying around. Beneath it was a rusted tin pail turned upside down, and beneath that he kept a jar of whiskey. He pulled out the jar and took a sip, stared at the blue sky, the wisps above him, a bank of dark clouds in the west. He took another swig and returned the jar to the pail and wedged a pinch of chaw in his lip.

He unbuckled his holster and pulled his gun out. He carried a standard issue Smith & Wesson revolver, a six-shooter with a rosewood stock. He kept the gun polished and loaded, fired off two dozen rounds once a week to keep his aim sharp, though he'd not had to fire it in the line of service in a long time. The Hillside murder was just the beginning, he feared. Even before Prohibition the town had had its share of bootleggers, and they'd made their share of busts, but the big runners were elsewhere—Charlotte or Asheville or East Tennessee. Castle was a sleepy town, and like much of the state it hadn't seen action since 1865. The mill villages were segregated, but in town there was trouble every so often. Jim Crow, the KKK, plenty of public whippings. But folks didn't lock their doors. A man didn't just walk into a place of business—no matter what business it was—and unload on two boys with his shotgun. Chambers returned his gun to his holster and laid the holster on the ground at his feet. He leaned back against the house to watch the cloudbank roll in until Alma called him for dinner.

The day was long already when Mary Jane came out of the woods from his afternoon at the river. His clothes had near dried, but his shirt was dark with sweat on his back. His shoulder and arm ached down to the bone, and he thought maybe it would be safe to stay another night with the widow. He found her sitting on the porch swing, gazing off at the sunset as he came up and sat beside her. When she didn't look at him for a moment, he asked, "What is it?"

"Go inside."

She stared ahead and held her lips tight together in that way she did whenever he or the boys were acting up, the way that always left him feeling like a heel. He rose and opened the front door and stopped. The inside of her house was wrecked—holes in walls, ripped up furniture, toppled over shelves, and scattered debris.

"The hell?" he said. He walked inside and took in the damage and knew at once who had been here. He hurried to the kitchen and saw with relief the fruit jars were untouched. To be sure, he pulled a few away and saw the three money-stuffed jars in the back where he'd left them. He returned to the porch.

Abigail crossed her legs and looked at him fiercely, which filled him with longing. Her hair was fading an elegant shade of silver, but her eyes burned like twin fires, clear and reflecting the sinking sun today. In them he saw what must have been a formidable woman in her youth, nail-tough and stoic, so that you never knew what she might be inclined to do. Those had always been the dangerous ones when he'd been young enough to go off sparking gals, and he wondered for a moment if this was what it was like to wind up married to one. He'd dated a few, but found them harder to break than horses. Case in point was his single, failed marriage, a six-week relationship from courtship to abandonment. Never again, he'd sworn, would he edge near love, yet here he was, a toe away from the abyss. He and Abigail had taken up a few months ago, their mutual need sparked by some nameless force. He and Shorty Bagwell had always drunk down by the river where he'd met his nephews, and one night Shorty had driven off and left Mary Jane by himself, and Mary Jane took it upon himself to sleep on the widow's front porch. She'd woken him up with a broom in his face, and the two had become lovers soon after. Funny how fate operated.

"The money's still there," she said.

"I saw it."

"Larthan."

"I figured. I can't stay here tonight. I got to get that money hid better and hit the road."

She stared back off at the plummeting sun. "You do what you need to do."

"I told you I've got a plan here."

"You all had a plan. What happened to the plan with Ernest and Lee?"

"Things have changed."

She cut her eyes to him. "And will things change again?"

"Honey, I don't know."

"You better find out," she said. "I told Larthan when he was here, when he was tearing up my house—my house—I told him you and he would get things settled before you came back. So you get things settled."

"I'm doing the best I know how."

"So far the best you know how has gotten two of you killed for nothing."

She looked away from him and began to sway. The chains squeaked as the swing moved back and forth, and he glanced up at the ceiling, half expecting to see a hook come loose from the violence.

He said, "Let me get this money out of here. I'll bury it over by the woods so if Larthan comes back he won't find it among the fruit jars."

She nodded.

"This is something I can do. It ain't much, but it's something. Probably best if you don't know where I bury it. I don't think he'll come back, but..."

He waited for her to speak, but when she didn't he grunted and left her for the kitchen. He slammed the mason jars against the counter, unscrewed one and pulled out a hundred dollars, folded the bills and left them out for her. Back on the porch, she held her fist to her mouth, and her eyes were crinkled. He stopped on the step, turned, and sat next to her again. She bit her knuckles as he put his arm around her, and she leaned into his shoulder.

"It's going to be fine," he said. "Trust me."

"I can't," she said, and it was like another piece of shot tore into his chest. He didn't say anything, couldn't speak and wouldn't know what to say if he could.

She took a breath and put her hand on his shoulder, said, "I should dress this before you go." She rose and brushed her dress and went inside. A moment later she returned with a roll of dressing, which she wrapped around his shoulder and arm, same as she'd done this morning.

"My Clara Barton," he said, and she laughed a watery laugh. "Thank you," he said.

When the wound was dressed, he carried the three mason jars to the shed, picked up a shovel, and moved along to the graveyard by the wood's edge. He looked back at the house and couldn't see the porch, couldn't see Abigail, so he set to digging. She wouldn't like what he was about to do, and he wouldn't be able to explain why he was doing it if someone came up and asked. Perhaps: he needed this money, his only bargaining chip with Aunt Lou, and Aunt Lou was his only way out from under Larthan's thumb. A train of events began with this money and moved in a logical sequence to a steady income and a free life with Abigail. To keep the money, he needed to hide it from Larthan Tull. Where was the last place Larthan Tull would look? Sick bastard that he was, he would have to be evil as a snake to look in the grave of the widow's son. Therefore, that would be where Mary Jane hid the money.

Dusk found him standing at the edge of the field, sweating and shirtless, the shovel resting on the mound of soft dirt at his feet. The meat of his shoulder was ragged from the stray pellets of shot. The wound had reopened as he worked and bled through the dressing. He laid the three jars in with the boy, two thousand dollars in each, and as he filled in the grave he was uncertain if or when their contents might be recovered. If the weight of the earth might crush the glass, leaving the paper money for the worms. Unto dust.

The air held the rich smell of fertile earth, the black soil seemingly ripe along with the crops. To his right were six more graves, each marked with crumbling moss-covered stones that jutted out of the dusty clay like dominoes, and before him the ground sloped through the woods, the valley's nadir swallowed up by the thickening pines and hardwoods now shadowblack in the gloaming. Sweat dripped from his hair and ran down his face, and water splashed on the hard ground where he had not been digging. His eyes bleary from the salt, his skin hot and wet and melting into the humid air like a drop of blood in clear water.

He watched the pink backdrop fade below the oak-hickory forest on the rise to the southwest. Firs coated the misty-covered crests to the north. Beyond the western trees soot coughed out of the mill's smokestack, and farther back, the high point of the hill country was Castle Mountain. Rocky knob for which this town was named, and to which he was heading. He knew he did not have much time, so he pulled the shovel out of the mound of dirt and studied the grave. He'd shoveled some dried leaves over the cut dirt so that after a rainstorm or two perhaps no one would realize the boy had recently been undug. Nothing he could do about the appearance either way now. The widow could have seen him from the house if she were looking carefully, but if she had seen where he'd buried the money she would have been over here to stop him. He started his hike back to the house.

In the clearing between the woods and the house, the cornstalks clacked together in the wind. The pulse of crickets in the field sounded like a coming plague. Old Testament times. He carried the shovel to the barn and hung it on the wall where he'd found it hours ago. Blood from his shoulder had soaked everything—his arms, his pants, the shovel—but each scoop of soil had brushed off the blood until the shovel was dry dirt and rust and nothing else. The sticky black dirt on his hands clawed its way up his arms like the loose branches of a hickory in winter, so that he looked like he'd been wrestling with Satan himself. Which he might as well have been.

He grabbed his shirt from the peghook in the barn and walked—briskly, but not running, there was no need to run yet—to the front of the house, where the widow sat on the porch swing, rocking slowly, her gray eyes cast toward the shadow of the hills to the west. A lamp burned softly inside the window beside her. Thunder rumbled in the distance, and then heat lightning set fire to the sky, followed by more thunder. Cicadas hissed in the summer air. He kissed her cracked lips, took in the puffs under her eyes, her worn-out brittle hair, and said, "It's done."

She gazed off the porch, to the blue dusk and the ridges of the hills in the distance.

"Look at me," he said. "Give me two weeks. Just keep telling them you don't know where I'm at. In a few weeks you won't have to worry about a thing. Neither of us will."

She turned from him, and he considered saying something more, but instead walked back to the forest, past the graveyard and onto the logging road that fell to the bottoms, to the valley flatlands and the river.

Clouds moved in from the west, and with them came the occasional burst of thunder. He would follow the river south away from the town, along land he'd known all his life. He needed a frame of reference until daybreak, and then he would be able to wend his way to the mountain without doubling back into the mouths of those who would be coming. The woods swallowed him, and his feet crunched on the unyielding dirt and roots and dried leaves that had been on the ground for eight months and still had not decomposed. Leaves that would hide the boy's exhumed crypt until Mary Jane could return. If he returned.

He could not see his hand in front of his face, but he knew this trail to the bottoms. He'd traveled it twice a day for years, the copper still set up by the creek, firing steam into the night sky, the machinations of which provided higher revenues from the corn than any legal market ever had. The river flowed through here less than a hundred yards from where the path opened to the bottoms. The sky cleared and the emerging stars lit his way through the kneehigh grass, crickets abuzz and brambles scraping his legs, the night moonlit, active, indignant.

He raged and shook with feelings with which he had no acquaintance, and he found the river and stripped out of his clothes and waded into the water, stumbled to his knees and submerged himself in these cool waters for the last time. His shoulder felt like it was being assaulted by a mess of hornets, and he could feel the water brush against his wound, rinsing it clean. He rubbed his arms, his face, and then he reached for his clothes. He rose and came out cleansed of the blood and the dirt and the sweat from the evening, but his soul still choked with dirt.

He scrambled from the creek, dressed and hurried along the river south, carrying nothing with him but the night and the approaching storm and years worth of memories that he wished he could bury in the hardscrabble land of red clay.

Willie continued to swim for a long time, kicked against the current, rode downriver and swam back up to where they sat on the blanket, watching the sun blaze as it lowered in the sky, as afternoon slowly gave way to evening.

Not long before dusk, he got out, put on his shoes, and draped his shirt over his shoulder.

"Tell them I'll be home before long," Quinn said.

"They won't care, so long as you're up in the morning."

"Bye, Willie," Evelyn said. She lay on her elbows with her ankles crossed. No sign of the anger or discomfort that she'd had when Mary Jane was around. Willie's heart leapt and his palms sweated as he nodded to her and scrambled up the banks.

Once on the tracks, his skin cooled as the beads of water dripped off and the film of water on his skin dried. The tracks were still hot under his soles, but he could feel autumn lurking even in the summer's peak. The heat on his back felt good. By the time he made it back to the highway, the sun was low in the sky, the hot white given way to a dying ember in the west. A car approached from town, and when he turned to look, he saw the face of Larthan Tull behind the wheel of a big black Studebaker, which made Willie's heart skip. He wondered if the man was coming for his daughter, or just out for a drive, but whatever the case, Tull passed him by and drove on past the fire road that would have led to the river. Quinn and Evelyn were safe for now. Willie kept walking.

He wasn't ready to go back to their dull, cramped home, so he stopped by the church and tromped into the cemetery to look at names and imagine ghosts. His family had moved to the Bell when he was seven for reasons unknown to him. His uncle Mary Jane came first, followed by his parents soon after. He'd been born on a cattle farm his family had owned for three generations. He and Quinn had started school there, but they'd spent most of their time running around the hundred acres of land, hiding in the corn, swimming in the creek, living in the free spaces, the hills and the woods and getting lost so they'd have to walk until they came to a fence and then follow the fence around until they regained their bearings. Those spaces didn't exist in Castle. They had the Broad River, and they often sneaked onto others' farmland, but even then Willie couldn't escape the tightness of the Bell. The railroad tracks, the roads, the odd car humming by, the dusty smell of the mill. He made do with the town when he played, but he always felt watched, never completely alone. He found some solace in the quiet churchyard, here among the dead. Proud water oaks and magnolias buffered him from the dust and the noise of the mill village. In the back of the cemetery, woods took over, a thick meshing of oaks and poplars, tufts of cedar limbs poking out.

Today clouds gathered where the trees met the horizon, an eerie blend of orange and gray, and a cool breeze passed across the yard and sent a chill along his back. From where he entered, the closest graves were the oldest, going back to the church's founding in the 1880s, the eldest members the first to die off. These graves were square stones on the ground, and often whole families piled up here—Eunice and Eulice Clark, who both died in 1898, Annabel Clark, who died in 1901, Walter and Arthur Clark, who died in 1916 and 1918. Then there were the Harrises, the Winstons, the Joneses. Willie hopped over these stones, not wanting to step on their bodies, to wake the dead. As he walked farther into the graveyard, the sun tumbled into the horizon so that the stones' shadows were long and dark and he could no longer read the names. Heat lightning rippled through the eastern clouds, thunderless.

But here was a plot for his own family. They'd left several of their kin on the farm: his grandmother, one of his uncles who'd died in an accident with the railroad, older faces who'd moved in and out and whose connection to the family Willie was never able to place. But here there had been deaths, too: his father's sister Maggie, who had been born dumb, two miscarried siblings, both dead before they had names, and his younger sister, Hazel, named for their grandmother, who one winter grew quiet and hot and died in the night. Willie had little memory of the miscarriages. His mother was pregnant, she was going to have a baby, and then she was not. There was no baby, she stayed quiet for a time, and then she was going to have another. Then again she was not, and the house had been quiet ever since.

"Who's there?" called a male voice from behind him.

Willie turned and in the twilight saw his grandfather limping through the stones, not bothering to slide around them, stepping right on the ones that lay flat on the ground. He was still dressed in his Sunday clothes, the brown slacks worn thin in the knees, a white buttondown shirt, and his faded brown jacket.

"Who's there?" he said again. He limped forward and bumped into a stone. He rested his hand on top of the granite, eased his body around, and stopped a few feet away.

"It's Willie, sir."

"Willie? Willie who? What are you doing here?"

"I was playing, sir."

"I'm sure, Willie, I'm sure." Abel's eyes were glassy and his hair was a mess.

At that moment the leaves behind them struck up a chorus of

chirrs that sounded like locusts, though it was only wind. Still no thunder, only the fading strip of orange in the west, twilight's bruise and the speckling of starlight. Willie shifted, looked toward the road. No lights in the church, but the houses on the hill were beginning to glow. The wonder of electricity.

"A sad enterprise, ain't it boy. The Lord'll smite us all."

"I guess," Willie said.

Abel leaned back and went to rest his hand on a stone, but he missed and stumbled and fell to his knees.

"I'm all right," he said, and waved Willie away.

"Granddad."

Abel looked up at him. Cleared of the long gaze, his eyeballs rolled around in his head and focused on Willie, and he said again, "I'm all right."

Willie reached for him. "Let me help you up."

The two walked around the church onto Pinckney Road and up the hill. Pellets of gravel on the road stuck to Willie's shoes. He walked at the ready, in case his grandfather were to fall again. Each step a conscious beat up Harvey Lane to the house. His parents were not far from bed when Willie and his grandfather reached the porch. His mother opened the door to let them in and said, "Daddy, what were you doing out there?"

"Oh, I was just out for a walk and ran across my grandson."

Susannah eyed him before turning to Willie.

"Go on, get ready for bed, boy," Abel said. He turned to Susannah, shook his head.

Willie's father sat at the table, and when Willie walked in he lifted his eyes as if the lids weighed as heavy as steel. "Where's Quinn?"

"He went off with the guys. Said he'd be home soon."

"He's not off with that gal, is he?"

"No sir."

His father eyed him a moment, and Willie was glad his shorts were wrinkled, obviously having been wet from the river. He didn't want to get caught in more lies than he could keep track of. He thought of his mother and grandfather in the other room, what they hid from his father.

The whistle would sound at five-thirty, so they went to bed at dusk, every day, same as the farmers. Joe rose and said goodnight, and Susannah trailed him. When Willie returned to the front room his grandfather had taken off his shirt and shoes and sat on his bed.

"Your brother coming home?"

"He told me he'd be in soon."

Abel grunted. "He better get in before the storm gets here."

"He'll be all right," Willie said as he crawled into bed. "Are you?"

"I'm all right. Go to sleep, boy."

Abel blew out the candle and was soon snoring.

The night was hot. Willie tossed on his small, creaking mattress for a long while, thought of Quinn and Evelyn and what they might be doing. The window was open, yet their house didn't catch a breeze. Noise from the street drowned out some of the noise inside. A dog barked. One of the neighbors cursed. A bottle smashed. The houses were too close together, and Willie tried to drown out the sounds of the night by burying his head in his pillow, but it was the same every night. Music, fights, sex, talk. He always heard too much, the creak of a board in the stairs next door when Caroline Mahoney came home too late after carousing around with some older neighborhood boy—Willie's mother whispering, "That girl, such a shame, it's like no one has any decency anymore"—and Willie wondered what she'd say about Quinn tonight. Or Jimmy Clark would get in a fight with his wife after he'd had too much to drink—"Goddammit, woman, goddammit"—followed by a shattering.

His grandfather slept soundly in the other bed, a scratchy and muted snore, the most peaceful he would be until next Sunday, his next night off. A car drove down the road, kicked up dust and cinders from the mill. Crickets, the river. When the storm arrived cool air would blow in and the hiss of rain on the dusty streets would eventually lull Willie to sleep. For now, boards creaked next door, the neighbor man coming home to his wife, coughing and slurring his words and coughing some more. He'd been off somewhere private, drinking shine at a neighboring house or on someone's farm. Men did that, even on a Sunday, that thirst, that need, too powerful to wait.

Willie listened to the coughing and the drone of the wife's voice, and then the coughing slowed and her voice changed. Both noises grew louder and that was followed by the rhythmic squeaking of the mattress. Although Willie's head ached from the constant noises, a new sensation muffled the headache. He thought of Evelyn, of what she and his brother were doing at the river. Evelyn, with her porcelain skin shimmering in the moonlight, the fabric of her cotton dress sleek along her body, perhaps damp with sweat in the night's swelter. He thought of her lips, which surely tasted of peaches, thought of running his hands through her hair, and of the smooth white skin where her neck curved into her shoulder. He pulled his head out from under the pillow where he'd been suffocating and took himself into his hand, and he tried to breathe softly so that his family wouldn't hear him. He wiped his hand on the sheet, rolled over onto his stomach, and buried his head in the pillow once again, and once again he tried to dream away the fervor and commotion of night on the mill hill.

Tull had to carry the load himself this week. Time was he carried the load every week, when he was first getting his business started and only had Depot and the black man working for him in town. Back then he and Mr. Watkins, his business partner and investor, eventually made some connections up in Charlotte, a way to sell more than Castle would ever need. Keep the demand high, keep prices up and money coming in. Those connections led to back street deals brokered under cover of starlight, or midnight meetings in the corn, crates of liquor unloaded west of the city. Then there was the occasional run-in with the law—he drove Watkins's Cadillac V8, sped through the country with sirens wailing behind him, ever more in the distance. In the mid-twenties, around the time Watkins passed on, Tull hired young runners, good customers looking for a discount. Mary Jane Hopewell had run for him in the old days, though for the past few years he was nothing but a drunk, more interested in that widow woman than in matters of business. Lee Evans and Ernest Jones had been with him going on two years now. They made a good pair and he was sad to see them gone. Not least because it meant running all the loads on his own until he found a replacement.

He drove into Charlotte's east end before midnight, through neighborhoods with shaded houses behind wrought iron gates, and he pulled up to number 102 and paused. A black man came and opened the gate and Tull drove up a gravel drive, parked under a hickory tree. The night was clear yet, but had the cool acid scent of rain on its way before morning. No moon that he could see, only the faint patter of the stars above the limbs of the hickory. He walked up the brick steps to the front door, rang the bell, and waited.

As near as he could tell, Aunt Lou had been living in this house forever, and Prohibition had made her the woman to go to if you had more than a passing interest in the liquor trade. Her father had been some sort of railroad tycoon, back when Charlotte was little more than a sleepy mill town like Castle, before the industrial boom of big businesses. Banks and stockbrokers in the 1910s and '20s, a resurgence of gold mining now that the banks had failed. But before all that were the railroads, the boom and clank of steel, the chug and smoke of the engines. While tracks passed through every hamlet and outpost in the piedmont, Charlotte was the central hub of the South. Knoxville, Atlanta, Richmond—they all connected here, and Aunt Lou's money came from her father recognizing what the trains meant for commerce and distribution. Rumors lingered even now that he'd had ties to the great J.P. Morgan himself, financier of the Southern Railway. Like Larthan Tull, like Spencer Watkins, Aunt Lou's father had been a man with connections, a man who always got his way.

Like a lone puppeteer behind the scenes of an elaborate show, the man dealt everything from rugs and jewels to opium and liquor. While her siblings moved on, went to college or married, Aunt Lou stayed home with her father, a widower who seemed uninterested in remarriage or incapable of falling in love again. Some folks thought the relationship between father and daughter unnaturally close, but

Aunt Lou—so named for a mess of nephews and nieces who had scattered throughout the Carolinas like Roman soldiers cast to far-flung outposts, Brittany, Romania, Judea—remained with her father until the end and then rose up and took over his operations. What Tull would have given to have been there when she met with her father's distributors and told them what was what, that she was reorganizing the operation to focus on only the most profitable arms of her father's business.

Here was this woman who looked like your spinster aunt, the kind of churchgoing lady who would offer you tea and pinch your cheek, in charge of shipping black market goods alongside the textiles coming in and out of the city. She didn't know the first thing about making decent shine, but she knew how to get it into the hands of customers anywhere east of the Mississippi and south of the Mason-Dixon. She stayed out of Florida, and she kept away from the Chicago boys. Otherwise, she was the man, and she was the one who reached out to Tull, sent a man down from Charlotte to Castle with a letter: *Dear Mr. Tull, Through some acquaintances of mine I have procured some of your soda plant brew and have a business proposition for you.* Not so much a proposition as a procedural explanation. What choice did he have? Anyone who went his own way wound up at the bottom of the Broad River, blocks of concrete around his feet.

The bolt clicked in the lock, and another man opened the door to let Tull into the foyer without making eye contact. The house had a musty opulence to it, as though someone with money adorned the walls and then shuttered out the light. Walnut-colored walls darkened the entryway, and a red Persian rug led down the hall. On the walls were violent paintings. A ship at sea being tossed by a storm, green waves lapping up into the bows and wind rocking the sails. A close-up of an old man staggering on a sidewalk, pitched forward and leaning one hand against a fence rail. A rat scurrying across a burnt wasteland riddled with the shadows of corpses and pocked with bullet holes and bomb fragments.

Tull followed the man down the hall to a yellow-lit dining room, where sat an elderly woman with a cup of tea. She smiled as he came in and took off his hat. Petite, gracious looking, you would never peg her for the largest supplier of liquor in the Carolinas. She had close-cropped gray hair, but her bright blue eyes shined like those of a comely farm girl without a care in the world. Her cheeks were red and rounded so that she somewhat resembled Herbert Hoover, if Hoover ever had a sense of humor. When she stood, she was no taller than five feet, and she spoke with the gritty voice of a woman accustomed to work.

"Evening, Larthan, fancy seeing you again."

He set his hat on the table.

"Sit down, sit down, have a cup of tea."

At those words, the man who'd let him in now upturned a cup on the table and indicated it with his hand. "No thanks," Tull said, and sat in the chair across from her. "Not this evening."

"What brings you up here?"

"I had some trouble in Castle this week."

"Ernest and Lee find them some gals to run off with, leave you to do your own business?" She chuckled as she said this.

"No, they got shot in front of my bar last night."

She squinted. "By whom?"

"I don't know. Sounds like a man named Mary Jane Hopewell."

She nodded. "I remember him."

"My barkeep said they had some kind of argument. Seems they were plotting to cut into my business."

"I'll be damned," she said, and chuckled again. She topped off her cup of tea, said, "Let that be a lesson to you, Larthan. Business is one thing, but you got to expect repercussions if you want to hold a monopoly. Next time you might have some more intelligent competition."

"Says the tycoon."

"Heavy is the crown," she said.

"There's more to it than that."

"Oh?"

"Mary Jane owes me several thousand dollars. He's been cooking up his own secret recipe, and I believe he might stop by here before it's all said and done. Try to convince you to go into business with him. In fact, word is he may already have reached out to you."

She took another sip of her tea. "No, I've not seen him since he drove up here with your load. Must be a few years ago now."

He believed her. He could see her eyes calculating her next move and knew this information had been news to her. He said, "Mary Jane's a nobody. He makes extra whiskey on his farm—good whiskey, I'll give him that—but not enough to distribute on any scale."

"Oh Larthan, you know I'll not be doing business with anyone else down there. You're too good to me for that."

They both knew she was lying to him now, that for enough money she'd have him killed and not lose a minute's sleep over it, but he knew she wouldn't leave him to go into business with Hopewell. Hopewell couldn't bring in the kinds of profits Tull did for her. Still, it had to be said. The man had five thousand dollars hidden somewhere, and Tull aimed to find it before Hopewell could invest it in something like a business deal with Aunt Lou. Once she got the money, Tull would never get it, and Hopewell was too stupid and inept to bring in enough profits to pay off Aunt Lou and Tull both, and Tull would be forced to kill him. Not that he had a problem killing the man, and the more Tull thought about it, the less he cared about the money. Hopewell was a dead man.

He said, "I got your load this week, a little extra. Might have me some new runners by next week, but supply might be a little low until then."

"That's fine, that's fine. Next time, I might call and meet Hollis out in the fields before stopping by. They got me under an investigation, and I suspect a murder down in Castle is going to draw some attention from the big timers."

"I'll keep an eye out."

"I know you will, darling. I know it. You never did worry me with how you handled the law. I know you'll lay low when you need to. You come on by any time you like."

She lit a cigarette and blew smoke toward the overhead light, which was his signal to go. He placed his hat back on his head and walked out the front door, the man Hollis following close behind. Tull backed out of the driveway, and the man followed him in a '29 Model A. Together they caravanned out of the clean, swept streets of the east end, away from the street lamps and quiet elm-lined avenues and out into the countryside south of town. They turned off the macadam and onto a gravel one-lane framed with tall rows of summer corn, on along the rutted and washed out path until they reached a clearing big enough for their vehicles. The gravel chirred as Tull slowed and turned in. When the Model A parked beside him, the headlights winked off, enshrouding them in near total darkness.

Tull got out and opened the trunk of his car. He'd upgraded from the old Cadillac to a gleaming black Studebaker Commander with a 354-inch engine that could outpower any other car in Castle County, and in the trunk was a hidden compartment for hauling whiskey. The back suspension was double framed to accommodate the weight of two hundred gallons of shine pressing down on the axle. The man stood beside him, a specter in the night, and he remained silent as they loaded the gallon cans of whiskey into the other car.

These were the evenings Tull was most comfortable with, loading shine under cover of moonlight, the wind in the corn and the chatter of crickets, the call of a whippoorwill. A V8 for a fast getaway. Somehow his business had gotten complicated of late. Brewing whiskey itself wasn't hard, you just needed raw ingredients: corn, sugar, yeast, water. Make a mash, let it ferment in a barrel, boil it through a web of copper pipes, collect the condensed alcohol in gallon cans, and it was ready to go. In his youth in Knoxville, the challenge was always finding an out-of-the-way creek where the revenuers wouldn't find you, but once Tull had taken over Watkins's soda plant in Castle, he had access to the ingredients and a natural cover in the plumes of steam that rose out of the plant. His secret was to add some cola to the brew, which gave it a bit of color, helped with the flavor, and stretched his supply.

No, the liquor side of the business wasn't that complicated. His real business was people. It didn't take that many to run a small soda plant—twenty could do it—and he made sure they knew not to ask too many questions about what went on in boiler room three. But when you could brew a thousand gallons a week, more than enough liquor for three counties, you found yourself in business with the likes of Aunt Lou, always having to keep your guard up, not only against the tiger in front of you but also snakes like Mary Jane Hopewell, slithering through the grass at your feet. Men like him had no respect for established businesses and must be dealt with, swiftly and harshly. Like a spot of rust in a machine, they must be greased and polished away so that the machine glided along without friction, as it was supposed to do.

After loading the Model A, Tull wheeled out of the clearing, down the gravel road and back toward Castle. In the rearview, the man's headlights veered off and for a time Tull was chased by nothing but darkness. He crossed the state line, and somewhere in York County a siren wailed. From out of the blackness a police car pulled in front of him and cut him off. Tull jerked the wheel and drove two wheels onto the roadside while the car bucked beneath like an angry bronco.

He skidded to a halt before the cruiser, flexed his jaw a few times, waited. A county officer got out and sauntered over. Pants hitched up high and his white shirt tucked in. A billyclub and a revolver by his side. He had a jolly-looking face, enough jowls that the line between his chin and his neck was merely a wrinkle in the flesh. The kind of man you'd want to serve you eggs and coffee in a diner.

"Evening, officer."

"Evening."

Outside the window, the waning moon and the stars lit up the night a deep and blazing gray, and the chatter and hum of crickets sounded like a chorus across the empty farmscape. Tull said, "What's the trouble here?"

"Name, please?"

"Jimmy Malone."

"Well, Mr. Malone, what brings you out tonight?"

"I was up visiting a sick aunt in Charlotte. Heading back home."

"Where's home?"

"I work in the Bell mill."

The officer looked up and down the length of the Studebaker. "Kind of late, isn't it? Don't the whistle blow at five?"

"Yes sir, but my aunt, she's sick."

"So you said." The officer stepped back and took another look at the car. "Nice car for a millhand. She registered?"

"Yes sir, I got the paperwork right here." Tull reached for the glove compartment but the officer tapped on the door with his billyclub.

"Why don't you step out for a minute?"

Tull thought for a moment about paying the officer off. These hicks all had a price, but Tull was in no mood to negotiate. The door creaked as Tull swung his feet out, planted them in the loose chert. A chill in the air, the scent of cedars and earth. A shelf cloud hovered low in the distance, an anvil in the dark. Wind tossed nearby treelimbs, turned the maple leaves upward.

"Since you work at the Bell, I reckon you've heard about the murder that took place last night?"

"Oh, it was terrible." Tull shook his head.

"The man that did it is somewhere out in the backcountry here."

"You don't say."

"Mary Jane Hopewell. You know him?"

"I heard about him, but I never met him myself."

"Never met him. Well. This state's been having all kinds of trouble lately. Bootleggers and murders and men on the run. You wouldn't be involved in any of that, would you?"

"Oh, no sir. Clean as a whistle, I am. In church every Sunday." Tull could feel lightning in his veins, and he realized he was watching his moment for paying the man off slide away, but he didn't care. Insects rattled in the fields, and the breeze blew against him. Somewhere, a toad bellowed. Off in the distance a spider's web of lightning spun its way across the sky.

"Why don't you open this trunk for me? I hate to call out a fellow Christian, but—"

"Oh, I understand, officer. Here." Tull walked around and unlocked the trunk. Inside were a spare tire and an iron.

The officer poked his head in, felt around with his hand, and glanced at Tull.

"Seems this liner is a little loose," he said.

The officer pulled the spare tire out of the trunk, the tire iron. He lay the iron on the ground before reaching in to pull up the lining of the trunk. Below it was empty, Tull having delivered his whiskey.

The officer said anyway, "Well, well. Mighty strange thing for you to have in a car. Trap door like this."

Lightning moved out of the clouds and streaked across the sky, flickered down in an angry, jagged shot. Cool rain began to sprinkle down on them.

While the officer still had his head in the trunk, Tull scooped up the tire iron from the ground. The officer pulled away and looked at him too late. Tull swung the iron into the man's forehead, and it was as easy as striking iron in a forge. Again and again until the officer's skull was stove in and sticky black blood pooled about the roadside, dampened the weeds that grew out of the gravel, spread into the grasses.

When he was finished, Tull wiped his hair out of his eyes and rubbed the iron over the man's shirt. Blood smeared across his back. Then he reached down and pulled the pistol out of its holster, a Smith & Wesson 38-44. Brand new, looked like it had never been fired. Tull got back in the car and drove off into the approaching storm.

PART TWO

L ight the color of blue dusk feathered into the room. Willie woke to the sound of his grandfather stirring and rising and limping outside to make water before enough light came out where the entire block would see him. Five months here and he still wasn't used to indoor plumbing. Perhaps there were things in a man that became fixed at birth, and people lied to themselves until they grew too old for it to matter. Willie closed his eyes and wondered what it must be like to be an old man. Abel was cut from an ancient mold, conceived right in a Confederate battlefield, the way men weren't made any longer. He could handle a rough mattress in a crowded room, he said, but he was seventy years old. There came a time. Willie wondered if the time were now. No one had noticed the old man addled and aloof when they came in last night. His father had shrugged them off and his mother—well, he didn't know what she made of it all.

The man had fainted before and she had promised him to silence. Months ago, he and Quinn and their father had been in the garden, and Willie had come in for a glass of water. From the kitchen, he overheard his grandfather say, "I'm OK."

"What happened?" asked his mother.

"I don't know. I was here, and then I felt dizzy, and then you were here."

"You ought to take a day off."

"I can't." He coughed a wet loose cough, as if he had gravel in his chest. "Best not tell Joe. You know how he gets."

Willie tried to sneak back outside, but his foot caught on one of the chairs, and the chair scraped across the floor. His mother ran in, and the two of them stared at each other.

"Willie," she said. "Come in here for a moment. It's all right."

His grandfather sat on the bed, and he smiled at Willie. "Hey, boy."

"Willie, your grandfather just fainted, but he's all right. You can't mention this to anyone, not even Quinn."

"Why?"

"Because if someone thinks your grandfather is ill, he'll have to quit work. Your father and Quinn, they both work so hard, and they've got a lot on their minds without having to worry about your grandfather. Promise me, Willie?"

"OK," he said, and it was like a wall fell between them. When he went back to the garden, he debated for a moment whether to tell his father, or Quinn, but he had kept quiet. Now he wondered if there were anything he could have done, if he could have changed the course of history or at least prepared his family for what was looming. Had he told his father, perhaps they could have saved up. Done something. Years later he would understand there was nothing to be done. No single trigger, no instigating event. Life carried on and then it was over.

As morning crept in Willie struggled out of bed, got dressed, and shoved at his brother. "Quinn," he hissed, but his brother lay there an unmoving lump. In the kitchen pots and pans clattered as Susannah heated up the coffee and boiled a pan of hominy. An oil lamp burned on the table. His grandfather sat there with the same bleary look he always wore.

Joe came in and asked, "How you feel, Abel?"

"Another day."

"That it is."

His father took a seat, pinched his lips and widened his eyes like he always did when he had nothing more to say. They waited on Susannah to finish with breakfast. Quinn came in a moment later, nodded at the family, and sat next to Willie. Their mother put the plates in front of them and sat down. After saying grace, Joe looked over at his eldest, the boy dragging like a stubborn mule. Shadowed and bloodshot eyes and a sleepy gaze. Up to all manner of sin.

"What time did you get in last night?" Joe asked.

"Not too late," Quinn said.

"Got them raccoon eyes."

"I'm all right."

They scraped at their plates a few minutes, their father clearly warming up for whatever lesson he wanted to impart. A man took on responsibilities, their father believed, and the boys needed to learn. Their father prided himself on setting that example. He'd had his hell-raising youth, which his sons had only heard tell of from their uncle Mary Jane, but in the years after the war, Joe's future was much less certain. Willie was not yet born, but the whispered tales suggested his father was bad to drink and hit the bottle with more fury than Mary Jane ever did. Whatever those monsters were, Prohibition was his salvation—that or the birth of his second son. "It's going to be a hot shift," he finally said.

"I said I was all right."

"Long day."

"Joe," Susannah said.

"The boy was out half the night and now he's going to work a long shift tired. He won't last long with that kind of lifestyle, and we can't afford for him to get hurt or lose his job."

"Ah, leave the boy alone."

"You stay out of this, Abel."

"Joe," Susannah said again.

"What? Y'all want to let this boy tromp all over the county? He can't concentrate, he'll get his arm sucked into a loom. Then where will we be?"

"It's a long life, son."

"Hell, I know it's a long life. I'm trying to make something here, so when I'm your age these boys won't have to be worrying about me. Maybe they can think about doing something else with their lives."

Abel said, "If my being here's a burden, you let me know. I can move along any time."

"And where you going to go?"

"Joe," Susannah said again.

"What happened to you last night?" Joe continued. "Who's going to take care of you, something bad happens out there?"

Abel shook his head. The rest of the family studied their food.

When the whistle sounded, the three men and Willie stood and put their plates in the sink. As they were leaving Susannah hugged her father and whispered, "I'm sorry, Daddy."

"It don't matter anyway," he said.

They walked down the hill toward the mill. Mist clung to the earth, but once the sun broke above the horizon and the dawn-pink sky caught fire, the mist would burn away and the oppressive day's heat would settle in, right as the machines inside the mill warmed to full force. They trudged through the iron gates where the mill waited for them like a prison, looming square and brick and tall, the fortress of Castle. Men trickled in and by six the rooms had filled for the day's labor. The clack and clank of the machines, the stale concrete, the smell of oil and sweat. Looms bobbed and battery fillers refilled bobbins of thread. A slight breeze from the fans blew hot air into the morning. Remnants of spit tobacco were sticky and wet and sour on the floor. As the machines heated throughout the day, the men sweated and stank, and lint fogged the rooms.

It was this life their father wanted to keep them away from. Scrimping. Looking at your budget and wondering how people got along. Freeing yourself from the company store. Your only options the mill or the military. The whole country was in bad shape. Land that a family had owned for generations suddenly became worthless. Their grandfather told the story over and again. "We borrowed against the farm if the crops had a bad season, but one year the credit just dried up. Bank said our farm wasn't worth what we owed on it." Abel found himself an old widower who couldn't pay his mortgage, forced to come live with his daughter's family. Joe and Abel had always had an uneasy time around each other, going back before the war, when Joe and Susannah were both farm kids. Then there wasn't a lot to do out in the country but ride around drinking, sneak off, and try to spark.

Joe and Susannah's courtship was the stuff of legend in the Hopewell household. Willie knew the story the same as he knew the stories in Genesis, how one evening Joe brought a bottle over to her farm, how the two of them sipped whiskey in the barn loft, giggled, and lay down together. It was just that one time, a first for the both of them, but she later had to go to her parents and tell them what was what. Abel rode over to the Hopewells' farm, his fedora low over his eyes, and a few weeks later Joe and Susannah were married. They lived in her childhood bedroom for two years. Quinn slept in a crib in the corner, and Joe worked for Abel for the same wage Abel paid every other farmhand.

When the war broke out, Joe joined the army and spent a year in a trench in France. Mostly days of boredom, the pop-pop of gunfire over No Man's Land far off or absent altogether, but the lines shifted and for a time Joe found himself shooting at muzzle flashes in the distance. He returned to South Carolina with memories he never planned to revisit, and the first thing he did when he arrived was go out with Mary Jane and get drunk. A regular occurrence until the beginning of 1920. Susannah was pregnant with Willie then, and the farm was failing. They'd moved from Susannah's childhood bedroom to a sharecropper's shack out of the main house, but it wouldn't be long before they'd have to leave Abel and the farm altogether for the mills. Joe had one last drink on January 16, 1920, the day before the Eighteenth Amendment kicked in, and he hadn't touched the bottle since.

Willie was born, then Hazel, and crops failed during two years of drought. Five mouths to feed, the children too young to do much. Susannah's mother was ailing, and Abel wanted to sell off part of the farm. Joe and Susannah followed Mary Jane to the Bell, left Abel and his dying wife to what was left of the farm. Days blurred, time measured only by the quick sprouting of the children. Susannah lost a baby, and then they moved into the house on Harvey Lane. Their daughter, Hazel, died of scarlet fever one winter after weeks of a strep infection. Susannah lost another baby, during childbirth, and this would be her last. The doctor tore up her insides trying to save her life. Ether that was supposed to go over her nose spilled into her eye and burned like hot grease. A smell Willie would remember every time the doctors came to the Bell to perform tonsillectomies, and the smell of ether emanated up and down the village. Then came days of coldness, days of fire. His parents argued and Joe worked longer hours, began saving, pennies here, pennies there. They scrimped on meat. Joe was in line for a promotion when Susannah's mother died of typhoid fever and Abel came to live with them. Although they hadn't been saving much for the past few months, they were OK for now, so long as everyone worked. Otherwise, well.

As the day wore on, rumor of murder out by the Hillside spread through the mill. In weave room #6, Joe and Abel sat at looms and watched a shuttle pass back and forth while their neighbor Mink Skelton repeated the tale again and again, same as he'd done after church yesterday. The men bickered over what was the truth, Mary Jane with his side business, the viciousness of Larthan Tull.

"You seen the sheriff yet, Joe?"

"He came to the house yesterday afternoon. Looking for Mary Jane."

"I hope your brother's long gone to Alabama by now."

"Knowing him, he could be anywhere."

Mink grew quiet, said, "Rumor has it Larthan's on the hunt for him as well."

"Wouldn't surprise me," Joe said. "Also wouldn't surprise me if Larthan was the one that did the shooting."

"You think he'll shut down for a while? Lay low?"

Joe spat. "He won't be closing down. Benefits too many people."

For a few moments the men worked the rows of looms in silence, so all you heard was the hum of the shuttlecocks. Then Mink cleared his throat and said to a weaver named Leuico King, "Did you see Larthan when you were at the Hillside?"

"Naw, he wasn't there. Never is, when I drop by."

"He must work at night."

"Maybe so."

Half the men in the mill bought whiskey off Tull, and although most had seen him around, few knew him well enough to call him Larthan to his face. For all the sins he brought into town, he kept them behind closed doors, as whispers in the night ever since the start of Prohibition. The story of how Tull and Watkins had gone into business, how they used the steam and sugar in the soda factory as a front for producing libations beyond Watkins Cola. Spenser Watkins was a local man and kept them all in good supply, be it soda pop, beer, or whiskey, but no one seemed to know what to make of Larthan Tull. Everyone heard tell of murders, a man on the run from federal agents, all manner of seedy connections in Tennessee. There were rumors of the mean streets and the Memphis underworld, and of the rain that carried rubbers and wastepaper as it sluiced through the winesoaked gutters of Knoxville. Men in dark suits and with heavy eyelids, Colt revolvers under their coats, even Italian thugs from Chicago. Who was this man who ran the bootlegging trade in the sleepy back alleys of the Carolina piedmont? A town now split between mint juleps in rockers on the front porch and slugs of rotgut in junkyards, between nine o'clock bedtimes after prayers of repentance and joy, and card games above the diner, the curses and whores and carrying on.

The men quieted as Willie came through with the broom, sweeping up lint and dust and tobacco spit on the floors.

Mink spat where Willie had just swept and said, "Boy, you must be getting to be a short timer around here."

"School starts in three weeks."

"Mmm," Mink said. "Hey, Joe, when was the last time you saw Mary Jane anyway?"

"Not since he plowed into that woman's flowerbeds."

The men laughed.

"We seen him out at the river yesterday," Willie said.

The men all hushed, and Joe said, "Say you did."

"Me and Quinn, when we went swimming."

"He wasn't brewing liquor out there, was he?" Mink said. "Getting you to run it for him?"

"Naw sir."

"Rumrunner Willie," Mink said, laughing.

"He say anything to you?" Joe asked.

"Naw sir. Just swam a while, put on his clothes, and left."

Joe narrowed his eyes at his son. Something must have lodged into place, like a bullet sliding into a fresh chamber, because he sat up and yelled, "Quinn!" He got off his stool and jogged to where his elder son was gathering a fresh batch of bobbins in the spinning room. Willie followed.

"Quinn," Joe said.

"Yes sir?"

"Did you meet Evelyn down at the river yesterday afternoon?"

Quinn glanced at Willie, who fiddled with his broom.

"Your brother didn't say anything. I just want to know if she told you anything about the Hillside Tavern. About her father and Mary Jane?"

"Not to me. Likely she don't know anything more than we do."

"Willie said y'all saw Mary Jane at the river."

"What's that got to do with anything?" Quinn asked.

"Boys, what happened yesterday? I just want to know what's going on with my brother."

"We were swimming," Willie said. "Mary Jane was there, that's all."

"He didn't say anything?"

The brothers eyed each other, and Quinn said, "He was just Uncle Mary Jane. You know how he is."

Joe nodded. Willie wished he could ask his father for advice. About Mary Jane and the whiskey trade. About Evelyn Tull and her father and Quinn. About why, last night, his grandfather showed up in the cemetery. Willie was caught up in a world of secrets, and though he might not know what to do about it, he knew that when the truth eventually came out, he would be guilty along with every-one else. There were things he couldn't say to his father, obligations he had to others, but it left him cut off from everyone. Quinn, his mother, his grandfather, Mary Jane. They all had secrets. Did you just learn to forget and let the world carry on around you? He went back to sweeping up the afternoon's accumulated dust. He thought of his uncle, lugging those two cans of shine away from the river. He thought of his grandfather's glazed eyes, of Quinn lying on the riverbank with Evelyn Tull. And he thought of the sheriff, his badge and his gun saying he was the law.

Chambers spent the last day of August driving around the countryside, smoking a cigar and pondering his next move regarding the Hillside murders. When he returned to the station the sun was long past its zenith and rocketing away from the still-blue sky. A long black Ford was parked out front. In the waiting room were two men in gray suits with slicked back hair and rounded, ruddy Irish features. Chambers pegged them for the feds he'd been hearing about before they said word one.

"Good afternoon, Sheriff," said the first. "I'm Agent Jeffreys, and this is Agent O'Connor."

"Gentlemen," he said.

"May we have a few words?"

"Step on back."

He led them through the doors past the deputy to his office. A map of the county on the wall in yellow parchment, a clutter of files on his desk beside the typewriter and a copy of Erskine Caldwell's *Tobacco Road*. A metal filing cabinet with the top drawer ajar.

"Have a seat," he said, and sat himself behind the desk. "So let me guess. You're here about Mary Jane Hopewell."

"We're here to defend the United States from evil and corruption," said Jeffreys. "Mary Jane Hopewell is part of why we're here."

"And Larthan Tull."

"That's another part."

They studied him, and he folded his hands and leaned back in his chair. The skin on his forehead was sticky, and he could feel a damp spot on the back of his shirt. "Well?" he said.

O'Connor crossed his arms and stared, like a limo driver or a bodyguard. Here but not here. Finally, Jeffreys spoke: "We're stationed in Columbia. There's a thousand murders in a thousand small towns across this great country every year, and ordinarily none of them make their way to the FBI. Our job isn't to step on the toes of the local police, or even the state police. But the nature of the shootings last week attracted the attention of some people up north. One of our divisions is responsible for patrolling the liquor trade in the southeast. Understand, we don't bother with small-time mountain shiners, for the most part. It's the national distributors we're looking to squelch out. Most of the big runners are over in the mountains—they've got an investigation going on in Lexington, one over in Knoxville. But O'Connor and I currently have an investigation up in Charlotte. You've heard the name Aunt Lou?"

"Sure," Chambers said. "She's famous."

"She's also elusive, and she must have a good system set up in her house because the few times we've gone in to try and bust her, someone's already tipped her off and her place is cleared out. We don't know how big her operation is, but we suspect she might be the single biggest supplier of illegal whiskey on this side of the Mississippi."

"She's not in Castle, if that's why you're here."

"But Larthan Tull is," Jeffreys said. "You see, Aunt Lou distributes. She has runners working for her and connections all over the southeast, but she doesn't brew it. She lives in the city limits. There's no place for her to brew it. Folks'd see steam floating over her neighborhood or see her buying corn and sugar and copper all in large quantities. But I've been in her house. She doesn't have anything that remotely resembles a still. We've searched it up and down. She doesn't make it herself, which means she brings it in from somewhere else, most likely several sources."

"So Larthan Tull is one of her suppliers."

"We think he's her biggest supplier," Jeffreys said. "We're pretty good at going around sabotaging stills along rivers and creeks, even in the deepest hollows, but, as I'm sure you're aware, there's something futile about that. Makes a man feel like he's wasting his time on small fries. Fortunately for us, and as I'm sure you're also aware, Tull has a better setup."

"His soda factory."

"Provides a pretty good cover, don't it? To make soda he needs to buy a lot of the same ingredients he'd need for whiskey, and no one's going to think twice about billows of steam coming out of a factory."

"We understand why you might want to turn a blind eye to his operation," O'Connor said, the first words Chambers had heard him speak. He had a gravelly voice, with an accent that Chambers had never heard before. Vowels elongated and bent out of shape. Not Irish, despite his name. Sounded German.

"A very blind eye," Jeffreys said.

"He's a respectable townsman," O'Connor went on. "A little liquor trade isn't that much of a disruption."

"Even though it's a federal offense."

"But the fact is, he's making more than a small town could ever drink. He's the largest supplier for one of the largest distributors in the country, and we aim to put a stop to him and her both."

As the two rattled back and forth, Chambers tried to follow what O'Connor was saying, minus interruptions from Jeffreys. O'Connor spoke like he was teaching children in Sunday school while Jeffreys grew redder and redder, until his face resembled a plum tomato, and he stood and leaned over Chambers's desk. "He's undermined the Constitution of the United States," he barked, and he beat his fists on the desk. "He's a menace to our entire society. A threat to women and children and good Christians everywhere. A stain on the map of our great country and an insult to God."

"Hey listen, fellas," Chambers said, standing as well. "My job's to keep order in this county, and I do a fair job of it."

"You do a fair job?" Jeffreys wiped the sweat off his reddened face, turned and paced a lap around the room. O'Connor still sat off to the side, unflappable, rubbing two fingers along his lower lip and gazing down at the desk. "A fair job," Jeffreys said again. "Will you listen to this guy?"

"Bust him, then," Chambers said. "You don't like how I've run my investigation, or how I've handled certain things, that's fine. Go on and arrest Larthan Tull, see if I care. Do me that favor."

"It would be a favor, wouldn't it? Your dirty work. Just like a redneck sheriff to not want to take up his responsibilities as a citizen of this great country."

"Easy, both of you," O'Connor said. He looked at Chambers with gray eyes and tired lids. His voice like a smokefilled box of rocks. Maybe he was older than he looked, not some thirty-year-old punk who'd never had to make a real decision. "Sheriff, did you hear about the patrolman that got beat to death the other night up in York County?"

"Yeah, I heard about him," Chambers said. The news had come over the wires, an officer bludgeoned with a blunt object, his firearm stolen. He'd been on patrol looking for Hopewell, and no one seemed to know what to make of it. Chambers knew Hopewell, knew that even if he did kill the boys in front of the Hillside, he wouldn't have murdered an innocent police officer. Chambers knew that.

"We think that's related. We don't know how, and I doubt you do either. Our job here is to help you and the other local police put a stop to this violence. Restore order."

"Somebody's got to," Jeffreys said, and O'Connor cleared his throat.

"We'd like to take out Tull," O'Connor went on, "but there'd be another one soon enough to take his place. We really want Aunt Lou, and we need your help to get her."

"Do you boys have a plan, or you just want to pile in my car and drive up and get her?"

"We would if we could," Jeffreys said. "That'd be new for you, wouldn't it? Going up and arresting the bad guy without hesitation."

"But we've all got procedures to follow," O'Connor said. "So we'd like you to help us. Keep an eye on Tull, his movements. Take notes if you can so in a few weeks we'll have a good idea of where he is and when, and what kind of schedule he keeps. We'd like to catch him in a run to Aunt Lou's."

"That's well and good, fellas, but I got to tell you, driving into town in that fancy strange car's liable to have already got the neighbors calling each other to gossip about you. I'll bet Larthan's already heard that the feds have stopped by the police station. There might have been better ways of keeping this operation a secret. Call maybe, instead of showing up."

Before Jeffreys could respond, O'Connor said, "We understand, but we don't think that'll be a problem. We plan to talk to him ourselves before we leave town."

"And say what, exactly?"

"Throw him off. Make him believe he's the one we're after. So long as he doesn't know we know about him and Aunt Lou, he'll think we're just passing through, hassling him. We do that on occasion."

"What?"

"Pass through and hassle Tull, ask to inspect the Hillside Inn, cite him for some violation or another."

Chambers tried not to let the surprise show on his face. These guys knew Tull, had been coming through town without him realizing it for how many years? When he was young and green in the world, he made all kinds of mistakes, usually when he switched jobs. At eighteen, he'd joined the railroad, headed west. Talked big with some guys about South Carolina until he'd found out they'd been through his state more times than he'd left his county. One of them had even spent time in the state penitentiary, and this knowledge had left Chambers hot in the face for three days, the world suddenly much larger than he'd ever been prepared for. And in Texas he'd worked on a ranch for a few months, forgot simple things like latching a pin to keep cattle in. Somewhere in all those years, before he'd moved back to Castle and married Alma, he'd learned humility.

His twenties a decade of discovering his limits well enough that his thirties, forties, and fifties were good years for him. He knew what he was capable of, and knew he knew, and moved with an ease about him because of that knowledge. But now, approaching seventy faster than he'd like to contemplate, it felt like he was regressing, the world passing him by and he just a dumb hick who couldn't keep up.

Jeffreys looked like he was about to say something more, but O'Connor let Chambers off the hook and said, "We best get on. On your desk there is a card where you can reach us. We'll call you before we make another move, but we'd appreciate it if you could start keeping tabs on Tull for us."

"All right, fellas. I'll be seeing you."

"Soon," Jeffreys said.

When they'd gone, Chambers put his feet on the desk and opened the bottom drawer of his file cabinet, where he kept a flask of whiskey for days such as this, but it wasn't there. A box of shotgun shells, some old receipts and scraps of paper, a rusted horseshoe he kept around for good luck, but no flask.

He slammed the drawer shut. "Those sons of bitches."

Mary Jane woke to the sound of dogs. He'd made camp on a bed of pine needles with branches of cedar for a pillow. Somewhere in the distance a hound bayed, followed by a chorus of throaty barks. He ran through the woods along the eastern slope of Castle Mountain. More of a tall hill than a mountain, but a definite peak among the piedmont landscape. The trees thinned at an overlook and he allowed himself to peer down the mountain. Lights flickered in the land below, half a dozen men with lanterns chasing the dogs. He moved on.

Soon he reached a creek, bubbling its way down the slope of the mountain, and he splashed into the water and ran against the current. The cold water bit against his shins and numbed his feet. Where the creek widened, he stepped on a stone, and when he stepped back into the creek he sank to his waist. Bone-cold water sluiced along and sloshed against his chest, so cold it jarred him awake. What was he doing out here? The men were probably out hunting, but something told him they were the law, and if they were the law he needn't fear them. It was Larthan Tull he was running from. But something told him Larthan Tull had a hand in the law, so an enemy of Tull was an enemy of the law. The current beat against him and he hiked up the mountain through the water, stepping on stones where he could, allowing his feet to sink into the sandy muck where he couldn't. As the woods thickened around him, the sound of the dogs faded.

After a time he stepped out of the creek and onto the mossy bank. The dripping water weighed his clothes down like irons on a chain gang. He wrung out his pockets, felt like his clothes were bursting sacks. Trying not to think of a chance encounter with a copperhead, he took off his shoes and upended them to drain out puddles of water. So wet and chattering from the cold in the dark, he slid into a dreamlike state whereby time passed on two parallel tracks, the real of the night and the dogs and his busted shoulder numb from the chill of river water, and the warm and fluid wander of thoughts as though his mind clung to the vestiges of some lost dream. The widow's bed, perhaps, a haven, a return to his free life. Time before the road, before the weight of responsibility for Ernest and Lee, before he'd found himself in a corner cell, the door guarded by Tull and his henchmen. The world was not a kind place to those forced to reckon with the here and now of their lives. Like the shot of a rifle, the irrevocable strike of the hammer against the firing pin, Mary Jane had been ejected from his world and now roamed without a center, with only a sense of loss.

When he'd dried his clothes as best he could, he focused on the real and tried to study where he was. Above him he searched for something recognizable in the sky. He found the North Star at the end of the Little Dipper, for all the good it did him. Ancient navigators may have read the sky's asterisms to find their way across darkened seas, but Mary Jane had never been one for navigation. He set on up the mountain, figuring he was far enough from the dogs that they'd lost any scent of him. Tree frogs and whippoorwills and rustling limbs created a racket, but there was no sound of man.

He stumbled into a clearing near the mountain's plateau. The trees fell away and starlight shimmered from a liquid sky. In the clearing were the burnt remains of a house, scraps of charred wood long gone, the fire a distant possibility. A few stray beams jutted from the ground, but the only thing whole, on the far side of the rubble, was the rock hearth, which stood untouched like the day it was made. In the heart was a fire and beside the fire sat a figure in the shadows.

Mary Jane crept closer and saw the man had no eyes. He wore tattered clothes and rested his hands on a cane. He faced blankly into the crackling fire and didn't stir, even as Mary Jane stepped into the rubble.

"Hello?"

The man turned to him.

"Sir?"

"The Lord sent you to me."

The man's face was grimy with soot, and the sight of the bleak eyeless sockets raised the hairs on Mary Jane's neck. Gone were the days you could trust a stranger on the road. Hard times had turned strangers into villains, drifters into thieves and bandits. Cautiously, Mary Jane drew up next to the fire, lay his satchel by the hearth, and sat on the ground.

"There's some beans left in the pot," the man said. "Ain't much, but you're welcome to them."

Mary Jane had subsisted on stolen fruit for two days, plucked tomatoes, apples, squash. His belly rumbled in protest, so he said, "I thank you. I'm obliged."

The man nodded. "The Lord will provide."

Mary Jane spooned hot beans from the pot, swallowed without chewing. The man closed his eyes and appeared to be sleeping. Through bites, Mary Jane watched him breathe. When he scraped the empty pot with the spoon, the man's eyelids opened, but if he was disappointed that he still had no eyes with which to see, his face didn't show it. He licked his lips, grabbed a stick at his side, and poked at the fire. Flames shot up and sparks swirled like fireflies before it all settled down to the coals.

"You're welcome to put another log on this fire for me."

He aimed with the stick at a cord of chopped wood.

When he'd completed his task, Mary Jane said, "You live here?"

"No, I come down from Tennessee. Name's Ephraim." The man cleared his throat. "I go where the Lord calls me, and last week he called me to this here mountain to pray."

"You and me both."

"You a Christian man?"

"Baptized in the Broad River when I was twelve."

"That's good. You're saved then."

"I hope so."

"Ain't no hope about it. You committed yourself to Christ, which is all you need for forgiveness."

"I've got a lot to be forgiven for."

"Doesn't matter. For God so loved the world that he gave his only begotten son, that whosoever believeth in him should not perish but have everlasting life."

"I don't know that I believe that anymore."

The man swished his mouth as though freeing food from between his teeth. He said, "Even Jesus had his time in the wilderness."

They sat for a time listening to the crackle of the fire. Mary Jane shifted, wishing he had a bottle of whiskey to help him sleep. The old man looked like he might be holding a nip of something, but all that talk of Christians and the Lord made Mary Jane suspect the man for a teetotaler. He stayed quiet and let his hands tremble and his heart beat too fast for him to rest. The fire warmed his wet clothes and made him more comfortable than he'd been since leaving Abigail. A glass of her special brew would go right nice, would help a man forget his troubles as he cozied up to the fire. Thoughts of Abigail, however, hurt his heart, to know what hurt he'd caused with his liquor scheme and what further hurt she'd feel if she ever learned what he'd done with those jars of money.

He'd been a midcareer drunk who couldn't seem to grow out of those wild days of youth. He'd watched his brother marry, have children, become a man, and although he didn't begrudge Joe a thing, he felt the disapproving eye of their father every time he contemplated his wasting life, which only made him drink more. In truth, he loved the thrill of it, finding those honky-tonks hidden from the eye of the law, those secret codes to gain entrance, those nights of one-upping his brethren inebriates with their war stories and their big talk. He grew older and one day found himself no longer the young buck at the bar, but rather the alderman of Lethe, the guide for boys like Ernest Jones and Lee Evans, Tommy Cope and Shorty Bagwell, boys who wanted to belong in the night's society and looked to him for the right social cues. Hell, there wasn't anything complicated about it. You showed up, embarrassed yourself a time or two by over-imbibing until you found that line and conducted yourself with great success in the likes of the Hillside Tavern. If you had half a brain, you even learned to shoot pool.

As the senior wild man, Mary Jane considered it his duty to do more than set the example, to stay out later and tell taller tales. His latent, unrefined entrepreneurial instincts gave him visions of his own whiskey empire. Larthan Tull did all right for himself, that was for sure, if that mansion he lived in was any indication. Mary Jane was a simple man at heart. All he wanted for himself was a steady income without having to pick up day labor. He loved to drink, so why couldn't he find a way to make a living at it? One rule about drunken schemes is that if you think of an idea in a stupor, chances are nothing will ever come of it. If you mention that idea to a friend, still nothing will come of it. But once you mention that idea to two friends, you've set the game in motion and there is no turning back.

That was how Mary Jane found himself in a fledgling business with two rangy mountain boys. Lee was a bucktoothed millworker who always wore the same pair of patched-up overalls and a shit-eating grin. Like so many mountain folk, the boy and his father had shown up at the Bell with the clothes on their backs, a Protestant work ethic, and no story to explain their origins. Ernest was even more of a mystery, dropped off like a dog in the country for Abigail Coleman to take in shortly after the sheriff had shot her own son. Ernest refused to speak above a whisper for nearly two years, and only recently, as his friendship with Lee blossomed, had he offered signs of a personality. Mary Jane loved them both as fellow strays.

"Come on, boys, we're going to make us some money," he said to them one night while they were drinking on Abigail's porch. The three of them enjoyed some of her special brew on a regular basis, a brew that helped him sleep easier than anything Tull cooked up, and made the next day more pleasant as well.

Ernest and Lee smiled through Mary Jane's sales pitch, how they could distribute Abigail's product as a select, high-end mountain shine. When he finished, he called into the house, "Abigail! Come on out here! We got us a plan."

At the end of his rambling pitch, this time embellished beyond what he'd cooked up with Ernest and Lee, so that he'd about convinced himself he was on way to being an outright millionaire, she said, "Y'all do what you want to do, but know this: When Mr. Tull comes knocking on my door, I'm going to tell him exactly where to find you."

"He's got more business than he knows what to do with. We're not opening us a tavern here. Why would he even care what we do?"

She mm-hmmed him and went back in the house, left him flustered and struggling to salvage his brilliant idea. He doubted old Mr. Tull, as she called him, would ever come knocking, but if he did, the least Mary Jane would need from her was her silence.

Well. She'd kept her silence all right, even while Tull ransacked her house. Building a business takes some effort, and, drunk most of the time though he was, he passed more and more time with her, less and less time at the Hillside. She went from tolerating him to— what? He wasn't sure how she really felt about him, in the deepest corners of her heart, but he knew how he felt about her, and it startled him to think how fast passion seized hold of you, like a conflagration of your very soul.

Dogs bayed in the distance, and the old man stirred and cocked his head, farther from sleep than Mary Jane thought possible. How to explain his own presence on this mountain, if the old man asked? It occurred to Mary Jane that you wouldn't find your way up here unless you were on the run or, apparently, were called by the Lord.

"I've got some business up in Charlotte," he said quickly. "In a few days."

Ephraim nodded, as if all were clear.

"I appreciate the supper."

"You're welcome to bed down for the night. It's not much, but it's a long ways to some place more hospitable."

"You know how far we are from Charlotte?"

"I don't reckon I've ever been to Charlotte."

"I know it's two hours by car from Castle, but we're a ways from town and I've got no car."

"That's a different perspective, being able to get in an automobile and go wherever you please. I remember when it was a day's ride if you wanted to get anywhere, less of course you already lived where you wanted to go."

"I've never thought much of it," Mary Jane said.

"No, I don't suspect most folks do. You in the war?"

Mary Jane nodded. Then he grunted his assent.

"You've been around the world then, and seen about all there is to see."

"I don't know about all that."

"No, I wasn't always blind. You don't need to feel sorry for me and what I haven't seen, because there's only one sight I aim to see, the only sight worth seeing, and no automobile nor ship nor airplane can take you there. People move so fast, they're losing their sense of direction. You say you got business up in Charlotte, which I respect. Every man needs a profession, but let me ask: what kind of business is in Charlotte that wasn't where you came from?"

The man had a gift for preaching, Mary Jane gave him that, but the twentieth century was no place for prophecy or soothsaying. He said, "I just need to meet with someone."

"Maybe someone needs to meet you somewhere else. Maybe you're going the wrong direction."

"If I was, how would I know?"

"It's all about having that sense of direction. Take me, for instance. I wasn't always blind, but now I see better than before because I know where I am and where I'm heading."

"I know where I'm heading. I just don't know the easiest way to get there."

"Everyone finds his own way," Ephraim said. "But few find the right way."

Ephraim quieted and sat before Mary Jane as though time were on his side and he could afford to waste many a night warming by a fire. He wondered how the old man came to find this place with no eyes, and how he settled in with a cord of neatly chopped firewood. He was sure Ephraim would reiterate the line about the Lord providing, as though all one needed to do was look up to the heavens and say, "Help me out, God, I need you."

From the foot of the mountain, voices carried up along with the sound of the dogs.

"There's some men down there," Mary Jane said. "Hunters, I reckon."

Ephraim nodded. "Likely the law on the hunt. They's a murderer on the loose, and they've got a dragnet over three counties to catch him."

"Say again?"

"Man beat a police officer to death up in York County on Sunday night."

Mary Jane laughed in relief. "Where'd you hear that?"

"When you don't have eyes, you keep your ears to the ground."

"I didn't mean—I'm sorry, I didn't mean no offense. Just I hadn't heard about a dead cop."

"Beat to death with a tire iron. Farmer found him the next morning, the bloated body already swarming with flies."

"They Lord."

"These are dark times we live in," Ephraim said, and he turned his head as though he could see Mary Jane with eyeless eyes. Between them the fire dulled to hot coals glowering in the hearth. "Men on the road with no direction, bad things is bound to happen. That's how sin works."

"I hope they get their man," Mary Jane said.

"He'll get his, in this world or the next," Ephraim said. "For he that doeth wrong shall receive again for the wrong that he hath done, and there is no respect of persons. The Lord knows your heart, and there is no escape."

Gossip was a way of life in the mill village. When the millhands weren't insulting each other or telling lies about their past exploits, the weather and last days were safe topics. But nothing as exciting as the Hillside murders ever happened in the Bell. Hence on Wednesday, three days after the murder, conversations repeated themselves in an endless refrain, hushed voices following the cotton from ball to cloth.

"The sheriff shut down the Hillside yet?" one man asked.

"Naw, Tull's got him paid off."

"Chambers wouldn't take a bribe."

"How else you explain it?"

"He's the law. You got to have evidence fore you can do anything."

"Hell, two boys shot in the street ain't evidence enough?"

"That's the thing, they weren't in the Hillside itself. Tull's a smart man. Boys get shot in his bar, he's liable to feed the bodies to some hogs before the law gets involved."

The men muttered their agreement. Everyone knew the kind of man Larthan Tull was, but no one really knew him. They might have bought whiskey off him, but he kept his cards to his chest.

"No, no," Leuico King said. "The man's not part of the mob. He comes from a family of mountain shiners."

"How you know?" asked Mink Skelton.

"Seemed like I heard him tell it one day at the Hillside. Said his great-great-grandpappy was servant at Mount Vernon. Got George Washington's recipe and then moved to Tennessee to start a business."

"You think Tull's brewing a recipe his family learned from George Washington?"

"That's what I heard, is all."

The men laughed at that.

"Anyway, it's not the recipe," Mink said. "Anyone with shine now can make a living. You got to have business sense. You got to have prospects."

"Tull's got more than prospects. I hear he reads minds."

"What you saying?"

The men quieted and leaned in as Leuico had his say.

"I'm saying, Tull knows things he ought to have no way of knowing. I don't think it was any accident those boys were shot in front of his bar rather than inside it."

"Yeah, if he did it, he pulled them out before he pulled the trigger."

"What I'm saying is, he could have made them disappear. Whether he shot them or Mary Jane shot them, didn't no one have to know about it."

"What are you talking about, L.K.?"

"I'm saying, things don't happen around the Hillside without Tull wanting them to happen. Any of you planning to make shine and try to cut in on his business?"

The men all leaned back at once. No, they knew better than to even consider crossing a man like Larthan Tull. Without knowing a thing about him, they knew he was the kind of man who would break fingers just for an inconvenience. They believed that any one of them could end up dead in the street if Tull had a notion, and the thought of that set them back to the looms.

Willie shucked at the dust with his broom. He liked the work in the mill, liked contributing to the family, liked listening to the old timers talk, and liked the break times when he and the other boys would play around the machines. But this week the mill had grown solemn, for one of the boys who had been shot, Lee Evans, was from the Bell village. Lee and his father lived up the street, a quiet pair of men. Harry worked in the weave rooms, and Lee had been a card hand, Quinn's job. Harry was out today. The funeral was tomorrow and the superintendent told him to stay home for the week.

As Willie passed through with the broom, his grandfather coughed and took him by the arm, said, "Don't let any of this talk scare you."

"I ain't scared."

Abel nodded and patted the boy on the back.

"Y'all ever hear anything from Mary Jane?" Mink asked awhile later.

"Not a thing," Abel said. "Joe don't think Mary Jane shot them boys, and I'm inclined to believe him."

"Mary Jane's always been real fun to hang around."

"He's got his problems, but killing some folks seems out of character for him. Course Willie here suggested Mary Jane might well have done it."

"Did he now?" Mink said, and they both looked at Willie.

"I didn't mean that," Willie said, and he felt hot in the ears thinking of Mary Jane out by the river, his shoulder torn up. Shame was funny like that. You remembered those moments, things said and done, lies told, secrets kept, and you felt the weight of them later, all the more painful for your inability to edit the past. He'd done wrong to think his uncle could be a killer, but, worse, he couldn't say he saw Mary Jane toting whiskey from the river, because if his uncle were guilty, to talk would be wronging him twice.

"Who knows what went down at the Hillside?" Abel said. "Bad folks gather there, and any one of them could have shot Ernest and Lee."

The men muttered in agreement. Abel leaned his stool on two

legs, holding onto the loom, stretching his back or puzzling over the work, when the stool tipped over. He shuffled one foot to the ground, and the stool clacked and squeaked beneath him.

"You all right, Abel?" Mink asked, laughing.

"I believe I've about had enough today."

"It's too early for you to be talking like that."

"My body's not made for sitting on a stool all day."

The other men laughed and one set his stool to wobbling in manic emulation. The old man only shook his head.

Willie kept his eye on his grandfather, thinking of the other night in the cemetery. The mill could be a dangerous place. You had to pay attention to what you were doing or you'd lose a finger. The men loved to talk about accidents, seemingly more than anything else, perhaps as a way to ward off the bad luck for themselves, or perhaps just one more way to while away the hours. Remember Myrtle Clark, the woman who got her hair caught in a loom last year? Lost half her scalp and made it back to finish her shift. Oh, that's nothing. Another man heard tell once of a supervisor in Spartanburg. Wasn't paying attention and got caught in a pulley. The pulley threw him into the ceiling and splattered his brains against a beam. Things Satan himself would have trouble matching.

When Abel righted himself, he caught Willie watching him and said, "You know, I imagine running whiskey's a tempting job for a young man. Glamorous."

"Maybe so," Willie said.

"There's easier ways to make an honest living. Maybe not in the mills, but not by running shine."

Willie nodded. He'd heard this before from the old man. You can find your way across the entire world, but you couldn't ever get out. You were always part of this life, still in the trenches. Just new towns, new names. And you don't know what you lose from it all until you're an old man looking back. "If you're not careful," Abel had said many times, "you might one day realize that everything you thought you knew about life, the code you lived by, was all wrong."

"Times are changing, that's for sure," Mink agreed. "Violence is taking over everything."

Abel coughed and rubbed his rheumy eyes, blinked a few times. "Hell, people always been like this. When I was a baby, my oldest two brothers were killed by Confederates."

"Where you from, Abel?"

"I was born right up on the mountain, west of Gastonia."

"They was killed by Confederates?"

"Home guard."

"God almighty."

"I was only two at the time, but that shadow's followed me my whole life." Abel trailed off.

Willie listened to this, pictured two dead men in the street in front of the Hillside Inn, two boys killed by Confederates on horseback in front of a burning barn. Last days indeed.

Afternoon swelter steamed up the weave room, kept the cotton fibers soft. An eerie mist in the air from the sprinklers. For a while the room was silent save the drone of the machines. The hum could put a man in a trance, something almost mystical where man and machine joined and became one entity. Amid this reverie, Willie set to sweeping again. He noticed the old man's eyes were watery and red. Abel stared fixedly at the loom with his mouth ajar. As soft strands of cotton danced between his fingers, he watched the threading of the cotton, the pattern of the warp and woof, as though he were being presented with a miracle, God's majesty revealed in textiles. Then he slid off the stool and clattered to the floor.

Willie yelled out and ran to his grandfather. He knelt by the old man, but other men gathered and someone pulled him away. Everyone in the room crowded in and pushed Willie to the back.

Quinn and Joe laid Abel on the bed while Willie and Susannah watched. Mr. Lowry had given all the Hopewell men the afternoon off. A doctor had come to the mill, pronounced it a stroke, and said Abel would need at least a month of rest, and perhaps would never be able to work again. With the other three there to steady him, Abel had been able to walk home. He walked up the steps to the house on his own, lay down, and turned to the wall.

Joe pulled Susannah aside, led her to the porch and into the front yard. Quinn and Willie followed to the doorway and listened while Joe told the story.

"The doctor says his body's just worn out. Says when you get to be Abel's age, the blood vessels get clogged like old drain pipes." Joe wiped sweat from his brow and stared off toward the mill. He said, "I should move up to second hand soon. We won't go into the hole even if he never works again."

Willie could hear the frustration in his father's voice and knew he felt cornered by events beyond his control.

"Daddy," his mother whispered. "God damn it."

"He told the doctor he'd had a few episodes before. Did you ever notice anything?"

When she paused, his father read her silence, said, "For how long?"

"Early June?"

"Jesus, Sue, we could have been preparing for this. We could have—"

"What? We couldn't do anything except wait."

"Hell we could have done—"

"Nothing. We were getting by, and we'll get by now."

"I was trying to do more than get by."

Joe turned and slunk into the coming night. She stood in the yard a moment to watch his fading silhouette before coming back inside where Willie and Quinn waited near the door.

"We'll be OK," she told them. She brushed past them and went to her father, sat on the bed, and laid a hand on his shoulder. "Daddy?"

"It was a stroke," he mumbled.

She brushed his silver hair out of his eyes and then rested her hand on his arm. "There wasn't anything you could have done," she said.

He turned his head away and, like he was recommending how far apart to space a few tomato plants, he said, "I could have died."

The brothers moved to the porch, sat on the rockers. Dusk came down like a curtain so that the rail and the bushes in the yard and the road and the trees all faded to a smoky haze of gray. The lengthening shadows made the world appear ghoulish and strange. A breeze blew through, and the cypress trees in the front yard bent like dancers, held that pose until the air stilled. Willie felt more alone with his brother than he could ever remember.

"Granddad's going to be all right," Quinn finally said.

Willie nodded, gazed at the ferns that hung from the ceiling above the rail.

Quinn continued, "I'm going to town. I'll be back, but if someone asks, you don't know where I've gone. Or tell em I couldn't sleep, that I'm just walking in the neighborhood."

Willie watched his brother, like their father before him, disappear into the night, leaving Willie alone on the porch. A breeze cascaded through the roofs of the pines across the street, a lonesome crackle of limbs, the drop of a cone against a neighbor's roof. The night was cool for the end of August. For weeks now, the days had burned around a hundred and the nights had remained in the nineties, a sticky mess, so the chill air was a relief. School would be starting soon, Willie's time in the mill come to an end until next summer, unless his father would change his mind about him staying on, now that his grandfather wouldn't be working.

Willie went inside and found his mother rattling in the kitchen. He sat at the table without saying a word and waited for her to speak, to say something that would clarify the day's events and restore order to his world. The room was dark save for the flame in the lantern, and in this light his mother looked old to him. There by the sink, pausing, with her hands resting on the counter in front of her, she stared ahead as though looking out the window. Nothing but darkness and spirits out there, he knew, and although she couldn't have seen anything, she looked anyway. Her hair was brittle and yellow, her skin a dusty ochre in the lantern light. Lines pronounced, crow's feet at her eyes, and grooves in her narrow cheeks.

"Momma?"

"Yes, Willie."

She continued gazing out the window at the darkness.

"How is granddad?"

"He's resting now, you just saw him," she said, and she turned to him. She walked over and put her hand on the back of his neck and rubbed the hairline. "Don't worry about him," she said.

"I'm not worried."

She continued to rub his hair for a moment, and he closed his eyes, relaxed with the comforts of his mother.

He said, "If I had told Daddy—"

"That wouldn't have made a difference. Your granddad was in bad shape, and there wasn't anything anyone could have done to prevent this."

"You told me not to tell. I didn't."

"I know, and I'm proud of you. Part of growing up is learning how to keep a secret."

"I thought secrets were bad."

"Generally they are. But there can be good secrets. Grown-ups think all kinds of things they don't say to one another. It keeps us civil. What you'll find out more and more is that we all have our things we'd rather keep to ourselves. Like your granddad's dizziness. It wasn't our place to go telling the neighborhood, so we didn't, and I'm proud of you."

She came around and leaned over Willie's face and kissed his forehead.

He sat at the table while she went back to the sink, folded a towel. "Go on to bed now," she said.

He rose and as he was leaving the room, she blew out the lantern and everything went dark. From his bed he heard her walk through the room and close her door. He lay on his bed, the room ashen and dim in the moonless night, and he pondered what his grandfather had meant by his code being all wrong. What code? Do unto others? Love thy neighbor? An eye for an eye? Honor thy father and mother, the commandment said, but it didn't say what to do when your father and mother were at odds, when honoring one meant dishonoring the other. Yes, he'd kept his secret, and his mother was proud of him, but did that make it right? What she said sounded true, we do keep secrets.

Where had his father gone? His brother? Mary Jane? The night was lonesome, a time when spirits would come out from wherever they came. The mill hill was civilized, everything on a grid, folks so close you were never alone until the day wound down. He remembered nights he'd lain awake at his grandfather's farm, before it was sold. Abel had lived up north on the other side of King's Mountain, and when the family would visit, Quinn and his brother would lie out in ticks in the yard, the house too crowded for the kids. Warm breezes and the calling of crickets. The days building forts in the cane patches, or crawling on hay bales, the nights for stargazing.

One time, though, he woke to the sound of something rustling in the brush in the field. He lay still and watched the tall grasses quiver, the moonlight so bright it might as well have been day. Some manner of beast, sure as the ground beneath him now, came out like a large cat and crept along the field line and into the grasses of the yard. Willie felt as though his body were in a trance as the thing moved along. He wanted to call out, to warn his family, to bolt off to someplace safe, but he couldn't move, was held in some deep paralysis the likes of which he'd never felt before or since. He could only watch as the cat-beast stood and hovered over his brother's body, only a few feet away now. As the beast rose up on two legs, its claws forked from its paws and a low rumble came from its throat.

But it didn't strike. It paused, and in that pause the screen door slapped shut. Willie's eyes flickered, and he saw his grandfather lumber out with a shotgun. When he looked back to Quinn, the beast was gone.

Quinn stirred when their grandfather came over, and the old man said, "Why don't you boys come inside for the night?"

"Did you see it?" Willie asked.

"I saw something, to be sure," Abel said as he led the brothers inside. "Don't worry, it can't get you inside."

"What was it?

Abel leaned the shotgun against the wall and said, "They say the spirit of an animal haunts this land. A remnant from way back, when all this was wilderness, and only Cherokee and Creek lived here."

Their grandfather sat with them in the living room as they unrolled their beds and settled once again. Quinn fell asleep instantly, unaware of the danger he just missed, but Willie was up for the night.

His grandfather said, "I never heard tell of a beast like that attacking anyone. I always thought they might be something of a superstition."

"That wasn't a superstition I just saw."

"I didn't mean you didn't see something," his grandfather said. "Go on and get some sleep."

Willie would never see such an apparition again, though he would remember that night on occasion and wonder how much of the memory he could trust. Perhaps people were predisposed to believe in certain things, and maybe he saw something that not everyone would. Maybe there were more things in this world than exist on the constant plane we all walk through in our daily lives. Maybe there was something beneath the surface that, if we listen, we can actually touch. Willie had no doubt of this underworld, but, except for some moments out in the country, he never felt in tune with it, almost as if those moments of sight were mere dreams.

Tonight he pictured his brother, once again unaware of the danger lurking in the country shadows. Quinn would be approaching the railroad tracks now, where Evelyn would meet him, twin figures in the darkness. Dogs howling in the distance. Trunks of pines clacking in the wind. The muted thump of cones falling in the dry leaves on the forest floor. Outside his window, the sky glowed, a sheen of white haze from the stars over the black void beyond. Willie imagined them walking on, both conscious of the unknown ground upon which they tread. Last year, Judy Singamore had gotten pregnant, and no one knew where the father was. Rumor had it the boy was with a traveling salesman, meandering across the state with a trunkful of books, and seemed to stay gone twice as much now that there was an infant in the house. Judy didn't have friends anymore, didn't see anyone from the school. Then there was Carol Evans, who eloped with Jimmy Lee Carter last spring, just a few months shy of their sixteenth year. They rented a house on the mill hill, Carol already pregnant and Jimmy Lee working full time in the mill, weekends as a carpenter's helper in town.

Quinn and Evelyn could run steady, but they needed friends around. If you didn't want to wind up in the same rut as your parents, married young and working in the Bell, you didn't go out on dates. Couples went to the picture show in a group and tried to sneak a moment together. A safety net in numbers. But Quinn and Evelyn ran in different circles, and Evelyn truthfully didn't have many friends. She was beautiful, but that wasn't the reason people were intimidated by her. Other girls' parents didn't want her coming over for sleepovers, and boys weren't about to ask her father for a date. Father and daughter had shown up in town when Evelyn was a child, no roots and not much of a story. Evelyn Tull: always outside the circle, a beauty who did well in school, who always went to church even when her father missed. She took piano lessons and could often be seen in a front window practicing Chopin.

In Willie's mind it was him walking Evelyn to the river tonight. He slid off the rail and onto the alternating ladder of gravel and tie. The woods thinned by the river, and although he didn't know what was coming he knew it would be good. They walked in silence, her hand tucked neatly into his. Willie could feel her softness, and it made him conscious of his own rough, cracked skin, blistered and raw from the machines. His dirty clothes, his home-cut hair. Her hand was cool in his, and he could feel the bones in her knuckles. Every time the fabric of her dress brushed against his sleeve or his arm, he felt a tingle. Her creamy skin appeared bluish in the starlight, her features soft. She didn't belong here with him, her blood a solid English stock, akin to aristocracy, he thought. Or maybe she had a drop of Spanish or Cherokee blood in her, some ways back, that darkened her hair.

At the river, they lay in the grass, and the grass was cool and dry beneath them. She lay back on the blanket they were about to unfold, and the flare in her eyes guided him to her. His body took control of him, and his hips rammed against hers. She bit her lower lip, and a moment later their lips meshed and he rolled on top of her. They pressed together until he burst. Then Willie relaxed and lay in the gray night, the stillness of the mill hill interrupted by the occasional creak of a board, or the shirr of leaves in the breeze.

Full dark had set in when Joe reached the edge of town. It was a little more than a mile walk from the Bell into Castle, but the road was flat and the weather was calm. Heat lightning flared far off in the east, but he knew it was headed elsewhere, that this region was dry tonight save the fog of humidity that would hang in the air deep into the night.

He arrived at the Hillside Inn and knocked. Three square knocks, the passcode for entry as pointless as the secret handshakes of the Masons. If you knew the right man to ask, or even if you just hung around the cotton mill long enough, no secrets existed.

"Who is it?" a voice asked.

"A weary traveler in need of brighter spirits."

The door opened, and after he entered the darkness Depot Murphy replaced the beam across the doorway. The barkeep was a stumpy man with arms larger around than his legs. Nearly bald, his head was burnt red as a cherry tomato and a few ugly white strands of hair curled along the side and back of his scalp. He shuffled back to the bar, said, "What say, Joe?"

Joe sucked his teeth, looked around. Two empty pool tables to the left, only one man sitting at the bar. The only light came from two bare bulbs jerryrigged to the ceiling and an oil lamp on the bar. Sawdust coated the planks of wood on the floor. Silence throughout. It was early yet, but there was a slight chance a few more would venture out on a Monday night, murder or no murder. He drew a seat at the bar, said, "Glass of whiskey."

"You got it," Depot said.

Without fanfare, he filled a glass with brown liquid and set it in front of Joe. The first glass of whiskey Joe'd had in twelve years. Prohibition hadn't curtailed the county's liquor trade, but it had helped Joe sober up. By the end of 1919, his firstborn was old enough to remember what he saw in his father. Joe remembered the curious look three-year-old Quinn had given him one night that Christmas when Joe'd stumbled in, fallen over in the living room, and laughed and laughed until he'd roused the entire family. He'd expected Quinn to cry like the baby he was, and for Susannah to rock him back to sleep, to give Joe a cold glare tonight, a talking-to tomorrow. Unpleasant, but forgettable.

Instead, Quinn had walked out of the bedroom on his own two legs and stared at his father. Perplexed, maybe, though not judgmental. Yet. The intelligence in his son's eyes had haunted Joe, the way Quinn had picked up on his father's weakness and seemed to understand the full story. Joe had woken to the memory of that look every day for more than a decade now, and the memory still filled him with shame. True, he missed the drink. It still was hard for him to sleep, harder still for him to come out to the Hillside Tavern on the few occasions he'd needed to find Mary Jane, to see a roomful of liquor being consumed like it was as legal as a Coca-Cola, and to walk away. But every time, he had managed to walk away, until now, when events finally outweighed the shame of that Christmas memory.

His hand shook as he held the glass. Before taking a sip, he said, "Sue's father had a stroke on shift this afternoon."

"That a fact?" Depot said.

"He's all right, but he won't be working for a while, if ever."

"That's a tough spot to be in," the barkeep agreed.

"How's business?"

"Would be better if there weren't bloodstains on the pavement out there."

"Sheriff came out to my house on Sunday. Said the rumor was Mary Jane had got himself involved here."

Depot began to wipe down the bar with a dirty rag. "You could say that."

"In fact, Chambers said it was Mary Jane who might have shot them."

"You could say that, too."

"You see it?"

Depot stopped. "Like I told Chambers, I saw Mary Jane come in here and march those boys out to the street, and then I heard two shots go off."

"I sure hate to hear my brother's messed up in anything like that."

"He didn't shoot me, didn't shoot anyone in the bar," Depot said. "Far as I'm concerned, whatever else that goes on, I don't much care to know about it."

Joe drained his glass in a single swallow. His throat caught fire and his belly smoldered. He closed his eyes, nodded. "Don't care to know about it, huh?"

Depot started wiping the counter again, said, "That's right."

"Well. Pour me another'n."

Depot brought him another, and Joe felt the liquor sidle into his blood. A hot calm, this was, much needed after Abel's stroke. The family had been OK until today, but now their future remained to be seen. They wouldn't leave Harvey Lane, that much was clear. Beyond that, who knew what the stroke would mean for them? Maybe nothing. Maybe everything.

He sipped his second shot of whiskey, relaxed into that old familiar stupor where the burdens of life fell away and your mind cleared. Funny how just a few sips could do that to you.

"It wasn't him," Joe said, thinking back on the wild days with Mary Jane, back when the brothers had first gotten back from France, when

Joe and Susannah still lived on the farm with her folks, and Willie and Hazel had yet to be born. Weekends, he and Mary Jane would go out regularly, and some weekdays too. Everyone has reckless years, he'd reasoned, and he'd earned some release in the service. Evidently, if the Roaring Twenties were any indication, the entire country felt the same. But Joe was never a part of that. Even after he quit drinking, he still tried to go out and have a big time. The end of the illusion came one night when Susannah was pregnant with Willie.

Joe was already working long days then, four to dusk on Abel's cattle farm, but he was still young enough that the work hadn't worn on him. He didn't realize he was starting the rest of his life. He was just working and having fun. He and Susannah could leave Quinn with her folks, drive into town and go out with Mary Jane and his girlfriend, a woman named Arlene that Mary Jane was smitten with, and might even have married had he been able to get it together. Instead he'd gotten drunk, pissed on himself, and run screaming into the night, leaving Arlene a crying heap on the floor, an unhappy Susannah leaning over her, rubbing her back and giving Joe a glare that said, "No more."

Joe put on his hat and strolled off after his brother. Least he could do was to make sure Mary Jane didn't tumble into a ravine somewhere or drown in some body of water. As he listened to his brother wailing in the forest, the clap of tree limbs, the rustle of brush, he knew he should be grateful to be sober, grateful that he would not suffer a hangover in the morning, grateful that he would not have to endure the shame of sobering up, but instead he wanted to be right there with his brother. Drunk. Blotto. Stinko. He waded through Mary Jane's blazed trail, darkness shading anything that might be there. The woods opened into a clearing with the burnt remains of some abandoned campfire. Mary Jane lay by the charred wood and stared up at the stars. When Joe reached him, his brother said, "Man, what a night."

"Let's get on back, Mary Jane."

Joe sat beside his brother, who said, "I ain't going nowhere. You remember when we used to visit Papaw and lay out under the stars? The whole mess of us."

"I remember." Their father sharecropped, their siblings all worked the land, but their grandfather had saved up and bought a square of land, more home to Joe than anything else. Land the family owned. Days long gone now. He'd hoped that by marrying Susannah and buying land from Abel, he'd be able to set up a life for his own children that he himself had never had, but the land wouldn't work with them. They sold out when the boys were younger and had paid rent to the mill owners ever since. But that night out with Mary Jane, he still had reason to believe his life would turn out differently. Only one child so far, and he was buying property from Abel. His life was on the rise, so he didn't agree when Mary Jane said, "Sometimes I think those were the best years of our life. Like we ain't never come back from those nights out in the country."

"Your mind's just warped from the whiskey."

"But that's the thing. The whiskey makes me think clearer. Like I'm more aware now than I ever am sober. I feel it, man. It's electric."

Rather than reply, and consider his own demons, Joe left his brother there, retrieved his wife, and went home to their sleeping son.

Someone knocked on the door of the Hillside, and Depot opened the door. Two men came in, one in his thirties and the other maybe sixteen. Judging from the crisp clothing they wore, they looked like they lived in town, and they walked over to the pool tables like no one owned them and no one would dare try to stop them. Depot brought them a half-empty mason jar and two glasses. The older one looked familiar to Joe. He had a buzzed haircut and bald triangles above his temples that were spreading back high on his forehead. His skin was tanned, and he had gray-blue eyes, a sharp jawline, a puffy nose. Joe stared, and after a moment he got up and walked to them. "That you, Lester?" he said.

The man looked up, squinted. "Goddamn, Joey Hopewell. How you been?" They shook hands and Lester looked at his friend and said, "This is an old army buddy of mine. We were in Germany together." To Joe, he said, "This is Moses Cope's boy."

"Little young, ain't he?"

"I'm eighteen." The boy's voice was hoarse and on the verge of cracking.

"I'm sure you are."

"Hell, Joey, long time." Lester lowered his voice and leaned in: "I heard about Mary Jane yesterday. Damn shame."

"It is that." Joe refilled his glass from the jar of whiskey, said, "Hell, let's get a game going."

"I'll drink to that," Lester said, already reaching for a pool stick.

They started a game of pool but didn't finish before another knock at the door interrupted them. Depot let another man into the tavern, his back dim in the shadow cast by the light at the bar. Joe leaned onto the pool table and shot. The cueball popped and sank the seven fast, and Depot said, "Evening, Sheriff. What brings you out?"

Joe leaned against his stool as the kid took his shot.

The sheriff sat at the bar, a big man, one you'd expect would be a lumberjack before a sheriff, broad shoulders stooped over, a thick beard covering the front of his neck, an olive green felt hat atop his bizarrely rounded head. He said, "I'm looking to talk to Larthan some more about them boys. He around?"

"He'll be here directly."

"How bout a drink while I wait?" He took off his hat and added, "Relax, Depot."

Joe sipped his whiskey and stepped back up to the pool table. The room was starting to spin on him, the table unmoored on the barroom floor. The kid stood behind him and pushed at his shoulder. He was drunk and slurring that Joe shouldn't miss this shot or else he was going to step up and whoop ass on him.

"Whoop ass," the kid said. "You ain't even going to get another shot. I'm a run the table."

He shoved off Joe's shoulder and stumbled back to the stool, missed, and fell into the wall.

"Hellfire, boy," Lester whispered. "You better straighten up fore that sheriff decides to take a closer look at you."

"Let him come. I ain't scared. Let him come."

Joe glanced at the bar, saw the sheriff hunched forward to talk to Depot. They weren't looking this way yet, but he knew the sheriff wasn't here to have a drink before calling it a day. It wouldn't be but a few more minutes before he ambled over here to try and see if Joe had heard from Mary Jane yet.

He sank his shot and rubbed chalk on the end of his stick and studied the table.

"Lucky break, but you better just make em all fore I come in there like some goddamn trench warfare," the kid said.

"What do you know about trench warfare?" Lester asked. "You wasn't even an itch in your pappy's cock when me and Joey was off in the trenches."

"I would have whooped up, though, just like I'm about to whoop up on this here pool table."

Joe took a slug of liquor and said, "You boys can learn something from this." The cueball zigzagged around the table, struck the one ball, and kept going. The one bounced twice and missed the side pocket.

"That's a shame," the kid said. When he moved to take his shot, he fell right over.

Lester howled. "Boy, you're drunker'n a polecat that's been guzzlin homebrew."

Lester helped the kid stand, and Joe cursed about his missed shot, eyed the bar. The sheriff and the bartender looked their way, so he downed the last of his whiskey. "Watch him," he said to Lester. "I'll get us another'n." He moved to the bar, aiming to get whatever the sheriff had to say to him over with. "How bout another pint?" he said to Depot.

"Seems that boy's had his share and then some. Thisn's for you and Lester, right?"

"Absolutely," he said. While Depot went for another pint, Joe turned to the sheriff.

"Evening, Joe," Chambers said.

"You taking a break after quittin time, or you investigating?"

"No word from Mary Jane, I suppose?"

"Not a thing."

"Mm. What a mess. State police are combing the county, got people set up in Columbia and Charlotte, but no one's seen him yet. You heard about that cop that was murdered up in York County?"

Depot set the pint in front of him.

"You have a good evening, Sheriff," Joe said.

"You do the same. Take care of your boy back there. He don't look so good."

"He's not my boy. Just some kid off the farm."

"Whoever he is, he ought to be careful what he says and when. I had fewer things on my mind, I'd likely walk over and see for myself what he's up to."

"I'll pass the word along."

Joe took another swig as he walked back to where Lester and the kid were racking up another game.

"Took you long enough." The kid grabbed the bottle out of Joe's hand. "Goddamn, what'd you do? You done drank half the bottle between here and the bar."

The kid guzzled from the jar and Joe sat back, accepted a cigarette from Lester. As smoke fogged up the bar, Joe closed his eyes and hoped his brother was safe. State police might not be as sympathetic as Chambers if they caught him first. Chambers at least knew the kind of man Mary Jane was. Troublemaker, yes. Killer, no. That gene didn't run in the family. He'd been in and out of work his whole life, and he made and kept the wrong friends from school, but there was a difference between drinking bootleg and playing bluegrass long hours on the porch, and killing folks to build your own whiskey empire. That was bad business, and Mary Jane didn't have a head for business, good or bad. One time when they were kids, Joe sold him a penny for five cents because the head faced the wrong direction. Head's supposed to face this way, Joe said, pointing to his right with the coin facing him. He turned the coin to face Mary Jane and said, "Lookit: It's pointing the other way," and Mary Jane handed over a nickel for it. Their father made him give it back and let Mary Jane keep the penny for the trouble. Joe hung his head and apologized, and later stole the nickel and penny both after Mary Jane went to sleep that night. By the next Saturday when his brother went to look for the change to buy some candy at the store building, he'd already forgotten Joe's hustle and never did mention to anybody why he didn't buy six cents' worth of candy like he'd planned on. Just turned red and said he didn't want anything, assumed he'd lost the money or maybe never had it to begin with. Joe didn't know.

It was after midnight now, and the three of them had a third of the bottle left. His breath smelled like rotgut, axle grease, a radiator. The whistle would be wailing in a few hours, and he had a twenty-minute stumble to get home. The kid slumped on a stool and nodded his chin to his chest, and Lester was shooting in all the balls, stripes and solids alike. Joe held the whiskey, the bottle warm in his hands, and felt a weight pressing down on him that not even these last drops of liquor would lift.

He slunk out of the Hillside and shuffled into the street, headed west toward the Bell. The night grew cooler by the minute, which helped clear his head. He kicked up rocks in the road as he walked, the crunch of his feet sounding out into the still night. Roadside trees gave way to cornfields, and stalks bumped together in the breeze. The familiar buzz of the night unnerved him in his stupor. The rattling of Satan's army coming to destroy his soul. Trench warfare, the cough of Howitzers, the hiss and whistle of bullets and canisters of gas. Fire and men screaming and clouds of dirt and dust spattering through the air. And when a battle was over, the eerie silence as the dead were counted, the wounded helped. Groans and coughs, a chorus of whimpers that seemed to emanate from the lot of them, one uniform cry of anguish. No one shouted in those still hours, the echo of the guns still ringing in their ears. The silence that was not silence.

A figure approached on the road, and a moment later Evelyn Tull emerged from the darkness. Her blue dress was stained black by the night, her skin like porcelain beneath the stars. When she reached him she kept her head down, her eyes on the road.

"Where are you coming from?" he said.

"Out for a walk," she said.

"A walk."

She didn't respond. He stood in the road, a few feet from the shoulder where she had paused, and in the starlight he looked her up and down. There was something familiar about her, the way she held herself, composed and graceful even in the middle of the night. She looked young. Not like his boys looked young, still boys. She was a grown woman, but young, her skin smooth and fresh and unlined. Unharmed by the ills of the world. He remembered Susannah in the barn loft being like that. Something whole about a woman as she entered adulthood, something that fractured as she aged. A smile less wide, eyes with less life. He suddenly felt a deep and untenable ache for this young woman, a desire to protect her from what he knew to be just around the corner. A cloud hovering above her, waiting for just the right moment to descend.

He tried to speak, slurred, "I told my boy not to be sparking you. That you wasn't one of us. But I can see why he might not listen to me."

He stepped toward her, caught his balance as one sluggish foot landed in front of him, then the next.

In the faint light, he saw in her eyes a flood of fear as she sidestepped away from him and scurried along the road. He tripped and fell to his knees, cursed at his clumsiness. He watched her pick up her pace, grab her dress, and nearly break into a run.

"Stay away from my boy," he called after her, but he was no longer certain whose sake he had in mind.

R are was the day anymore where Chambers could sit on the porch with his wife and rock away the afternoon. It was something he'd always longed for, time when they could relax and reflect on the fruit of their lives. Not everything had come to pass that he may have planned on, that they may have planned on, but all told it had not been a bad life. She was out there now, chewing on her nails and rocking slowly. Often she enjoyed reading outside, but today she was simply staring, which struck him as faintly ominous. He watched her through the window and wondered what she was thinking about. Perhaps nothing. She had the blessing of a still mind—not an empty or a slow mind, but a tranquility he'd always envied.

This afternoon he needed to get on to the station to check in with the state police and their dragnet, to see if there was any word of Mary Jane, any chance he could soon put the awful mess behind him. Instead, he poured two glasses of iced tea and joined Alma on the porch.

She looked at him a moment before taking the glass. She said, "I didn't reckon you'd be staying home this afternoon."

"I can't join my bride at the homestead?"

"It's been a long time since I was a bride."

"You'll always be my bride," he told her, settling into a rapid rock beside her. The bones in his left arm signaled yet another storm this evening, as though once the good Lord decided the county deserved water, He would provide in abundance. Chambers pumped his fist, unable to complete the grasping motion. He said, "I do have to go back in."

"Won't look good if the voters catch the sheriff idling on the porch."

"Not when younguns are getting shot in front of an illegal tavern," he said, ignoring her sarcasm.

She sat still and waited for him to speak, which he would eventually, but for now he just wanted to rock. She had more on her mind than peace and tranquility this afternoon, and he was content to let that lie. In the early days of their marriage, he pestered and pried, but he'd learned that most of her blue moods would cure themselves with or without him. Signing the paper at the church meant you were together always, so what choice did she have but to come around?

After a while he said, "You know, I always did like Mary Jane. We've had our run-ins, me and him, but he's not a bad man. He always knew when to stand back when a bar fight was brewing, and he tells a good story."

"You're thinking he might not be guilty of anything?" she asked.

He reached over with his aching arm and took her hand, glad to feel her sliding away from whatever shadow had passed over her this afternoon. "I remember one time, way back before Larthan Tull ever set foot in this town, I went camping with my brother James out on the river and went on a regular bender. I disremember what for, we just had us a few days off, I reckon. I think you and the boys were visiting your momma."

As always, he grimaced inwardly at the thought of their dead sons. If Alma noticed, she didn't show it.

He went on, "Mary Jane was probably only eighteen at the time, younger even, and he came up on us in the afternoon, trout fishing. Even though James and I were two old drunks, Mary Jane sat with us about three hours shooting the shit. Good kid. Anyway, I've been thinking about that time a lot lately. I don't see much of James anymore, and it makes a man nostalgic to grow older. Things are changing so much around here, I feel like all I do is pine away for something that used to be. Or maybe it never was. Maybe I'm mis-remembering the past. When I was young I couldn't wait to be older, and now I'd give anything to be young for a little while again."

When he finally quit, his wife smiled and squeezed his hand. She said, "Do you have any idea how foolish you sound? You men never can allow yourselves to be content, can you?"

"I'm content enough," he said, and he understood that Alma was not out of the shadow after all, that she'd merely been biding her time, waiting for it to go away on its own. But he'd pestered her, as always. That was one piece of wisdom he'd learned: Nothing ever changed in a marriage.

She went on, "There's no such thing as content enough. You're either content or you're not. You can be happy enough. You can be content and happy enough. Or you can be unhappy, but content. Or you can be discontent, happy or not, which is what you are."

"So am I happy or not?"

"It doesn't matter. You're discontent, Furman. Probably always will be as long as you're off chasing those bootleggers. You know why women can be content without ever thinking of happiness?"

"Why's that?"

"Because we're practical. We can accept things the way they are, even if we don't like them, and we can move on. You're like a child, you and all those men out there. Always dreaming and scheming and mourning some part of you that you feel like you've lost, and you're ignoring the world around you."

"What am I ignoring?"

"Me, for one thing. You've been running all over chasing after men who don't really matter. What are you avoiding here? Why do you stay half the night down at the station when they don't need you?"

"I'm here now," he said.

"Yes, but for how long? Forget your job for a while. Let Larthan and Mary Jane and the rest of them take care of themselves. Let the feds come in and burn their operation down and take them all to Columbia. Enjoy yourself while you still can."

"Just up and quit?"

"Why not? Our land's paid off. We can take in a tenant and do just fine for ourselves."

"That's tempting, but I can't do that."

"What's stopping you?"

"I owe it to somebody to see this thing settled. What if Mary Jane's innocent?"

"What if he's not?"

"If he's not, half the police in the state are out to find him over that murdered patrolman. He'll be lucky to see trial if some of those fellas catch him. Lord knows what would happen if Larthan gets ahold of him. But if he is innocent, I feel like I owe it to him to see him cleared."

She quit rocking. He held his breath while he waited for whatever she might say, whatever judgment she might pass. He knew she put up with more than her share of his grief, especially since their sons had died. Life with a badge, keeping the peace, enacting justice, all of it just a game, he knew, a way to stay busy and keep going. To feel useful in a meaningless world. Alma knew that too, which is why her opinion of him mattered so deeply. If she thought he was a fool who was wasting his life, he likely was.

But she surprised him today. Rather than suggesting he retire, she squeezed his damaged hand again and said, "You never were one to shirk your responsibility, even in a lost cause. It's what I love about you."

She resumed her rocking. He took a sip of tea, drained the glass to cool his parched throat. He set the glass on the porch beside him and stood to go. She gave him permission with a glance and a smile, so he said, reluctantly, "I've got to get on."

The agents showed up at the Hillside earlier than usual, but they'd been in town long enough for someone to have tipped Tull off and for him to have gotten the building clean, so that he sat waiting for them on the porch when they arrived. This was an old routine for this pair. Stationed in Columbia, Jeffreys and O'Connor made a loop up the Broad River, through Castle and on up to Gastonia, over to Asheville and down through Seneca, along the Indian maiden Issaqueena's trail to Ninety Six and back to Columbia, busting up stills and collecting money and information along the way.

Tull knew them well enough to know they weren't going to bring him in. He also knew they were after Aunt Lou, which they didn't know he knew, but which didn't concern him much. The buck could be passed, but in his line of work, as long as someone was up or down the chain, those in the middle didn't have to worry as much. He stood on the porch of the Hillside and sneered at the agents as they pulled into the grass on the side of the road.

Jeffreys gave O'Connor a look that said, "This is going to be fun."

O'Connor didn't acknowledge it, just stared at Tull relaxing on the porch, his boot kicked up on the wall, chomping an unlit cigar between his teeth. Tull spat. "I heard y'all were at the sheriff's office. That's new for you."

"Just cooperating with your local law enforcement," O'Connor said. "You know the drill."

Tull sneered. "Come on in. Maybe I missed a can somewhere."

The agents entered the Hillside and were met with the stench of cigar smoke, old wood, vomit. The room dank and empty other than the three men, gaunt and hollow in the dim light like lost souls ferrying across the River Styx.

Jeffreys nosed around the bar, and O'Connor stomped on the wood floors with the heel of his shoe, tapped at the baseboards with the welt until he heard the muted thunk of a loose board.

Tull sparked a match, and a cloud of fire and smoke blotted his face as he relit the stogie.

O'Connor pried up the baseboard. Beyond it was a latch that pulled up a trapdoor in the first floor, and he shined a flashlight down into the crawlspace. A ramshackle crate over loose dirt, empty now though you could see the lines of dust where gallon cans of liquor had been.

"Little late, boys."

O'Connor set the trapdoor down and stood up. "Maybe one of these days we'll come straight here, rather than dallying about town."

"Now why would you do that? It's so much more fun to make a game of it."

"He thinks we're playing a game," Jeffreys said.

"Apparently," O'Connor said.

"Do you think it's a game?"

"I don't think it's a game."

"I don't know about you, Roy," Jeffreys said, "but it makes me feel like maybe I'm wasting my time here."

"Why would you say that?"

"Here we are, slaving away to protect our country from the likes of this man, and he makes a mockery of us. Makes a man wonder what he's got to show for his years of service."

"Hey, buddy, don't despair. I'm sure Larthan here's got something for us. To make us feel like we're not wasting our time."

"You think?"

"Yeah, sure. What do you think, Larthan? Do you think we've wasted our time today, coming all the way out here?"

Tull blew smoke across the room and grinned, but when he widened his lips the rest of his face remained steady. "OK, gentlemen," he said. "What brings you out here today?"

"I don't know, Roy. Should we talk to him now?"

"Why not? He seems ready to play ball."

"You think?"

"Sure. Look at him, he's smiling, he knows we're not here to arrest him today, he's having fun."

"Just a game for him."

"No, no. He'll talk and sleep easy tonight," O'Connor said. While the agents went back and forth, O'Connor had kept an eye on Tull, who remained still and puffed on his cigar.

Jeffreys glanced behind the bar, saw a biography Tull was in the middle of reading. "Stephen Field?" he said. "From the Supreme Court?"

"I admired him as a younger man."

"What do you know about the law, Larthan?"

"You'd be surprised," Tull said. "Justice Field believed the liberty of contract was implicit in our Constitution."

"You don't say."

"And implicit within liberty of contract, gentlemen, is the notion that the federal government has no business interfering in the transactions of men."

"Listen to this," Jeffreys said. "A real smart guy, he is."

"Sounds like it," O'Connor said.

Tull folded his hands across the bar and said, "Gentlemen, I'm a busy man. You want to talk, let's talk."

Jeffreys sighed. "All right, Larthan. What can you tell us about Mary Jane?"

"He's a drunk. Came in here last weekend and shot up two of my workers."

"Why?"

"Lord knows." He leaned his elbows on the bar and clasped his hands together. "Why does anybody do anything? He's irrational. Maybe they beat him in a card game. Maybe they sidled into his favorite whore's bedroom."

"Who's his favorite whore?" O'Connor asked, grinning.

"Woman out in the country named Abigail Coleman. Widow woman he's been living with."

"Would she know anything you're not telling us?"

"If she does, she wouldn't tell me. I went out there on Sunday to try to find him myself, and she beat me off with a broom."

"Rumor going around is she and Mary Jane were brewing whiskey out on her farm," O'Connor said.

"They may have been. I don't keep up with who all brews what in this town."

"I'm sure you don't," Jeffreys said.

O'Connor glanced at Jeffreys, then back at Tull. "Larthan, the rumor is you were the one who killed those boys, and tried to kill Mary Jane, too, only he got away. Rumor is they were cutting too deep into your own business, and you felt the need to put them in their place. We were called in because the county rep believes all this to be related to the whiskey trade."

"Well, now you can tell the county rep you came in and searched my place and talked to me, and you don't believe the two are related, because they aren't. Mary Jane Hopewell is crazy, and a drunk, and he may have been brewing whiskey on the side. But any connection between my employees getting shot in the street and the underground whiskey business in this state is pure fabrication. Nothing but coincidence."

"Coincidence."

"Runs the world," Tull said.

"We'll take that back with us," O'Connor said.

"You do that."

The agents walked out of the Hillside and stood on the pavement up the hill. The afternoon sun fired against them, and O'Connor held his hands to his hips and scanned the landscape. Farmland out there. Trees beyond the Hillside and across the road empty fields, cattle grazing on the horizon, a farmhouse sitting low to the ground in the distance.

Tull watched them from the window and grinned. This was what he lived for, life under America's rug. Yes, coincidence does indeed run the world. It explains why one man ends up behind a bar while another ends up in front of it. Why one man makes liquor, another man drinks it, and a third altogether tries to put a stop to the operation. Coincidence explained how Tull wound up here, snarling behind a cigar and smug in the knowledge that the two federal agents couldn't do a thing to him. The knowledge that he was above the law.

He sucked on the cigar until he had a good inch of ash drooping from the end, and then he rose from the stool and picked up a broom, swept some of the dust off the floor. The trouble with being on top in business was that you always had to remain on the lookout. People wanted to cut him down. The feds he could handle, pay them off or give them a teaser of someone farther up on the chain. The county sheriff didn't even need that much of a bribe. In a way he felt sorry for Chambers, an old man out of his element. Wanted only to be left alone to finish out his last years before retirement.

He picked up a pool cue and hit the remaining balls on the table into pockets.

The seven in the corner, the three into the side. The cue ball into another corner.

Chambers had come out here the night Ernest and Lee had been killed, and you could see it in his eyes that he'd rather have been at home in bed. Poor guy. Tull figured he would file a report and let it drop, but Chambers had surprised him, sniffed around town, visited Widow Coleman, interviewed the neighbors. But then again that was to be expected, for while Chambers wasn't much, he was honorable, and townsfolk would expect him to come up with something. Stop this killing. Shut down the Hillside if you have to. What they didn't realize was that they needed a man like Larthan Tull. He alone was willing to take on the responsibility of providing liquor to Castle County. It gave people a release, without which the county would have far bigger troubles.

Tull lay the cue stick on the table and reached for his hat.

At the sheriff's office he found Chambers standing on his desk, cursing at a light bulb that wouldn't screw in straight. Tull watched in amusement as Chambers sighed and squinted, his mouth agape, until the sheriff finally noticed him.

"Larthan."

"Furman."

Chambers wheezed as he stepped off the desk. "I was just—"

"I got you."

"Take a seat."

Tull sat.

"What can I do for you?"

Tull reached into his pocket and withdrew a bottle of whiskey, wrapped in brown paper, and handed it across the table. The sheriff took it.

"I figured Jeffreys would find whatever stash you had in here and swipe it from you."

Chambers unscrewed the cap, pulled two shot glasses out of his desk drawer, poured the amber liquid to the brim of the glasses, and slid one over to Tull. They drank. After swallowing, Chambers said, "Couple of cards, they are."

"Ha, you right about that."

"How long you known them?"

"They come through about once a year, nose around for an hour until I pay them to go back wherever they came from."

"Greedy and corrupt," Chambers said, and he swigged his shot.

"Don't say it with such disdain, Furman. Where would the world be without the greedy and corrupt to get things done? It took greed to get us out of Eden, and corruption to get us saved when they hung Jesus Christ."

"The point isn't the corruption. The point is we lost Eden, and it took Christ to get it back for us."

"To hell with Eden. You know what Eden was? Eden was a married couple sitting around bored with each other. It takes a little trouble to stir things up. How often do you and your wife like to just sit around and eat fruit all day? Sounds dreadful, doesn't it?" Tull reached for the whiskey, refilled the glasses. "Besides, if everything was paradise, you and me'd be out of a job."

Chambers slugged the second shot of whiskey, and Tull could read his thoughts, could see the sheriff's wife asking him to go ahead and retire, and he could see Chambers hanging on lest he face the boredom of his last days slowly withering away.

"I can see what you're thinking, Furman. Don't beat yourself up, thinking like that. No man wants to spend all his days with his wife by his side."

"What about you? Don't you ever wish you had your wife back?"

"I was never married."

"What about Evelyn's mother?"

"Evelyn's mother was a whore I lived with in Knoxville. And I paid off her pimp to live with her."

"But she's also the mother of your child."

"I love my child, make no mistake. I'm in business for Evelyn. But her mother and me, that didn't mean a thing. She was just a bus stop on my way to Castle."

"And Evelyn?"

"What about her?"

"She's growing up, Larthan. I know, it happens fast. Don't you ever think about slowing down, spending time with her before some boy up and decides to marry her?"

"No man's going to touch her."

"Why? Because she's a bootlegger's daughter? Some day there'll come a man who doesn't know who you are, or doesn't care. He'll come into town and steal her from this paradise you're taking for granted, and by the time you figure it out she'll already be gone."

Tull sat back and stared across the desk. "What are you saying? Do you have designs on her yourself?"

"Hell no," Chambers said with a laugh. "I wouldn't know what to do with a young woman, even if I wasn't married. But I was a young buck once. I remember what it's like. And I'll tell you another thing, I was a parent too. Even if your child doesn't walk out of Eden, the world will come to her. That's how life goes. You can't fight it."

"I'll see you, Furman. Keep the whiskey, and let me know if the feds come back."

"Don't get all offended," Chambers said as Tull stood. "Sit down. Let's talk serious for a minute."

The sheriff poured two more glasses of whiskey and Tull sat.

"Maybe we ought to figure out the Hopewell business," Chambers said.

"What about it?"

"You know I can overlook what you do for a living. Hell, at least you're organized about it. But I can't overlook a murder. People in town—even the whiskey drinkers—want to know they're safe, and when people get shot in the street, no one feels safe. I've got people calling me up from Columbia for answers, and now the federal agents are coming in. They're all blaming it on your business, so they expect me to do something about you."

"And what are you going to do?"

"For now, nothing. You say Mary Jane shot those boys, and there's no evidence for anything else. But now they're hounding me about a highway patrolman got killed up in York County."

Tull paused. The Smith & Wesson was still in the glove box of his car.

"You know anything about that?"

"Not a thing."

"Me either. I don't believe Mary Jane does either, but those two feds are convinced it's all related."

"Everything's related, Furman, and nothing is. That's just the way the world works. Folks do what they have to, to get by, and your job as lawman is to see there's restraint. Of course, restraint goes against our very natures, but we need it for our survival, and therein lies the paradox."

"Just do me a favor and lay low for a while."

Tull grinned. "Ain't easy, is it, Furman? Just like being a kid again, and your parents tell you not to hang out with the boys who rule the neighborhood."

"My brothers and I did rule the neighborhood."

"Then don't worry about the feds. You just sit tight. Keep ruling the neighborhood. I got some more business to do today."

Tull left the sheriff bemused at his desk and stepped into the dusty street. He got into the car and started the engine. The streets were empty today—Thursday—and he couldn't judge why. The only person about seemed to be an eyeless man shuffling along the sidewalk as if he had no place in particular to go. Tull watched him lope and stop and lope again after feeling around with his cane. The man turned his head to the rumbling Studebaker, and for a moment it was as if, in place of those black sockets, he had eyes that bore straight into Larthan Tull's soul.

The piedmont unfolded from the base of the Blue Ridge toward the Carolina coastline like a carpet, gently sloping across a patchwork of hills and valleys, cut through by rivers and rail lines, and stippled with mill villages. Tall ryegrasses lined the dirt roads in the upstate, dusty two-lanes that ran near the railroads, village to village. From the mountains, deciduous forest overtook the landscape, sweetgums and white oaks and tulip poplars, and farther east the forests thinned out, and jerseys and holsteins grazed in yellowgreen meadows, rows of pines in the distance. Somewhere the whistle and clatter of a train broke the stillness. A flock of crows squawked and flew in a V away from the noise. The tires of an old black Model T kicked up dust on the two-lane. The smell of late summer blooms blew on the breeze, and the flowers colored the dusty green landscape—the sweet white blooms of Confederate jasmine, feathersoft pinks and oranges of the mimosas, the bloodred trumpet creepers.

All through the day Mary Jane traversed this countryside. At midday he settled in the arms of a sycamore, the smooth bark cool and the wide leaves shelter from the blistering sun. A cluster of other trees nearby, their branches twining overhead to keep him in the shade. He rested his eyes, and in the afternoon haze he dreamt of the blind man from the mountain, marching up Main Street ringing his bell and calling for the end of the world: "The Lord will smite down those who aren't saved. Follow me to the river, brethren, and wash your sins in holy water."

In his dream sinners came out of their proud houses with snakes' tongues and fire in their eyes, the living dead following the piper still tolling his bell through the streets of Castle. Sutures across their cheeks and foreheads, bare skin spliced to bare skin. Night fell on the town. The sun blackened and the moon filled with blood and a cloud of fire swept through the alleys like water from a burst dam. Mary Jane found himself alone in a jail cell awaiting his creator. Depending on God's demeanor, he would have words. He would have words.

He woke and moved on through a piney wood, roughly north, stopping once to pick blackberries. In the late afternoon the woods opened to reveal, in the distance, score marks where the crests of the Blue Ridge met the sky. A washed out and grown over dirt road led from the clearing into more pines and sloped down into a valley. A rusty tow trailer lay in a glade of sedge and red clay, grown over with dead brown vines beside rows of rocky tilled earth, sprinkled with sticks and broomstraw. Across the glade a boulder jutted out of the ground, and beside it he found a nice resting place, a circle of loaming soil and pinestraw. He rested against the boulder and sat in the soft earth, pulled a peach out of his bag and ate. Juice dribbled down his chin. His hands grew sticky from the soft sweet flesh.

Later he built a fire. Embers sizzled into the evening as a storm rolled in, and in his dream a figure emerged in the forest, a husk of a man whose firehot eyes could only be those of the devil.

I know who you are, Mary Jane said.

The man sat beside him, helped himself to a plate of cold beans, and chewed thoughtfully before asking Mary Jane about his family. His voice grated like a train skidding to a halt on a trestle: *You come from good people, Mary Jane. Why did you leave them?*

I couldn't help it, Mary Jane said. *Trouble came to us, and I had to move on.*

Trouble came because you called for it. You left Ernest and Lee dead in the street to save yourself, and you left Abigail to follow through with your selfish plans. Men weren't made in God's image to gallivant around like you're doing now.

I'm going to Charlotte to make things right.

Just like that?

Just like that.

And you believe it will all work out? Mary Jane, you're a hustler. That's who you are. You've left behind a trail of suffering, and before you is a long, narrow road. Godspeed, if you think you can walk it, but making things right now won't account for the sin you've already caused.

Mary Jane felt hollow inside, like he'd been bruised right down to the soul. Christ given for his sins, hung from a cross, suffered, died and buried. That knowledge was a heavy burden for a man to carry, for all of us come up short. How many have to reckon with their sins? To atone? To ask for mercy? He said, *Jesus will forgive me.*

Jesus? What do you know about Jesus?

He died for my sins.

He took lashings two thousand years ago, so that's two thousand years of souls he might have saved. I'm here to tell you there'll come a time when the Lord'll grow weary of forgiveness. His creation has done some damage and wiped the good name of His son through the mud. All in the name of Jesus. Ha!

So God's promise doesn't apply because I was born too late?

Have you ever tried to explain Noah's Flood to a child? the man replied. *In the good book God has done some wicked things.*

So has man.

And so has man. Such is human nature. We were made to fall, but what is God's nature? Father, son, and ghost? God wasn't made to fall, nor to forgive. He simply is.

So why does sin matter? Mary Jane asked.

Rather than answer, the man left him there and the night wore on. Rain came and went and the fire hissed until it was cold. Nothing moved in the darkness around him.

The next day he walked along a damp road without eating and stopped when he heard the squeak and hiss of a tractor-trailer pulling into the lot of a filling station. He followed the sound to a cleared-away patch of dried yellow grasses, clover, and concrete. An old country store set up in the middle of nowhere, no signs to indicate where he was or how far was the nearest town.

Inside, he stood in line to buy a bottle of Coca-Cola. The afternoon heat burned the dust in the air. In the back of the dry room, a woman held a miniature dachshund in her arms, and three old men with raspy voices stood around her, discussing its blackness, one man preferring brown dachshunds, the other two admiring this one. The cash register clanked as the clerk tendered the sale.

Mary Jane set his bottle on the counter and asked, "How far is Charlotte?"

"I'd say it's about forty miles, straight shot to your left up the highway. You on foot?"

"I was, lest I can get a ride."

"It'd take you two days to walk it."

"I'm going to set here and drink this Co-Cola and see if I can get a ride."

The clerk rang up the drink. "You set here and you don't have to pay for the bottle." Mary Jane paid with a dollar, and when the clerk handed him his change, he said, "Shouldn't take too long fore a trucker coming in will stop."

"Appreciate it," Mary Jane said.

"God bless."

In the back of the room, the crowd around the dog had quieted. Mary Jane felt their eyes as he stepped into the hot outdoors. The sun seared against the dust and the pavement, and he sipped the drink until the bottle was empty, and then he lay it in the shade by the building. The sugary syrup stuck to his teeth, and he wished for a real drink. Some days were worse than others, but he'd always liked to drink, ever since his days as a soldier in the war. His father had never approved, said it would lead him into the kind of trouble he was in now, and Mary Jane couldn't figure how his father had made such a prophecy so many years ago. His brother had drunk plenty back then too, but their father'd seemed to peg Mary Jane as the one who wouldn't be able to quit, who would ride it head on to the devil and come out ruined. Well. Here he was, on his way to Charlotte to face that devil. Making a deal with Aunt Lou would earn him enemies, especially Larthan Tull. That was assuming he could make a deal with her, and of that he was less sure now that he was several days on the road. Why he hadn't just killed Larthan Tull before he left town he couldn't say, but when he returned from Charlotte, that business would be his first order. And then any man who dared step in his path.

A car rumbled to a halt, and an attendant hoofed over to greet it. Mary Jane listened to children bickering in the back seat, didn't smile or wave, only continued to sit still until the family drove off. The broiling day made him faint, but he remained in the shade until he heard the hiss of another truck pulling in.

The driver was a sandy-haired kid not much older than Mary Jane's nephews. His shirt and pants hug from his lanky body like a boy dressed in his father's clothes, but when Mary Jane came over and asked where he was heading, his face wised up and hardened.

"I'd be obliged if you could get me a little closer to Charlotte."

"I'm not going all the way into town. Where you need to be?"

"Myers Park, eventually."

The driver froze with his tongue behind his lip.

"Anything to help keep me from being on the road till next Sunday."

The driver hesitated as though torn between common sense on one hand, the bandits on the road who would slit your throat and take everything you had, and on the other hand—not compassion, exactly, and not exactly respect for his elders, but the uncertainty of youth in the face of a grown man who knows what he's about. Mary Jane recognized that look as the same one he'd gotten from Ernest and Lee as he'd described his godforsaken plan to enter the liquor market. He took advantage of the kid's hesitance and climbed into the cab. "Much obliged," he said.

After he'd paid for the gas, the kid climbed into the driver's seat without looking at Mary Jane and started the engine. The truck jerked onto the highway as the kid mangled the gears. He got up to speed and seemed unconcerned by the curves and narrowness of the road. Their windows were down, so the wind and the engine created a deafening roar. Mary Jane nonetheless felt obligated to make conversation.

"Where you coming from?" he said.

The kid glanced over at him.

"I said where you coming from?"

"Georgia."

"I had an uncle in Georgia. Whereabouts?"

"South Georgia."

"Mm. My uncle was in Macon. I don't rightly know where that is."

The kid made no reply. The steering wheel wobbled loosely in his hands. Mary Jane studied him as he sped onward. He looked about Ernest and Lee's age, had that same scrawny look, a dust of freckles on his soft skin. Amazing how everyone not your age looked the same. Although the kid was trying to look tough over there like a working man, Mary Jane could see he was just another lost soul trying to make it in this world. The kid could easily have been one of Mary Jane's Hillside prodigies. Apparently, he'd never had a wild uncle like Mary Jane, or else he would have relaxed a little and maybe even shot the breeze.

Mary Jane closed his eyes and tried not to picture the truck missing one of these hilly curves and rolling right into an abyss. The warmth of the air blowing onto his face and the soft padded seat made him drowsy. Before long he was remembering his last night with Ernest and Lee, bonded by conspiracy, drunk off Larthan Tull's rotgut, playing cards in a booth.

Depot was sweeping the tavern, and when he passed near their booth, he said, "I hear you boys have some liquor brewing out at the widow's place."

"We might have a sup. Why, you want some for the bar?"

Depot shook his head. On the next pass with the broom, he said to them, "Tull know you've got a side business going?"

"Likely he does."

Depot nodded and swept on. A moment later he called, "Why don't you boys step out with me?"

"Hell, Depot, we're in a game here."

"Come on."

Mary Jane saw the shotgun before the boys did, and he knew what was coming the same as if he'd read the story in the newspaper: Three murdered outside the Hillside Inn. Ernest and Lee looked up and saw the score as well when Depot cocked his head toward the door and said, "I can't have you hurting my boss's business."

Ernest laid the cards on the table and eyed Depot as he walked away, Lee following, then Mary Jane. The night was sweltering, and Mary Jane, in what he felt would surely be his last moments alive, didn't pray or take in the beauty to savor the evening air. Instead, as he marched off the porch, he noticed a slimy slug that clung to the railing. As they walked up the hill to the road he thought that was one nasty creature. Where'd he come from? What was he doing up there? Those would have been his last thoughts, that banal musing on an ugly, insignificant creature.

The barkeep didn't say anything more to them. Once the four of them were standing in the road, Depot pumped the shotgun, aimed, and shot Lee in the chest. Lee's body spun as he fell to the roadside. Depot pumped again and fired at Ernest. The shot sprayed into Ernest's jaw and looked to take off half his face. Stray pellets bit into Mary Jane's shoulder, knocking him back.

He hunkered over and, without thinking, dove down the hillside and tumbled into the ravine. A third shot kicked up dirt at the hill's edge, and Mary Jane rose in the bottom and scrambled through briars and brush, not looking back.

The driver slammed the brakes and jolted Mary Jane from his daymare. The kid wheeled the truck to the side of the highway, kicked up dust as the rig eased to a halt.

"You said Charlotte?" he asked.

Mary Jane caught his bearings, saw a crossroads, meadowed hills, cattle, and a barn in the distance. Nothing resembling the great city.

"I'm heading north from here, but that road will take you the rest of the way in, maybe five or six miles to the city limits."

Mary Jane rubbed his eyes, pinched his nose. He thought about asking if the kid would take him on a detour, but the kid kept his eyes straight ahead, as though he were holding his breath until this stinking sinner got out of his cab. He'd done his Christian duty and learned his lesson. What lesson was that? Mary Jane wondered. Don't pick up a stranger or he'll fall asleep on you?

"Obliged," he muttered as he got out of the cab. The kid maneuvered the truck back on the highway and grinded the gears as he tried to floor it and speed toward wherever he was going, leaving only dust in his wake.

Mary Jane looked about him again and began to walk down the road the way the kid suggested. Meadows gave way to tobacco fields, their leaves yellowgreen under the blistering sun. He passed one shack after another, the men lazing in the shade not even upturning their hats to investigate this lone traveler. He passed a dead mule that seemed to have been hit by a car. The mule stank and flies gorged on its open sores. After a time he came to a mill village, the familiar puff of steam from the factory, the dusty streets, the cluster of houses a mirror image of the Bell.

No one was in the streets, but he could feel eyes watching him from the houses as he walked through. If this was anything like the Bell, strangers came in often but they didn't remain strangers for long. They either adapted to the community or left in a hurry. Likely the community knew before the stranger did whether they'd get along. He approached the mill and flagged over a man in the yard.

"I'm trying to get to Charlotte," he said.

"You looking for work, you found it here."

"Naw, I'm trying to get to Charlotte."

"You got another five, six miles to go fore you hit the city limits."

"You sure about that? Trucker that gave me a lift told me the same thing five or six miles ago."

"Where you coming from?"

"South Carolina. I come in on this highway."

"He must have dropped you way out."

"Wasn't nothing there but a few tobacco fields."

"Must have gone out of his way to get you there, because they's a hundred miles of nothing out there."

"He said he was passing by Charlotte."

The man scoffed. "This road'll take you into the city. Another five miles, you can catch a streetcar wherever you're heading. You looking for work, though, likely won't find anything more promising than the mill here. They're about the only ones hiring these days."

Mary Jane thanked him, wiped his brow, and walked on.

Willie had a dog named Charlie, some kind of collie mix with matted brown fur and sickleshaped nails crossed on each front paw. Charlie was about four years old and had shown up one day awhile back and the family began feeding him. He slept in the yard and would wander the streets as a vagrant on occasion, but somehow he always came back. He took to Willie because Willie, being young, was always interested in the dog and went out to play with him three or four times a day. The neighbors grumbled behind closed doors because the dog kept impregnating the bitches around town. Population control for animals meant tying a litter of puppies in a sack and dumping them in the river. Mean enough, but necessary for a good society, and the people of Castle County, at least in the city and the mill villages, believed they lived in a society. But some kinds of meanness you just can't account for.

On Thursday afternoon, four days after the murder, Willie and

Charlie the dog were out playing in a field in the Upper Flat. Willie had him running after a stick, which Charlie ran after so fast his ears tucked back behind his head. He stumbled when he reached the stick, flopped over himself, snagged the stick, and sprinted back.

Willie worked six-thirty to three-thirty, a shorter day than his father and Quinn by two hours, and these afternoons were lonesome and slow, especially now that his grandfather was out of work. Abel lay in bed all day, tended by Susannah, and the house had taken on the tone of a hushed prayer for Abel's convalescence. Anything louder than a whisper drew the cold eye of Susannah, and maybe a wallop to the back of the head.

Out and back, out and back, went the dog.

Until one run back, the stick right in the middle of his teeth, a rifle shot popped and the dog yelped, fell over, and skidded to a halt.

Willie stared at his dog, lying in a heap ten yards off. He looked around. The sun pounded against the hillside, a relentless blaze. The trees and shrubs were all still like images trapped in a photograph. No one was near. He ran to the dog and pulled Charlie into his lap. A groan from deep in his throat like some atonement for all the sackfuls of puppies he'd caused to be thrown in the river, like there was some maker in the world of dogs and Charlie was about to meet him. Charlie wheezed his last and then he quit and Willie held his dog, the tangles of fur and flesh, and wept.

What should have been a long weep was cut short by laughing on a nearby ridge. A boy approached with a twenty-two Marlin thrown over his shoulder. He wore shorts and a coonskin cap. "That's a dead dog," he called. Face-freckled and obstinate, peach skin. His head hinged back, and he laughed like a billygoat's bah and said, "I killed that dog."

Something rose up in Willie, a thing he didn't understand in this world, and he clambered out from under the dog and ran toward the boy. Air shot out of his nostrils and a buzzing filled his head. Peach Skin quit laughing, but it was too late, for Willie was already scooping stones out of the red clay earth and hurling them at the boy.

One missed, but the next connected with his head. Peach Skin's eyes bogged out and he turned to run, not even thinking that he might have the upper hand by holding a rifle.

Willie chased him down the hill, hurled more stones that popped off the boy's back. He leapt over shrubs and slid on the hillside and onto pavement. Peach Skin occasionally glanced back, and at the edge of the village, his coonskin cap fell off his head. By the time they entered Down-the-Street, Peach Skin was sobbing and Willie was an unstoppable fury. He picked up another rock and launched it at the boy, but it missed and banged against the store building.

Peach Skin ran in. When Willie followed, one of the mill attendants stopped him at the door. He grabbed Willie by the shoulders and held him in the street. "Whoa, son," the man said. "What are you doing?"

"He shot my dog."

"I never," Peach Skin said, peering out of the doorway. Onlookers had paused in their tracks to stare at the scene. A woman with a sack of groceries, a black man in a fedora who leaned up against a post and tried not to appear at all interested in the affairs of white folks.

"He shot my dog," Willie said again.

He struggled in the man's arms, and the man said to Peach Skin, "Son, why don't you hand that gun over and we'll check on this boy's dog?"

Peach Skin looked for a moment like he might defy the grown-up, but the man straightened himself up. The boy hung his head and brought the gun over.

"All right, son, where's this dog?"

As the onlookers went back to their routine, the three of them walked out of town. It came out that Peach Skin's real name was Parham, and that he came from a family of coal miners from Eastern Kentucky who'd drifted south after a mine had shut down a few years ago. It was unclear whether they lived off the land in the forest or had found refuge in a shantytown. Either way, it was no life for a man willing to put in his day's labor. Willie knew the mill would take care of you to some degree, as long as you were willing.

When they reached Charlie, the dog was already stiff with rigor mortis. The same stick he'd been chasing lay nearby, still damp from slobber. The mill attendant shifted his hat back on his head, looked at the boys, nodded to himself.

"You don't know I shot him," Peach Skin said.

"You want to tell me who else might have done it?" the man asked. He circled the dog, poked at him with the barrel of the rifle, and made a face. "I tell you what," he said. "We can keep the police out of this, and you can pay this boy five dollars for the dog. I'll give you your rifle back minus the shells, and everyone goes home. Or we can call Sheriff Chambers over to determine what kind of legal penalties he'd see fair. I reckon you ought to know he wouldn't take kindly to a boy killing another boy's dog, specially a boy without a permanent residence. Might send you to the county lockup for a few days to teach you a lesson."

In reply, Peach Skin toed the dirt. He stared at the ground with his lips pouted until the man said, "Well?"

"If I was to admit it, I ain't got five dollars to pay."

"I could spot you, give this boy five of my own dollars and hang onto the rifle until you've worked it out. We can always use more sweepers at the mill."

Peach Skin looked up, said, "Seems like I don't have much of a choice, doesn't it?"

The next day, Peach Skin was a sweeper in the Bell, same as Willie. Along rows of machines, through the fog and dust and heat, they and other boys traded by each other, Willie and Peach Skin smoldering. On Peach Skin's first day, the Hopewell brothers took a smoke break behind the mill, leaned up against the shaded bricks by the rusted-out green dumpsters. The chainlink between them and the world jingled when the wind picked up. Beyond it a field of waist-deep ryegrass angled north, and blades of grass cut through the fence and jabbed into the mill property, closecropped weeds and dirt inside the complex, grave-colored and cinder-covered gravel closer to the pavement itself. The backlot tinted an ochre sheen like the sepia of motion pictures or the faded amber of an old daguerreotype. The noise of machines never far away, the call of men's voices.

"How long's he here for?" Quinn asked.

"I don't know. Till he earns that five dollars for the attendant that's got his rifle."

"That'll be at least a week, assuming the man don't charge him interest."

"That's solid math."

"Shut up. I'm thinking we need to get him. You don't just go around shooting dogs. I don't know how they did things wherever he's from, but that won't work here. He needs to know that."

"What are we going to do?" Willie asked.

"I don't know yet. But I'll think of something."

Willie waited on his brother's word, but in the interim Quinn seemed more concerned with Evelyn. Only a week they were together now, but already the boy was smitten beyond all else. Couldn't wait to get out of the house at night to sneak off with her, and Willie could tell that whenever someone spoke with Quinn, Quinn's mind was off with Evelyn. He'd reply in monosyllables—yep, nope, mm—and his eyes would flutter around like he was thinking: "I got a woman here somewhere, where's she at?" Only trouble was his woman was in town and under the thumb of Larthan Tull. Willie had never met Tull in the flesh, only seen him from a ways off, but he'd heard enough stories about the man that a ways off was too close.

On Saturday afternoon, Quinn surprised the family by taking his paycheck into town after work and driving home in a rusted, ten-year-old Model T. When he parked the machine in the yard, the bucket of bolts rumbled, hissed, and coughed before it quit running altogether. Steam hissed from under the hood, and the engine pinged. Willie was out first to see it, followed by his mother and father.

Quinn hopped out and waved.

"Oh Lord, what'd you do?" Susannah asked.

"Got me a car, Momma."

He wiped down the hood with the sleeve of his shirt. She put her hand to her forehead like she was about to faint from a spell and said, "I see that."

"Where'd it come from?" Willie asked.

"I bought it off a guy in town. Ed Sothesby had one for sale, Larry Scruggs's uncle."

"How much you pay for it?" Joe asked, walking over and running his tongue across his gums.

Still wiping the hood, Quinn replied, "I bought it with money I've been saving."

"How much?"

"A hundred and twenty."

Joe spat.

"But I've been saving that money for a long time. Outside the family money."

Joe walked around the side of the car, kicked at a tire. "That's a lot of money," he finally said. "I reckon we could use a good car, but this thing won't even get us to town."

"Hold on, now. She needs some work, but she'll run."

"She won't run a hundred and twenty dollars' worth."

"I'll fix her up."

"You know how much it'll cost to fix this thing? You be better off taking it right back to Ed Sothesby and getting as much of your money back as he'll give you. We can find us a car this bad for half the price."

"What do you know about a car anyway?" Quinn asked.

Joe sucked his teeth, popped the hood. Underneath was a rusting four-cylinder engine with oil dripping out like water on cave walls. He said, "You think this car is going to get you somewhere with that gal, but I told you last week, Evelyn Tull is trouble. Trouble without a car, trouble with a car."

"Daddy, will you leave it alone?"

Joe shook his head and turned to go inside, followed by Susannah.

Willie walked around the car while his brother studied the engine. Willie had never ridden in a car before. They never needed one because everything they ever wanted was near enough to walk. Their grandfather thought automobiles were some manner of sin, but their father just preferred to do things the way he always had. The boys—and all the boys they knew—were dreamers.

"Daddy's right," Quinn said. "I am going to have to do some work on it, but there's no way to get this car for cheaper. Just needs some work, is all."

And Quinn did work on it, beginning that afternoon. Willie helped him change the oil, lay on his back against the rocky ground, the ground hard and rough against him. "Hold this," Quinn said, and handed Willie a plug before oil poured from the belly of the car. "I got to get this distributor adjusted." Quinn fumbled with a socket, trying to figure out which size would fit. Grease stained his fingers in the heat of the day.

"How you know all this?" Willie asked.

"I don't know. A man just knows this stuff."

Willie didn't know this stuff, and he wondered if this was just some kind of magical knowledge bestowed on you when you reached a certain age. He watched his brother and tried to take the knowledge into himself. Damaged gaskets in the carburetor. Some problem that dealt with the manifold. New spark plugs. The list continued so that by the time the sun began to plummet toward dusk, all they'd managed to do was change the oil, tinker, and make lists of all that was wrong with the rickety automobile.

"She'll run to town and back," Quinn said, "but it's going to take some time before she'll be ready to carry me any farther."

Quinn wiped his hands against his overalls, adjusted his hat. Willie sat on the bumper with grease imprinted on his skin as though he'd been tarred. Dirt under his nails, in the lines of his fingers, a stain of grease running up his arms. The smell of gas and oil and rust.

"Damn, this is going to be a chore," Quinn said.

"It'll be worth it, to have a car."

"Hell yes it will. Then I can take Eve out anywhere, anytime. We might up and get married, move up to Charlotte."

"Really?"

"Really."

"You only been sparking her a week."

"Brother, sometimes it only takes a moment to know where your destiny lies. Might have to put fate off a few weeks while you repair your car, but then the world is stretched out for the taking."

Willie imagined the globe in last year's classroom, tried to picture it stretched out and flat, the continents oblong and bleeding into each other, New York and Europe and China all like stepping stones, and he could see Quinn and Evelyn dressed up for society, driving the new car, Quinn in a top hat and Evelyn in a cloche, Quinn's head back and laughing as they wound down a road toward the city, toward sunset. Quinn could work in a skyscraper and carry a briefcase. Evelyn could be a movie star. They could smoke cigars with President

Hoover, dally about town like Clark Gable and Greta Garbo, beautiful and slick and rich. Was that where Quinn was heading? And how could Willie get into that life?

"I got a plan for the Parham boy," Quinn said.

Willie turned off the running picture show in his mind, looked over at his brother.

Quinn wiped his hands on a rag, leaned against the driver's side door, and propped his foot on the runner. He lit a cigarette. "We'll get him Monday," he said. "This is what I need you to do."

West along Highway 9, Chambers drove past the Bell and into the open piedmont farmlands. Trees in the wilderness guarded the south, and to the north was nothing but stretches of fields, cattle, corn. He turned onto a dirt road and headed north to his brother's house, the house where they'd grown up. It was a single-story beige stucco with a slate-colored roof, crumbling barns and proud magnolias in the yard, pastureland beyond, the grass yellowed and spools of hay baled in a checked pattern across the field. From a distance he could see his brother sawing a piece of wood next to a swing in the side yard. Hunched over, determined. After their daddy had died, James had been the one to stay and take care of Momma, and he'd somehow never found his way to leaving. Liked it here, Chambers guessed, and he could understand that. Some days Chambers wished to change places with his brother, though if he did that he figured he would see sides to this life he couldn't from the outside. He drove the cruiser down the gravel drive and parked by a holly bush.

James hadn't quit sawing even to look and see who was visiting. He stopped when the board was in two pieces, and only then did he look over at Chambers. He squinted through thick glasses, grabbed both pieces of wood he'd just cut, and leaned them upright against the swing's supporting posts. "Furman," he said.

"Hey, James."

James went back to work, propped another board on the sawhorses, began cutting, the zzzzt, zzzzt, zzzzt of the sawblade the only noise save for Furman's own breathing.

"What are you doing here?"

"Been awhile. Thought I'd come for a visit."

"I heard about all the trouble in town. I bet Alma's not taking kindly to your working all hours."

"She wants me to retire. I might look into opening a bait shop or something down on the coast, when all this is over."

James put the saw down. "Just like that?"

"What more can I do? People are blaming me for all this violence. They were perfectly happy to let Larthan lie, but with bodies in the street and feds in town."

"You can't fight that. You step down, someone else'll come up and learn the same lesson. They'll keep electing someone else, hoping things will get back to the way they used to be, but there's no going back. Maybe times were never that good. Just people wishing, is all."

"It's time I let someone else bear that cross," Chambers said.

James turned back to the wood and picked up the saw again.

"What are you making?"

"Need me a new rocking chair on the front porch."

"Something wrong with the one you've got?"

"Nothing wrong with it, except it's the only one."

"You getting greedy?"

"I need two, in case I get company."

"That's nice of you, little brother."

"I wasn't talking about you. Billy Henderson just died the other month, and his widow's up there by herself. I invited her over any time she feels like she needs some company."

Chambers nodded. "I remember her."

James studied the board he'd just cut. "She's nice, and it gets lonesome out here."

"I remember," Chambers said. And he did. The smell of honeysuckle and ripe earth brought him back to the time of his youth, when he lived out here in the yellowed country, the wind combing the landscape, the pines and cedars creating soft beds of needles in the forest. Home is what it was, and he missed it. A part of his soul was left here, sundered from the rest of him that had moved on. He used to climb a magnolia tree in the side yard. That tree was gone now, but others had replaced it. They looked so small now, so fragile, when in his mind's eye they were giant fortresses where he would escape as a quiet eight-year-old. He would ascend to their peaks and survey the land, the cattle and the horses, the corn and the garden. As the sun began to set, he could already tell it was getting dark earlier even though it was only early September. Lonesome times, always had been. When he was a boy in those magnolias, the evening sun stung his eyes and made him crave sleep. Now as an old man, the sun was almost unbearably sad, the color of nectarines over the piedmont. So much time lost out here, a whole way of life gone.

"You want some tea?" James offered. "I've got a fresh pitcher."

"That'd be nice."

"Set on the swing there, and I'll bring you some."

A moment later James returned with two glasses, and he sat in the rocker next to the swing. They stared over the pasture. The cows were lying down, a sign of rain. It had been a long time since Chambers had needed the rain the way a farmer does, but he remembered the strain a late-summer drought could put on someone who relied on the land. This year had been a blessing overall, and with luck it meant an end to the downturn. Maybe the violence would abate with the next wave of cooling rains. He hoped so. He was still sheriff for a few more months, and he wanted to leave on a note of hope rather than forking over trouble to the next man. Get this mess cleaned up. He relaxed and drank his tea, sweet and cold. The swing rocked gently, and the two brothers sat in a comfortable silence as the afternoon grew later still. What did they have to say to each other now? Years had passed since they'd been close. James had stayed on the farm and Furman had left. James's wife had died in childbirth, and Furman's wife was still alive. James had children spread out across the upstate, and Furman's boys were buried in Europe. Each man would give up something of what he had for a piece of what the other's life held.

"Why are you here?" James finally asked.

"I don't know what to do, James." He drummed his fingers on the swing. "About all this. I wonder if I got it all wrong, or what I might have done differently."

"Jesus, Furman, are you listening to yourself? Put Larthan in a corner, the way he's been putting this county in a corner for years. You've been sheriff for long enough now, you ought to know that. You remember a few years ago, when the drought killed everything in the state? You know how hard I prayed for a few drops of rain? And those folks in Washington are telling us how to live without even the first clue of what our lives are like. I could make more money selling my corn to Larthan Tull than I ever could out on the market, and in a time like that he owned me and all the other farmers out here. Had us in a right spot."

Chambers peered at his brother. He knew farmers sold corn to Tull, but this was the first he'd heard of his own brother mixed up in it. He considered that some of the whiskey he himself drank was born in part from James's crop. Still reliant on his family, something not even the free market could put an end to.

"Don't look at me like that. There's laws from God, there's laws from man, and there's the law of the economy, and those things don't always agree, especially when you've got a banker to pay."

"I know it."

"No, you don't know it. You've got a steady paycheck, and all you have to do is make sure the rest of us follow the rules someone else makes up. You've spent your whole life running away from the truth."

James rocked furiously and his eyes bore into the landscape as though he weren't looking at the land at all, but rather watched a reel of the past seventy years of human history pass before him, and he was disgusted by what he saw.

Chambers knocked on the swing, said, "I got to get on."

"I guess you do."

He rose and ambled over and got in the cruiser. The sun was falling fast out of the sky, coloring the west pink and casting long shadows from the electric poles and magnolias. He drove toward the sunset like a man seeking the last remains of a life long gone, as though if he could only catch up, he could regain all that he'd lost.

J oe sat in the kitchen while his boys worked on the car in the yard.

"That boy's fixing to get himself into some trouble he won't get out of," he said.

"There's only so much you can do," Susannah said. "You remember what it was like when you and me were courting."

"But your daddy didn't run liquor trade. You daddy wasn't a killer."

"Quinn knows enough to stay out of real trouble."

"He doesn't know enough to recognize real trouble when he's in it." Joe stood and said, "I'm going out for a while."

"Where you going?"

"To town."

"Maybe you need to think about recognizing trouble yourself."

He nodded at Willie on his way out and walked on down the road. So much pressure in that house, ever since Abel's stroke. His father-in-law lying in bed all day, Joe's oldest boy off with the boot-legger's daughter. Years ago, Joe had decided to take some responsibility for his life, to quit drinking and work to support his family, back when Mary Jane was still out honky-tonking every night, spending one night a month in the county lockup. The life of his brother wasn't one he wished for himself, and was one he feared for Quinn, but in some back corner of his psyche, in some leaky jail cell that housed all the unfettered emotions of a child, he felt envy for Mary Jane. His brother, on the run now, had lived free in spirit while Joe had toiled away in the mill.

Mary Jane had been trouble since day one. Two years younger than Joe, he seemed to have no boundaries growing up. He played pranks and lied about things he'd done, and their mother had always forgiven him. Their father was a tough farmer, and seemed determined to force his sons to earn his respect. Neither boy had done a good job as children—Joe always sensed his father thought them soft. The man had been born in a war, had served his country and made his living on the farm. Joe fought for his approval, eventually going off to fight in Europe. After his father's death, all Joe could do was regret never earning the man's approval. Worse, he was working for Abel, a father-in-law all the more difficult to please. It drove Joe to pack up his family for the Bell, and now here they were, their roles reversed, Abel in need, yet Joe was still unable to provide. Do men ever live up to the figures from the past?

Mary Jane had never sought their father's approval. He had their mother's love and undying attention, and he was free from the shame of masculinity. Joe envied his brother that. He'd given up his mother's affection in a vain effort to be seen as a man, rock-stable, and a part of his adult soul still missed her, the quiet farmwife who went to church and prayed regularly and took care of her family. Not unlike Susannah. Meanwhile, instead of growing up and then chasing after some vestige of his childhood, his brother had simply never grown up to begin with. Never held a steady job, never started a family. Any money he got—whether from painting houses or sharecropping for a season—he spent on liquor and card games, which then led to nights in the crossbar hotel. Mary Jane wasn't a mean drunk, he always smiled and told stories, but he'd get behind the wheel of a car or get into the wrong car and end up in some spinster's flowerbed. Or he'd flirt with the wrong man's wife and land beaten up in a ditch somewhere. Sheriff Chambers would pick him up and cart him in until he slept it off, and more often than not Joe had to come to town to bail him out. That was some kind of life.

But something had happened to Joe this week, whether it was his brother on the lam or Abel laid up in bed. The life Joe had made for himself was a tight box, and for years he'd always appreciated the order. Ever since he'd begun courting Susannah, Abel had made clear that Joe wouldn't be getting a free ride, that if he wanted to marry Susannah Washington, he needed to straighten his spine and learn the value of a good spit-shine. The army had taught him the value of keeping on schedule, but it wasn't until the battles broke out that he actually understood the reason behind the military regimen. Trench warfare was a nasty, brutish thing, and he found anything he could do to structure his days since helped keep his memories at bay. It had taken the eighteenth amendment for him to kick the drink for good, or at least until now. This week all the order around him had come undone. The box constricted his breathing, and he felt pains in his chest that only liquor seemed able to cure, as though the alcohol loosened up something in his body and allowed his blood to flow freely. A few drinks made it easier for him to breathe, and easier for him to sleep. The problems with Mary Jane and Abel and Quinn, they all diminished after a drink. It was dangerous, he knew, but these were dangerous times.

The sun tumbled from its four o'clock perch as he shuffled along Highway 9, a scrim of dust fanning out behind him.

On his way to the Hillside, someone called, "Hey-oh."

He turned and saw Shorty Bagwell limping behind him.

"Joey Hopewell, what say?"

"Hey, Shorty. When they let you out?"

"Long enough ago for me to develop a thirst."

"I'm heading that way myself."

"No fooling? Didn't know you were a drinker."

"I'm not, but it's been a week."

"Sheriff told me about Mary Jane."

Joe shook his head.

"I know it," Shorty said.

The two walked along the dusty road, rocks of red clay crumbling beneath their feet. A slight breeze blew through the tops of the roadside water oaks and pines, but no breeze reached them at ground-level, the air a thick swelter, the day on fire. Neither man spoke while they walked along. It was close to five when they sauntered into the Hillside.

"That you, Shorty?" Depot said when he unbarred the door for them.

"I'm out."

"I see that."

Lester and the Kid were playing pool, and Joe bought a jar of whiskey and brought it over. "Well, well," Lester said. "Two times in one week. You're starting to take after your brother."

"Yeah, yeah. Maybe it's in the blood."

"Hold on," the Kid said. "I'm about to run the table."

He leaned over and struck the cue, and the ball bounced over the lip of the table and rolled across the bar.

"Shorty, this boy's been dominating all week," Lester said. "Must have taken a pretty penny off Joe here the other night."

"I'd believe it," Shorty said. "Joe, when was the last time you played pool? Before the war?"

"Must have been. I was playing terrible next to this pro."

"Y'all laugh," the Kid said, his voice hoarse and cracked. "You old men'll still be playing here when they close, but I'm just killing time till tonight."

"You got a date?" Lester asked.

"Maybe so."

"Watch out now," Lester said as he bent over the table to take his shot. "Little man might be getting some."

"That's right. I'm going out with Caroline Mahoney."

"That the middle Mahoney girl?" Joe asked.

"No, her younger sister."

"She must have been ten years old last time I saw her."

"She's filled out since then, probably even had her monthlies by now," Lester said.

"Going for that young stuff, eh Kid?"

"Hell, he is the young stuff."

"She's old enough," the Kid said.

Lester sank the eight, and shook his head. "I hear she's already made her way through a couple of young bucks in town. Boys older'n you. You think you can compete?"

The Kid said, "Only difference between a virgin and a woman is you don't know if a virgin'll like it. With a woman, you know."

"That's pretty profound there," Joe said. "Where'd you figure that out?"

"Profound nothing," Lester said. "She'll be comparing him to those town boys. The woman might like it, but when she gets itchy and sees Kid here don't measure up, she'll find herself some other man that does. A woman's a crafty devil, and don't you forget it."

"Tell that to my oldest," Joe said. "He's in deep with a town girl himself."

"Seems like I heard something about that," Lester said. "Kid, you know anything about Quinn Hopewell?"

"Naw, he and I don't run in the same circle." The Kid picked up the stick and leaned over the table.

"Wait a second," Shorty said. "Did you say Caroline Mahoney?"

"That's right."

"Hoo-hoo, boy, she and I went rolling together a few weeks ago."

"I'll be damned," Lester said. "Kid, you ain't got a shot in hell, now that this stud's taken her to the barn loft."

"Oh yeah, I remember her now," Shorty said. "Whoa buddy, she's a quick one. Shouldn't be tough if you want to knock her box."

"You're just funning me," the Kid said. "Don't be talking about my new girlfriend that way."

"Girlfriend? How long you been going out?"

"Tonight'll be the first, but I might make a steady commitment here."

"Good luck to you," Shorty said.

After the Kid left, Lester asked, "You really go out with that young girl?"

"Hell naw, I just wanted to get a rise out of him."

The men laughed and carried on with their game. They closed down the bar a few hours later and stumbled out. On their way up the hill to the road, Shorty bumped up against Joe and said, "Shoot, I never knew you was this fun. You ort to've been coming out with us all along."

"No reason I can't start now."

The men trudged up to the road, the air still blazing hot, the sky hazy and the crescent moon peering through a break in the clouds like someone grinning from the heavens. The three men set out for town, Lester advertising whiskey at his house and Joe tight enough to want to find some trouble, Abel and Quinn and Mary Jane long forgotten. He said, "Why don't we try to find the Kid, see how his night is going?"

"Where you think he's at?"

"Where do all youngbloods take girls they want to spark?"

There were only two places young men could be counted on to bring a young woman in Castle, one being along the river near Abigail Coleman's farm and the other being across town by the city pond.

"He's probably at the pond, but that's a long way to go if he ain't," Lester said. "I say we try Coleman's farm, cause that way if we don't run into him we can at least stop by and see about getting a drink from the widow."

They set off along the railroad tracks toward the Coleman farm. Dark chattering in the woods, umbrella foliage overhead. Along the tracks they shushed each other whenever one tripped on a tie and landed in the trackside underbrush, guffawing underneath, a silent cackle. The night air was warm. One or two stars winked through the clouds, and cirrus wisps streaked across the sliver of moon. No sound from the woods except the three men shuffling along. Near the trestle, they sobered enough to hunker down, and in the starlight they could see a couple necking on a blanket by the riverbank.

"Cawaw, cawaw," Shorty called.

Joe and Lester snickered, but the couple on the blanket was too deep in their endeavor to notice a rumble in nature.

Lester squeaked out, "Ay-ay-ay-ay," in a high wail that no couple could ignore no matter their ecstasy, and the three men ran down the slope like incarnate savages and fell upon the young smoochers in their embrace so that they had mere seconds to pry themselves apart to confront their would-be assailants.

Only when the men neared did they see this couple was not the Kid and Caroline Mahoney, but rather Quinn and Evelyn.

"The hell," Quinn said.

"Sorry, boy," Shorty said. "We thought you was someone else."

"Good, then you can get the hell out of here."

"Now hold on here."

"Go on, you perverts. I'll kill you, you don't get out of here."

Joe said, "That's no way to be talking, son."

The boy squinted at him.

"You don't recognize your pappy?" Lester asked.

"God."

"You got that right."

"Daddy, what are you doing out here?"

The liquor still swirled in Joe's head. He knew this was the moment for him to put a stop to Quinn and Evelyn, that maybe now was a time to right his life, this last week a detour, a stumble from grace rather than an actual fall, but something turned inside him. Quinn had him on the defensive, asking what was he doing out here, a question Joe couldn't answer. He said, "Shorty just got out of jail today. The three of us was celebrating."

"Evening," Lester said, still agog from the melee and the whiskey. "Ma'am," he said to Evelyn.

Shorty said, "Hey, you all ain't seen anyone else out here, have you? We're looking for a kid—what's his name, Lester?"

"I don't know. Kid, I reckon. Cope's his last name."

"He had a date with the youngest Mahoney girl, left us at the Hillside to get his shoes shined or what have you."

"We ain't seen no one."

"That's all right. We figured we didn't see him, we'd hit up Widow Coleman for a drink. You welcome to come with us."

"Not tonight," Quinn said, still eyeing his father.

Joe sighed. "I wonder what your momma would say, me and you out here like this tonight?"

"She wouldn't like it."

"I reckon not," he said. He leered at Evelyn, standing petite beside his son, and he felt a stirring in him, remembered for a moment what it was like to be Quinn's age. He thought of Susannah in the barn loft, thought of Evelyn on the highway the other night. He put his arm around his son and said, "Hell, I reckon we're both in trouble then. Hopewell men, trouble's in our blood."

"I should be going," Evelyn said, backing away.

"Don't rush off on our account. We were just leaving."

"You go on with them," Evelyn said. "I can find my way home."

"You can come, too," Quinn said. "You don't need to rush off."

"My daddy thinks I just went to the pharmacy for a soda, and they're long closed. I need to get on."

Joe watched his son walk off with Evelyn.

Lester said, "Your son sure is taking a risk, ain't he?"

Shorty said, "He wouldn't be no kin to Joe and Mary Jane if he didn't take risks like that."

When Quinn returned, the men had a campfire blazing, three logs lit and orange sparks zinging into the night. They'd procured a jar of moonshine from the widow's stash, and they grew somber, reflective. Joe was still drunk from the bar and nearly asleep by the fire when his son returned. He waited in apprehension, for Quinn had never seen him this way. Something new for the both of them.

"There he is," Lester said.

"What are you doing back here?" Shorty asked. "Pretty woman like that, it'd take me half the night to say goodbye to her."

"He knows what he's doing. No time to waste, gets right down to business."

Quinn sat next to his father, and Joe eyed him as he passed over the jar of shine. His son grimaced as he took a sip, the liquor no doubt setting fire to his throat. He coughed.

"Whoa now," Lester said.

The logs were ashy and scales of glowing coals coated their undersides. Joe added another to the fire. The damp wood crackled, hissed. Billows of smoke swirled around the men.

After a time, Shorty said, "Did you at least give that gal a goodnight kiss?"

Quinn smirked and took another sip of the whiskey.

"Oh, he did! Look at him!"

"You're in trouble now," Joe said, his voice thick and slurred. "You better think of a plan for when Larthan catches you."

"He won't catch me."

"The hell he won't," Lester said. "Likely the man already knows."

"He don't know."

"That man's not all human. I've heard tell about how he knows things he couldn't have no way of knowing."

"He's just a man," Joe said.

"I've heard he's supernatural."

Lester said it so earnestly that all of them quieted and let the words hang in the air. Smoke blew into Quinn's face, and he coughed. Then he and Joe burst out laughing.

"You don't believe me?" Lester said.

"Shit no," Quinn said, waving at the smoke. "You're drunk as hell."

"You watch yourself, youngblood, and you too, Joe. Two Hopewells pissing off Larthan, he's liable to take a dislike to your whole family."

"That may be," Joe said. "He's a mean son of a bitch, and I don't approve of Mary Jane running whiskey for him." He turned to Quinn: "Or you dating Evelyn. I don't approve of it. But damn, Lester, there's a difference between a mean son of a bitch and the Devil himself."

"You can deal with a man," Lester said, "but when the Devil comes to collect, your days of wheeling and dealing are over. Now you tell me, when Larthan Tull shows up at your door to collect, can you deal with him like a man, or does he collect like the Devil?"

At the mill, they all stored lunches in a row of cubbyholes in a front closet, and Peach Skin's lunch was easy to spot. He brought it in a rusty lunchbox that had a hole corroded into one side of it. The guys teased him about it, but he kept saying, "My father gave it to me, my father gave it to me."

Willie hadn't slept all weekend in anticipation of today's vengeance, but this morning, when the deed was to be done, his bowels were knotted and his knees were weak. Quinn had agreed to do the hard part, to find a dead rat in town and slice it into small slivers. During a break in the day Willie was to sneak into the closet and put a few slices of the raw rat meat onto Peach Skin's baloney sandwich.

All morning he swept the weave rooms, he kept his head down and brushed with the broom while the other boys joked and horsed around. In room #6, his grandfather's chair was empty, no one yet to fill the slot. It seemed likely that Abel would finish his days on his bed in the front room of their house. Quinn worked in the card room, where Willie didn't go, but he did sweep past Peach Skin once early in the day. This was his third day on the job, and he had four more to go until he could get his rifle back. Watching him, Willie lost his nerve. The men ragged on Peach Skin so badly—first about his lunchbox, then about his Kentucky drawl, then just to rag on him. Willie felt sorry for him and wanted to back out.

But at ten o'clock, Quinn found him on break.

They shared a cigarette outside, in the shade of the building's east end. A wire fence separated the mill property from a pasture, the grass beyond the fence wild and unkempt, there solely for grazing cattle, whereas the grass on the mill's land was littered with dust, bone dry, gravy brown, and trampled near to death.

They watched the mill boss's Packard cruise up from town, slowly, and turn into the graveled drive of the mill. Quinn stood with his foot propped against the mill's wall, and Willie sat Indian style in the broken earth. His legs were greasy and chafed from the way the denim rubbed against him, and he thought maybe he'd be better off becoming an Indian when he grew up so he could walk around in the summer heat with nothing but tiny drawers and a feather in his head.

"I don't want to do it," Willie said.

Quinn took a puff and stared off into the farmland. "We're already rolling. It's happening."

"I can't."

"Yes you can."

"He's having a hard enough time."

"Good. He deserves it."

"Maybe he doesn't."

"Jesus, Willie, he shot your dog." Quinn smacked the back of his head. "What's wrong with you?"

Willie thought of Charlie, limp and bleeding, and of Peach Skin's harsh laugh, and he nodded.

"Atta boy," Quinn said, and he handed Willie a folded-up newspaper. Inside were the bloody slices of rat meat, which smelled rancid and sour when Willie peeked at them. Across the meat was the tail, the prime indicator that, yes, Peach Skin, you bastard, you are eating a rat sandwich.

His brother exhaled a plume of smoke, flicked the cigarette into the dust, and pushed off the wall. Willie scrambled to follow him into the mill. He slunk into the front closet and lay several slices of the stinking rat meat between the two slices of baloney, and his hands shook with the dastardliness of the deed. He placed the tail over the top and let the end dangle out of the bread so that Peach Skin wouldn't have to take more than one bite that he could still spit out before realizing his lunch was ruined. They weren't trying to poison the poor boy. This was just the first in a series of pranks to make his life miserable.

The Hopewell brothers didn't tell anyone about their plan, but they did make sure to get a good view of Peach Skin while he was eating his lunch. Their father ate quietly across the cafeteria, not noticing what the boys were up to. Peach Skin sat with one of the foremen—a burly, cold man—and pulled out his sandwich.

The brothers had to contain their laughter as they watched. They only expected him to unwrap the sandwich, smell it, investigate, and gag. But instead and to Willie's surprise he chomped down like he hadn't eaten since lunch yesterday. Which he might not have, given his family situation. They'd drifted to town after the Depression was in full swing, already poor and no buffer to keep them from getting poorer. Peach Skin's father was out of work, hadn't even come looking for a job, so who knew how the family subsisted.

Peach Skin consumed half the sandwich without even looking at it and not even chewing that Willie could see. Willie watched on in horror, and remorse returned to his soul, heavy and laden with a guilt no preacher would ever be able to assuage.

Peach Skin finally must have spied a piece of the tail because he quit chewing in a hurry. He opened the last of the bread, saw the bare and ringed tail, wormlike in its curls and nakedness, and spat out a mouthful of the bloody, unchewed food.

He moaned and twitched, stood up and screamed something awful: "Rat tail, rat tail!"

Turning, he stumbled away from his lunch, that rusty lunchbox, and ran into the mill. Men at their looms watched him, some of the younger men muttering, "They Lord," the older men not even turning from the machines, so used were they to the antics of children in the mill.

Peach Skin rounded a corner and tripped over his own feet and fell onto one of the idle machines. Men scrambled up and a melee ensued, napkins swirling and men cursing and Peach Skin screaming up to high heaven about the rat in his sandwich. The Hopewell brothers laughed and laughed and soon, when other men figured out what had gone down, the entire crew laughed at the poor dusty kid from Kentucky.

When he recovered from his spill, Peach Skin reared up and assaulted Willie. The two boys clambered around the weave room, among the dust and spit. The men shut down their looms, and the machines ground to a halt. Men yelled. The boys grunted. After rough hands pried the boys apart, an eerie silence filled the room.

Mr. Lowry, the mill boss, stood in the corner and waved for them to follow him to his office. He shut the three boys—Willie, Quinn, Peach Skin—in there. Through the window, Willie watched his father and Mr. Lowry talk. Joe frowned and glared in at the brothers with a look likely meant to instill fear. Mr. Lowry was wide and tall and wore a white button-down shirt so that, standing beside him, Joe appeared tiny, grimy, and meek. Back at the house, Willie knew, his father's authority would return, but for now he pitied the man and felt a deep shame for feeling that pity. He looked away.

Quinn hunched over and stared at the floor in boredom. Peach Skin's eyes flicked back and forth between the two brothers, and then he said to them, in a calm voice, "You boys know you're going to pay for this."

Quinn spat on the floor by Peach Skin's feet.

"I'll put a hex on your entire family," Peach Skin said. "You'll see. You'll be begging for a rat sandwich before I'm through with you."

"Yeah, yeah. I've heard that before," Quinn said.

Peach Skin pointed at him and said, "You think I don't know all about you?"

"What do you know?"

"About Evelyn Tull? You think everybody here doesn't already know about you and her? Doesn't even matter if I put a hex on you. You're already cursed."

PART THREE

Mary Jane roamed through Charlotte under cover of night. He'd been on the run more than a week now, tired and grimy from the long road and wrong turns. Water puddled in the wet streets of the east end, the Tudor houses in Myers Park, clear brick towering over well-kept lawns and curving streets. Light gutter trash and gas lamps. The quiet shuttle of streetcars. Not his district, but his destination. Tony suburb home of the mill owners, bankers, and utility leaders the rest of the city worked for.

At number 7 he stopped and examined the house, the downstairs windows still lit up though it was nearing midnight. All the neighbors had work in a few hours, office jobs, but Mary Jane knew this resident's business, and she didn't set foot in an office. His boots crushed blades of fescue, and then he stomped his feet dry on the porch, clacked the brass knocker three times, waited.

A moment later a kid answered the door—twenty-three,

twenty-four maybe, a snarl and a thin mustache. Older than Ernest had been, probably arrested and sent to the army, made it out and realized he wasn't cut out for real work anymore, got involved in the liquor trade. The kid stared at him until he said, "I'm here to see Aunt Lou."

"Who are you?"

"Tell her Mary Jane Hopewell is here. She'll know my name."

The kid eyed him another moment before closing the door. When he returned he didn't immediately invite Mary Jane in, instead asked, "What is it you want?"

"To talk to Aunt Lou."

"About what?"

"Larthan Tull."

The kid opened wide the door and bade him enter. The hall was dim, but even in the low light Mary Jane could see the well-polished brass fixtures, the shellacked floor. A light glowed beyond a door at the end of the hall, and he hung his coat on the rack and followed the kid to the back of the house. Inside the kitchen, Aunt Lou sat at the table, her hands cupping a mug of hot tea. She was small and trim and looked nothing like what he'd been expecting. She resembled his mother, God rest her soul. One would expect her to be a wealthy widow living off the pension of her dead husband. You certainly wouldn't peg her as the local moonshine tycoon.

"Didn't think I'd ever meet you face to face, Mr. Hopewell. I'm getting old enough now, I'm not sure how long I'll be in business. Been a long time since I've needed to meet any farmers out your way, it being the drive that it is. What brings you out here?"

He knew he looked a sight, wearing the same set of clothes for nine days straight, sleeping in ditches and mountain hollows, riding in smoky trucks. His shoes were worn thin, his skin was covered in soot, and he hadn't eaten in three days. Sallow and sunken and cut up from brambles, his village-soft back sore from sleeping on too many hard places after too many years in a comfortable bed. "You haven't heard from Larthan Tull's boys in the Studebaker this week," he said.

"That's right. I suppose you're going to tell me why, seeing as that wasn't a question."

"Larthan's barkeep shot them a week and a half ago in front of his bar. Tried to shoot me too, but he missed."

"I see."

"He's probably after me now, and I want him taken care of."

"Who? Mr. Tull or the barkeep?"

"Both, but I'd settle for Larthan."

"You'd settle, huh?" She took a sip of tea, and her eyes never wavered.

"You know he runs the show," he said.

"Indeed, and I understood the issue to be your selling shine to me. Seems there's a mix-up in Mr. Tull's ranks, but I'm not sure it helps either one of us to run with that confusion. Do you?"

"I've got a better business proposition for you, provided you can take care of him."

"Explain to me what you mean, 'take care of him.'" She paused, and this time it was his eyes that never wavered. She went on, "And what makes you think I can do that, even if I wanted to?"

"I don't want him dead. I just want him to leave me alone. I came into a lot of money recently—it didn't belong to Larthan, but he felt otherwise and now he's after me. He'd slit my throat in the night or do like his barkeep done to my friends, tear off my jaw with a shot-gun and not think a thing of it. Probably sleep like a baby afterward."

"I'm not interested in the condition of Mr. Tull's soul," she said. "I can't say I particularly blame you for how you feel, but I still can't figure out why you're here. Way I see it, you've done nothing but disrupt my business with my best supplier. And Mr. Tull is my best supplier." She nodded her head as she spoke to make sure he understood her. "So right now—and you'll excuse my directness—I don't see anything in it for me whether he kills you or not."

"That's what I want to talk about. That money I've come into, it came from whiskey I've been brewing."

"Yes, yes, I get it. You've got good whiskey and want me to sell it."

"Larthan bought my corn for nothing, turned it around for profit. I cut out the middleman, sold a few jars of my own. A better product, sold for less, still gave me more than what Larthan was paying. I couldn't make it on as large a scale as him, but it's quality shine. I was thinking we could do business."

"What are you offering me today that Tull can't already provide?"

"I've got capital."

"Mr. Hopewell. Surely you know we live in a free society here. Free enterprise, free exchange. The same principles apply to whiskey as they do to Coca-Cola. Since the government doesn't want it sold, we don't have to pay taxes on it. That's the only difference. I'm merely a vendor here, your local general store, if you will. If you want to enter this business, that's up to you, so long as you realize you're trying to enter a competitive, unregulated market with Larthan Tull. Competitive means I'm going to keep selling his whiskey unless someone offers me that kind of quantity at a lower price. Unregulated means he can do whatever he wants to keep his business running smoothly. He can kill your family. He can kill your wife. He can kill you. You understand?"

"A monopoly is the death of free enterprise."

She finished her tea, studied him a long while, so long that his knees quivered and sweat misted on his skin. He saw now why she was so good at her job. Then she grinned and said, "I can talk to him this week, but understand I'm not about to lose my best supplier."

"That's all I'm asking."

"Come back on Friday then. I'll think it over and see what I can do for you."

Tull's day was thus: He rose early and drove into the factory north of town. The rough industrial neighborhood, where his former employee Lucas Mackey used to live. Although Lucas was long dead, his family still lived up here, what was left of them. Shotgun shacks and a mess of kids scurrying about in the street like fleas.

Inside the steaming factory, they still produced soda, less than in the peak years before Prohibition, but enough to put on the pretense of legitimate business. In the back boiler they brewed whiskey: mixtures of mash in barrels, a row of submarine stills in which the liquid boiled, shot up through pipes to condensers, and dripped out in gallon cans for delivery. He still remembered the turnip stills of his youth, men in the backwoods under cover of moonlight, the scent of pines, the call of a whippoorwill.

Today was the first Tull had been in the boiler room in a few days. First the business in Charlotte, his meeting with Aunt Lou, and

then his time running the books at the Hillside, and then his deal-
ings with the lawmen. With all that was going on, these weeks had
been a time to lay low. Nevertheless, business continued to operate.
As the chief executive of his tiny empire, Tull had responsibilities in
every area of the operation.

Depot Murphy had been with him for years now. When the barkeep had first shuffled into town, his lazy eye had made him look
dumb, which had not instilled confidence in Tull about the man's
wherewithal. But Tull knew the type of man he was—broken down
from a long history of defeat in the Appalachian coal mines, drifting southward in search of an honest job, desperate in the way Tull
liked his employees to be. Tull set him up to man the stills, and after
Lucas Mackey passed, Depot became Tull's right-hand man, a good
worker who knew how to keep his mouth closed and wasn't averse to
using his muscle to strongarm someone behaving out of line at the
Hillside. Kept the operation well oiled and took on more work than
he needed to—the factory, the Hillside. Now Tull had one more job
for the man.

Depot was sitting on a stool stirring mash when Tull walked in.

"Hidy," Tull said. "Everything good?"

Depot grunted.

Operations were easy now, and required little more than checking
water levels and temperatures. Alcohol boiled cooler than water, so it
was a matter of keeping the burners in that magic range to separate
the two liquids. The bubbling mash smelled like a hog's gut, and although the room was well-ventilated Tull wouldn't want to spend his
days here. But he figured it wasn't any worse than a coal mine.

"Who you got running the Hillside this evening?"

"I left the kid in charge."

"Which kid?"

"Tommy Cope."

"The boy that's always running the pool table?"

"He's a good worker."

"I see," Tull said. "I got a call from Aunt Lou the other day."

"Oh?"

"She needs another load tomorrow, and I can't make it. You think
your old coupe could handle a trip to Charlotte?"

"Be glad to," Depot said.

"In fact, tomorrow I've got another task that needs to be done up in Charlotte. The price for it's negotiable."

"Is it?"

"It is. You might find it worth your while for more reasons than one. Let's talk tomorrow."

Depot nodded, and his eyes drooped so that his face appeared like that of the dead.

This was as long as Tull could stand to be in the boiler room. He quickly moved from there to the office, where stacks of papers lay for him to weed through. The day-to-day grind of owning a business, legitimate or not. His business had slipped beyond his control lately, so he needed to close himself off and think through his next move. He'd received a phone call from one of Aunt Lou's henchmen yesterday, who confirmed that Mary Jane had indeed made it to Charlotte, and had made some kind of futile offer for her with the five thousand dollars he'd scrimped from his bootlegging. The henchman had practically gloated that Mary Jane had sat there and tried to explain to her about competition and the benefits of selling a smaller-yet-high-end batch of his brew alongside Tull's mass-produced swill.

Well. Mary Jane was as good as dead tomorrow, but Tull could feel the foundations of his empire shaking, not because of some peon drunk who occasionally ran whiskey. But the scope of the situation, all the whiskey he made and the breadth of his operation, all the angles and crevices where danger lurked, all that pressed against him some days, to where he needed to sit and think. Mary Jane, Ernest, Lee. They were just the first, and he'd contained them almost without a hitch. Then there were the feds, but he paid them off with cash or information. There was Sheriff Chambers, a good man, and a good man was ordinarily hardest to deal with unless you wanted to kill him, but the sheriff wasn't interested in anything more than his retirement. Eventually, though, someone would come along who wasn't interested in retirement or money and who wasn't a bumbling fool.

When he got home that night—Thursday—Evelyn was in her room. He sat on the porch with a cigar and watched the light fade from the sky. September was already beginning to cast its autumn shadow even though the days still boiled. Wouldn't be long before the leaves fired up and then browned, those sad afternoons where the sun seems to be in a perpetual state of setting. Last days, the husk of life.

Around the corner on Main, a junkyard Model T was parked with the engine off. Tull couldn't see the face of the driver who sat smoking, his arm out the window, newsboy covering his eyes. There would come a time indeed.

When Evelyn came out and said, "Bye Daddy, I'm off for a while," he knew. He puffed his cigar and watched her stroll around the corner. She glanced back before slipping into the passenger seat of the Model T, and together the two of them drove off. He stubbed the cigar on the porch and drove down to the Hillside to check on business.

A light glimmered inside the tavern, a warm beacon in the cooling night. He slid down the hill from the road and banged on the door. A moment later Tommy Cope let him in. The teenager had been a fixture here for some time, and Tull thought perhaps he might not have to look for a new barkeep after all, so long as the kid had some manner of judgment and discretion. The bar was empty for now—it was early yet—but Tull asked anyway, "How's business?"

"Slow," Tommy said as he returned to his station behind the bar.

"I see that."

Tommy poured him a tumbler of whiskey, and Tull drained it.

"Leave me the bottle," he said.

Tommy nodded.

After swigging another shot, Tull said, "You know the Hopewell family?"

"I do. Me and Quinn were in the same class at school. Matter of fact, his daddy's been coming in here lately."

"That a fact."

"Strange, too. Lester told me the man hadn't had a drink since the start of Prohibition, but he's been here regularly. Plays pool like a pro."

"Trouble at home will drive a man to drink," Tull said, and he poured himself another shot. "Quinn's been seeing Evelyn lately."

Tommy's face whitened.

"Though I reckon you heard about that."

"Seems I might have heard something about it."

"I guess word travels fast on the mill hill."

"That it does."

"Goddamn Hopewells. What a family for her to get mixed up in."

Tull drained the last of the bottle, and Tommy cleared the jar. "You want another'n?"

"Yeah, one for the road."

Tommy handed another across the bar, the lid still on.

"I'll see you, Tommy."

Tull headed back for the house. The liquor had gone to his head already. He'd drunk more of it—and faster—than usual, and the road blurred in front of him. He parked on his lawn and stumbled up to his porch and fell into the rocker. Crickets hummed nearby, a steady pulse to measure the irregular clocking of time. He unscrewed the lid from the mason jar and sipped at the whiskey and waited for Evelyn.

Past midnight, a car parked at the end of York Street and dimmed its headlights. Tull debated marching up to the car and starting something here and now, but before he found the energy to stand, the passenger door opened and Evelyn got out. When she reached the porch she started.

"Oh. Daddy. I thought you'd gone to bed by now."

"I had some business, so I thought I'd wait up." His voice sounded hollow to his ears, as if he were under water. The mason jar sat on the porch, half empty, and she must have seen it, too. "Have a seat," he said.

She sat.

"Where were you tonight?"

"Out with some friends."

"Which friends?"

"Barbara and Helen Ann."

"Barbara and Helen Ann."

"Yes sir."

"Who drove?"

"What?"

"Who was driving the car you just got out of? That junky Model T with the dirty boy in the driver's seat."

She didn't answer for a moment. Then she said, "He was just giving me a ride."

"The Hopewell boy."

"Yes sir."

"I've told you before, that family's trouble."

"It doesn't mean anything."

"Then it shouldn't be anything for you to stay away from him."

"Daddy."

"Don't let me see you with that boy again. I know you've been sneaking off with him. I didn't know he had a car, or at least that's the first I've seen of it. But you keep that up, he's going to be trouble."

"Goodnight, Daddy." She stood up to go.

He slurred, "You have choices."

"I'm sorry?"

"Choices," he said again, clearer now, and he leaned forward until he fell from the rocker. There against the rough wood, he whispered, "You don't have to."

She opened the front door and left him there on the porch.

"I mean it," he called, and in response she shut the door softly behind her.

He lay on the porch and listened to the continued chirring of the crickets.

A fly landed on his neck, and when it bit him, he moaned and swatted it away. Another bit his ankle where his pants leg had rolled up. This was undignified, he knew, but he'd been here before. He shifted and rested his head on his arm and slept.

Overnight he had a dream, and on Friday morning woke at dawn knowing where Mary Jane's money was hidden.

"You damned depraved son of a bitch," he said, and he went back to sleep.

When he woke later in the morning, he couldn't believe how he'd missed it. Mary Jane had the money. He was wanted by the law, so he could only spend a little bit of it on the run or risk getting caught. And he had to know men would be after him. The law, sure, but he would know too that Tull would come for him as well. He would know there was a good chance he wouldn't make it out of those backwoods alive. He had a family, and he had his mistress, and of course he would want to take care of the widow should something happen to him. He would owe her that, at least.

So. He wouldn't have the money on him.

Tull had sent a few boys out to shake down the widow once again after he'd spoken with her. They'd ransacked her house, same as he'd done, pried up floorboards and ripped out walls, kicked the dog for good measure, but they hadn't found a dime. They'd combed the grounds for fresh cut marks, but in all the acres they hadn't seen a lick of evidence that a hole had been dug. Well, they'd found what seemed to be remains of one hole, but they'd dismissed it, because what kind of man would do that? Tull knew. The same kind of man who was desperate enough to rip off Larthan Tull in the first place, and audacious enough to go on the lam rather than simply pay what was owed. He must have known Tull would kill him either way, but still.

Tull had reconciled himself to the spectacle Depot had created when he'd shot Ernest and Lee that night. Not at all what Tull had meant when he'd said the men would need to be dealt with—he'd envisioned sealing their feet in cinder blocks and dropping them into the Broad River—but if you were going to drop the bodies in the street, at least get them all at once. Mary Jane was a louse, a scoundrel, a drunk, and an inept businessman who maybe did deserve a public bullet through the heart, but Depot was now a dead man for his ineptitude in letting Mary Jane go.

Tull went inside, where his daughter was already up and scrambling eggs. Coffee boiled on the stove. She kept her back to him.

"You're up early," he said.

"You slept in." She scraped the skillet, tossed the eggs.

"I've got some business to take care of this morning. Might take me all day." He wanted to apologize, to make some kind of amends for last night, but he had only hazy memories of the night before. Instead, he said, "How far does the apple fall from the tree in that family?"

"What?"

"The Hopewell boy. I know his people. His uncle's a drunk, slower than molasses in January, and his daddy's an all-around fool, from what I hear. I was just wondering about that boy's mental acuity."

She slammed the skillet into the stove, pulled biscuits out of the oven.

"I got to get on," he said.

He grabbed a biscuit, forked some egg into the middle, and set out for the widow's farm.

September this year was a dry, hot, dusty, weary month full of ticks, fleas, and mosquitoes. All the dogs in town stopped every few steps to scratch their bellies, and many of the children did the same. They'd be going back to school soon, but until they did they all hung out around the downtown diner, and all of them looked the same nowadays, dirty, smug, lively, and small. Tull drove across the railroad tracks, down the dirt road to the widow's farmhouse, and parked in the yard. Without bothering to summon her, he marched in a sure-footed line to the barn, and when the door caught against the dirt, he kicked it in. He grabbed a rusted shovel from the wall and walked to where the woods began. The Coleman family plot. Three graves of small children who never saw their tenth birthdays, a few more graves of old relatives long forgotten, nary a headstone reminder, just small rock plates.

On the end a wooden cross marked the final grave, the widow's son, the soil dark and still loose on top. He planted the shovel in the earth, stomped it deep, and plowed. The earth upturned easily. The smell of humus and decaying leaves rose to his nostrils, but he continued to dig. Heat smothered him and jaundiced the nearby grass, and although he dug in the shade a sweat broke out on his forehead by the third scoop. The wood of the shovel's handle slipped in his damp hands. Indian summer, the muggy preamble to the annual harvest. A flash of his own youth, quiet and sullen and working with the old man in the womb of the mountains, where sunrise gave way to sunset with no real day in between. As Tull cut the shovel into the soft ground, sweat darkened his clothes and dripped to the earth. He hadn't dug very deep when a door slammed in the house and the widow came running across the yard in a blue and white checkered dress, yelling for him to get off her land, go on, get out of here, he ain't got the right.

She clawed at his arms, tried to rend the shovel from his hands, but he heaved her back. She fell to the ground, and beneath her sour look he could see fear.

"It's here, ain't it?" he said, and he returned to digging.

"I don't know what you're talking about."

"I'm going to find it, Mrs. Coleman."

"Leave my boy alone. Haven't you done enough? Can't you let him rest in peace?"

She stood and tried once again to wrench the shovel from his grasp. Again, he struck her down. He blinked to keep himself in the here and now, and then he knelt and pinned the shovel to her neck. "I'm not the one you should be asking these questions to," he said.

She spat tobacco juice at him. He watched it arc and land on her dress between her legs. "I didn't choose for my boy to die," she said.

"None of us chooses death," he replied. "I've been running from the grave since I was fifteen years old, but there's no accounting for when choices we make lead to results other than what we intended."

As he spoke, his heart thumped deep in his chest and he felt short of breath, like he'd been running full speed the past thirty years and had only now paused to take the measure of himself, only to find his body hadn't caught up. He still held the shovel to her neck, and for a moment he considered bearing down until she choked to death. She met his eyes without fear. What would be the use? He rose and pulled a hand-rolled cigarette from his shirt pocket, struck a match on his boot, and sucked at the flames until the cigarette was lit. She remained in the dirt at his feet.

He went on, "Intentions are meaningless, Mrs. Coleman. Incentives are everything. You ought to know that by now."

"Where was the incentive in all this?"

"Isn't it always money? That's the only thing we're running around here for, isn't it? Money or power? If you're lucky, the fates line up and you can have them both." He resumed his digging. The cigarette dangled from his lips.

"I don't have any money," she said. "Look at how I live. I sold half our farm to pay my bills."

"And you sold your crops to me when the market wouldn't pay enough."

"That's right."

"But it still wasn't enough, so dear Mary Jane decided to sell his whiskey."

"I don't know anything about that."

"Now fate has brought me to this moment, to what's buried here with your son." These were simple lessons his old man never learned, his father always believing some almighty would bring rain if only he prayed hard enough, if only he'd repent. But to cede to the supernatural, to deny accountability and wait for grace to save you—that was foolishness and it did more than one hopeless farmer in. Aloud he said, "Poor choices, is all, and now fate is directing its own course. I am your fate, Mrs. Coleman."

"I don't believe it," she said. "There's no cause."

He stopped. "Cause? A cause assumes a reason, and if you want to discuss reasons, we can talk about greed. Otherwise, there is no reason. There is no cause. We can't just operate according to the will of another, or else what would that make us? My daughter and I, we're grappling with these same issues. What would it do to my self, to my soul, to give up to some cause?"

"What are you talking about?" the widow asked.

But he was no longer listening to her. "I suppose they only tell you so much at the Baptist church: Jesus will return, so give your life to Christ. That is all ye need to know. They'd have you separate reason from religion, but it wasn't always that way. Our religious men used to think about the world. This soil, this earth, what it means to be flesh. But you can bet Christ actually will come again before these backwoods Christians ever accept he was just a man."

His mind continued spiraling in on itself. The father abandoned his son in the flesh. The son left to toil and suffer for the whims of the holy spirit. Tull's father was built like a boulder, and like the towering mountains themselves, he humbled a stringy boy just trying to make his way in the world, a boy long off that farm now. Ma was dead. Pa was dead. Little Larthan was the mountain now, never to reconcile with them. Empires rose and fell around you in half a lifetime, and still you continued to dig for that ever unredeemable something, that lost piece of your soul.

He shook beads of sweat off his face, said, "Here's a question for you. If I'm digging up your son as part of some grand design, the game of some great clockmaker, what does that make my actions?

Do I actually have any choice in the matter? Seems to me we either have our freedom or our meaning, but we can't have both."

By this time runnels of tears streaked the widow's face. Dirt clung to her damp skin. She propped herself up with her arms and watched compliantly as he continued to dig. "Why are you here?" she said, her voice like worn-out sandpaper, her resolve crumbled to dust. "Why won't you leave?"

"And where is that clockmaker, anyway? We call him our father, but I'd never thank my own father for giving me this life, any more than Evelyn would thank me. We're all of us alone here, out of dust and unto dust, and our days pass away under the wrath of that malignant creator who set us here to suffer, to chase after—"

He stopped and, as though knocking to gain entrance, he beat the shovel against the lid of the coffin.

"This is what it's about," he said. "All cause and all design result in the power of our hands to do whatever work we may."

She sat by and silently watched as he scooped dirt from her son's grave and uncovered the pine coffin, the outer layer of the wood already decayed from the unrelenting earth. The coffin was made from hewn wood, nailed tightly together, and his boot thunked against it as he stepped into the grave. Ma is dead, pa is dead, but the mountain and the mountain's shadow still remained. He pried up the lid with the shovel, and the wood creaked and splintered beneath him. Inside, the boy was nothing more than bones, the cloth of his blue suit ripped and ragged and eaten through by worms. Beneath the bones lay three mason jars, each stuffed with cash. Tull reached for the jars and held one over his head. The fire of the sun at high noon shone down on his grinning, maniacal face, and at that moment a shadow fell across the land as a lone cloud winked over the sun, black in the chiaroscuro of the sky.

Out of ideas and restless at the station, Chambers paid another visit to Widow Coleman. He knocked on her door in late afternoon, and at first no one answered him. Then the door opened and her harried face peered out at him through the crack in the door. Her eyes were bloodshot and a tangle of matted hair hung in her face. The absolute image of the grotesque. Beyond her lay only darkness.

"Ma'am."

"What you want? You find him yet?"

"No ma'am, but we're looking. Have you not heard from him?"

"I ain't since he left here. You just missed Larthan Tull."

"What was he doing here?"

"Grave robbing."

"Come again?"

She stared at him a moment. "You all want the same thing. To find Mary Jane."

"Maybe you could step out and we could set here on the porch?"

She opened the door and strode out to the nearest rocker without looking at him. She walked like she'd been shot in the back, like each step sent a tremor across her body. In the light of day she looked a decade older than even a few days ago. The mills aged a body quick, but something was deeply wrong with her.

He walked around to the far rocker, sat down next to her, and said, "Why don't you tell me what's going on?"

"I can't help you, Sheriff."

"I'm the one trying to help you."

"I'm just fine here." She clasped her hands in front of her face and gazed off toward the tree line across her farm. She bit her knuckles and rocked violently. The rocker's runners drummed against the porch boards.

"I know I've never been good news for your family, Mrs. Coleman, but I want to help you."

She kept rocking. "Why is it men think they can help? You never let a person just be."

"You sound like my wife."

"I'm sure she knows what she's talking about. You sure don't seem to be listening to her."

"I try."

"You think you try? I highly doubt it." The widow was shaking now, like Chambers was the one who came in and took Mary Jane out of her life, like he was just here to harass her like Larthan Tull, whatever she'd meant by her grave robbing comment. True, Chambers had done more than enough damage when he'd shot her son back then, and he believed that gave her the right to be angry with him forever. But did it give her the right to comment on his marriage? To say he wasn't trying hard enough with Alma?

He said, "Don't you want me to try to bring Mary Jane in before Larthan finds him?"

She slowed on the rocker and seemed to calm down, which made him even more nervous. Emotions weren't like a light bulb. You didn't turn them on and off with a switch. They lurked, and often they came back more dangerous than before, like a reformed drunk who hits the bottle again.

"It don't matter now," she said. "Larthan's only after one thing, and he got it from Mary Jane, so he'll leave me alone."

"What thing?"

"What else?"

"Money."

"Mary Jane buried a pile of it with my boy, fool that he was, and Larthan came over and dug it up." She clenched her jaw and stared at him with a murderous fire in her eyes. "He dug up my boy. Mary Jane never had the right. None of y'all did."

"Where is Larthan now? I need to find him."

"Probably gone off to Charlotte. That's where you'll find Mary Jane, if you really want to bring him in. He's off trying to make a deal with Aunt Lou, and don't even know he ain't got his money to trade with any longer."

She stared back off across the field to the edge of the woods, where the family plot lay, and raised her hand to clench the front of her dress to her heart.

Chambers got up to go, said, "I got to send a wire to Charlotte."

"You do what you have to," she said, turning back to face him. "Just don't bring Mary Jane back here. He ain't welcome any longer."

She resumed her rocking, furiously, the toes of her feet rising in unison and dropping as her shoulders hunched forward with each rock. She said, "You ought to go home to your wife and forget about all this."

Rather than reply, he got into the car and headed back to town. Things were falling into place: the murder at the Hillside a product of competition between Hopewell and Tull, both jockeying for some kind of business with Aunt Lou in Charlotte. Chambers had never met Aunt Lou, but her reputation was well known. Why any man such as Mary Jane Hopewell would want to get involved with her was beyond his comprehension, but if something was going down, others needed to know about it. It was about two now, and he figured they had about a day to get something organized.

At the station, he got on the phone with the sheriff's office in Charlotte, and had to leave a message with the deputy: "You make sure you tell him, something's about to go down with Aunt Lou."

"I'll tell him," the kid said.

"I mean it."

"I said I'd tell him," the deputy said, and hung up.

Chambers then called Agent Jeffreys. The Columbia office gave him the number of a boardinghouse in Castle.

"Something's going on," Chambers said when he finally got ahold of the agent.

"Can you meet us at the diner on Third Street?"

"I'll be there in five." He hung up the phone and gazed at his desk. Paperwork piled high in the box, all his menial duties on hold while he roamed around town chasing after bootleggers. Maybe this was it. Maybe it would all be over within a week. He would be plenty glad for Larthan Tull and Mary Jane Hopewell to be sent down to the federal penitentiary in Columbia, leave Castle to its good citizens. He opened his desk drawer and pulled out the bottle of whiskey Tull had brought the other day. He unscrewed the cap and drank straight from the bottle. He set the open bottle in the drawer, out of sight in case someone walked back to his office. Then he pulled his gun out of his holster, spun the chamber, and returned the weapon to its place on his hip. He took another sip of the whiskey. The liquor bit at his throat and warmed his chest, and he wondered what would become of the whiskey trade if Larthan Tull were sent to prison. Would that be it? Would the county dry up, their problems solved? He kindly doubted it. Doing away with the supply doesn't do a thing to the demand. Before long some upstart would be storing liquor in his hencoop. He took one last swig of the whiskey before closing the bottle back in the drawer and moving on to the diner.

The agents were waiting for him, side by side in a booth, still in their transparent black suits.

"Fellas," he said. He sat. Haggard, run-down, feeling like maybe the widow was right. Time to pass off the case to these boys, let them do what they would with Larthan Tull. He needed to spend some time with his wife. Go ahead and retire. Clean up this last mess and move on. He'd done his duty. The next man could carry on.

"What's the story, Furman?" Jeffreys asked.

"I don't know if there is one, but I believe something bad is about to happen."

The waitress came over.

"Hey, Birdie," he said to her.

"Sheriff. What're you having?"

"Just coffee."

"Just coffee? You ought to get you some eggs."

"How's your dad doing?" he asked.

When she was gone he said to the agents, "Her momma poisoned herself about two months ago."

"You don't say," O'Connor said.

"I went to school with both of them. I think George beamed all his life that he was married to a woman named Pearl. Happiest couple I ever knew. Not a mean bone in either of em's body. But then he got a heart condition last year, and they just sort of stopped coming out. Sad news, what happened to Pearl."

"You ask him if he poisoned her himself?" O'Connor asked.

"Hell no. George wouldn't do such a thing."

O'Connor looked at Jeffreys, shrugged. "All kinds of meanness out there," he said.

"Good God, fellas," Chambers said. "I know there's meanness, but there's also decency. I don't know who your neighbors are, but here most folks are genuine Christians. They want to do what's right, work hard, and be left alone."

"Hence a man like Larthan comes to power."

"Basic principle of economics," Jeffreys said.

"He's just serving the needs of the community," O'Connor went on. "Free enterprise. Giving people what they want."

"Your invisible hand at work."

"Come on, Furman," O'Connor said. "Haven't you read your Adam Smith?"

"Larthan's not selling meanness here. He's selling whiskey."

"There's a difference?"

"I believe so."

"That's mighty innocent of you," Jeffreys said. "Seems like your town is getting away from you."

"The world's passing us all by," O'Connor said.

"Tell us what's going on."

"Thanks, Birdie," Chambers said when she set his coffee in front of him.

He turned back to the agents again. "I don't know if anything is happening, I could be imagining things. But I was out at Widow Coleman's house today."

He told them what she'd told him, Tull digging up the cash, a potential meeting between Mary Jane and Aunt Lou.

"That's it, Furman?" Jeffreys said. "That's what we're here for."

"It's still conjecture."

"She told you Mary Jane's likely to be cutting a deal with Aunt Lou—"

"Trying to."

"Trying to cut a deal with Aunt Lou."

"But she wouldn't go for it," O'Connor said. "Even if Mary Jane had the money, Larthan's her best supplier, and she's too good a businessman to disrupt that."

"Mary Jane doesn't know that," Chambers said.

"Then he's a fool. But how does that help us?"

"Do you think Larthan would go up there to meet with them?" Jeffreys asked.

O'Connor scoffed. "Why would he do that?"

As the agents discussed between themselves the potentials and what-ifs, Chambers sipped his coffee. When his eggs came he peppered them and hunched over his plate.

Jeffreys said, "We still don't know when he meets with her, or how supplies get there."

"Furman, you found out anything more about that?" O'Connor asked. "Who runs his liquor up there? Where do they go?"

"Mary Jane used to run for him, and the boys who got shot. I don't know who's doing it now."

"What do you recommend, then?" O'Connor asked.

Chambers buttered his toast, ate half a slice, decided he'd had enough. "Hell, I don't know. I believe something's going down soon, but I can't say what or when or where." He pulled some change out of his wallet, left it on the table for Birdie, and said, "I'll leave you fellas to it."

"Where you going?"

"To get some rest."

"You look like you could use it," Jeffreys said.

"We'll call you if we find out anything," O'Connor said.

Outside Chambers stood on the pavement for some time, contemplating what to do next. He considered taking the widow's advice and going home to his wife, but instead he drove out into the wilderness, way past the Bell and on into the woods. He turned off the highway and onto a dirt road at a crossroads, and the dirt road soon became rutted and washed out, a mere logging road so that his cruiser soon reached the place where it could go no farther, the log of a poplar lying across the road. He got out and sat on the log, the wood a hundred years old, thick and hard and covered in lichen.

The sky was the color of a peach, the evening sun a gentle reminder of time lost. He'd been alive long enough to see this land get developed, from a mere outpost to a proper town. The railroad ushered it all in, the machine like a god, coughing up smoke and clanking along its rails, arms pushing the wheels, its body a serpent, as if man were still in the garden, bringing about his own fall in modern times. What was his fruit this time around? Whiskey came to mind, the root of the knowledge of good and evil. Castle County like the land of Canaan, the Broad River our River Jordan. A Civil War at home, a Great War overseas. Skyscrapers in cities and a multitude of tongues across the land. How long before the destruction of Sodom and Gomorrah? Stoking a campfire at night was enough to bring about thoughts of brimstone raining down as fire. The dying sun in the west. Blood running through the streets and the end of days. Chambers mourned the world he was leaving, although he had no children to leave it to. Perhaps that would be a blessing when the sons of other men went off to some other war, or came up against something no man could understand. On that day, the Chambers line would be a memory at best, the blood turned to dust and ash in a burning land.

Aunt Lou's servant had dropped Mary Jane off in front of a cheap boardinghouse downtown with five dollars to get him through the week. Locked away, sober, he shook with memories of time past, from days of fighting out on Main Street at sixteen through years of too much whiskey and carrying on, years of death and trench warfare. So much life had to offer, and so much time took away from you. Now, on the run from God knows who all, Larthan Tull and Sheriff Chambers and the Castle County dragnet and even his closest family, Mary Jane's heart thundered in his chest with the thought that this was all he had left, that he'd abandoned all the promises of life in his younger days. Sleep came difficult, if at all, in the boardinghouse, so after two nights he went off in search of something to drink.

He found alleys with all-night lights and raucous blues and men chasing a dreamless sleep in the bottle of an unbonded whiskey, lost women taking advantage of the men's nature and their loosened wallets and providing services no man's wife would even dream of considering. Mary Jane made his way to these darker provinces with only a dollar to his name, enough to get him through a night but no longer. He would need an advance from Aunt Lou, he decided, as he sidled against a wall in an unnamed establishment lit with guttering oil lamps that shuddered throughout the room, like campfires, revealing huddled figures who kept their secret shame to themselves. No roadhouse honky-tonk, this. No place for wild times with the likes of Shorty Bagwell. No, this was some new arena, the likes of which did not exist in Castle County.

After ordering a whiskey and parting with half a dollar, he scanned the figures for signs of life. He was about to gulp his drink and move on to some merrier place when a girl materialized before him. She wore her hair back and had a powdered face, a fashion he could never understand, why a girl of no more than seventeen would want to age herself. She was more lean and supple than any woman who had shown an interest in Mary Jane in years.

"What brings you out tonight, cowboy?"

She sat across from him and nudged a booted foot up next to his leg.

"What you shaking your head for?" she asked.

"Don't know," he said.

"You don't know what you're shaking your head for, or you don't know what brings you out tonight for?"

"Neither, I guess."

None of the other figures in the room seemed interested in their exchange. The only one who seemed alive was the barkeep himself, propped against the bar and staring into the darkness like a sentry.

"I like a man who's not afraid to say what he don't know. Most people in this world, they just want to convince you of things they don't know a thing about."

"I'm not most people, I guess."

She laughed and rested her chin on her hand. Her foot tapped against his in such a way that she might believe she was kicking the table leg. He held up his glass of whiskey only to see he'd finished it. She saw it too and leaned in, put her hand on his forearm, and nodded toward the barkeep. She whispered, "That's my father over there."

"He the owner? And he lets you hang out here?"

"What's he going to do about it? Send me off to somebody else's bar to get into trouble?"

He thought of his nephew and Evelyn Tull down at the river, and he considered what future Larthan had in mind for her once she got a few years older—and what future this barkeep might have in mind for his daughter? She still had her hand on his forearm.

"Don't you worry about him," she said. "He lets me do what I want. He's got enough to worry about with the law. Let me get you another drink."

She returned with two more glasses of whiskey, both filled generously close to the brim. With the drink in hand, he was no longer interested in her. She laughed when he drained the glass without taking it once from his lips.

"You better take this second one," she said.

"You don't want it?" He already had his hand around it.

"You go ahead. I'll get me another in a few minutes. Where you coming from anyway?"

He almost said the truth, but he caught himself. "I come over from Tennessee."

"Tennessee! Whereabouts?"

"Outside Knoxville, a mountain town that ran out of jobs."

"It's happening all over. You found anything in Charlotte?"

"I've got some good prospects here."

"Yeah?" Light glinted off her watery eyes and sent a current through him. Ancient instincts from the days of caves and primitive fire.

"Matter of fact, I had a meeting this week to set myself up in business."

"You don't say."

"Should be right successful here in Charlotte."

"You mind if I have a sip?" She took the glass from him and raised it to her lips, set it down as graceful as a movie star. He inhaled and raised the glass himself.

Later he found himself in an ill-lit alleyway wrestling a man among a pit of swine. A gamble over a free drink, a drunken entertainment, distraction from a lonesome bar. His mind was too far gone to keep straight the how and why of his circumstances. He only wanted to pin the man down with the pigs while other men cheered them on.

"Get him, Ray," someone yelled.

A tangled-eyed boy grinned and chuckled and waved his hand as though casting a spell on the two wrestlers. The night was cloudy so the alley was dark and disorienting. The man before him paddled his hands as though climbing up a steep mountainside, his mouth ajar, his beard scraggly like he'd hacked it himself after half a pint some long afternoon. A railroad drunk, a brawler.

"Take him down," someone else yelled.

"Spill his guts."

The two men circled each other amid the din, and Mary Jane struggled to focus his mind on this newfound task. Then something that felt like a heavy sack slapped the back of his head and knocked him into the bearded fellow before him. The man's hands reached up. Mary Jane struggled to remain on his feet, but the world spun so that man and beast and building and cloud wisps patterned across his eyes. The crowd booed and cheered, and the silhouette of a man wielding a billyclub smothered out the light.

Later still Mary Jane lay in a copse of trees beyond the lights of town. He wanted to sleep but two figures kept prodding him, rifling through his pockets, rolling him over as though he were merely a lazy hound who'd settled in the wrong corner of the room.

"He ain't even got a dollar on him," a man said.

A woman replied, "Did you check his shirt pocket?"

"Hell yes, I checked everything."

She cursed and said, "Don't look at me. He must have been about to stiff us at least five."

"A wonder y'all even stay in business."

"Most of em come in after payday with a pocket full of money to spend. How was I to know?" Her voice lowered, softened. "Come on, sergeant. It's early yet. We can find us a way to settle this."

"Your daddy's not going to like you reaching into his till."

"Maybe I don't need to reach into his till. He doesn't need to know everything that goes on in his business."

"I should hope not."

The man let go of Mary Jane's lapels, and Mary Jane fell to the ground with a thump.

"You ain't even going to arrest him?"

"What good would that do for me?"

The two left him bleeding and nearly blacked out. He lacked the energy even to roll over to a more comfortable position, so he just lay on his stomach with his face against the bitter dirt. After a while rain began to patter, then pour, and water pierced the copse of trees and splashed him awake. While the rain cooled the still and humid air, it quickly turned the dirt to mud around him. A shivering, stinking mess, he rose and shuffled back toward the light of civilization.

Among the main streets again, still not sober but no longer falling-down drunk, he tried to regain his bearings. If he could find the bar district, he could find his way back to the boardinghouse. His mind fumbled for the address or for the name of its proprietor, but it was all a fog beyond the dull ache of an ensuing hangover. He wandered on, into a residential district with shotgun housing somehow even more oppressive than a mill village. Rain flowed through the gutters. Hinges squeaked. Trash cans rattled. Late-night revelers or vagabonds, perhaps, scrounging for scraps among the working poor. His body ached up and down from the night's drama, but he felt immensely relieved to have escaped the clutches of that mendacious tavernkeeper's woman.

The night was not finished with him yet. He rounded a corner and there, swinging his billyclub like he was practicing for the circus, was the crooked policeman, who also must have extricated himself from the woman. He caught Mary Jane's eye from the next block over, and you could see the transformation: curiosity to recognition to shame and anger.

"You there," he called.

But Mary Jane was already running. Still disoriented from the drink, he splashed through watery streets and into an alley, unsure of whether the cop was following, and he was not about to slow down to find out. He hurdled a low fence and landed in a backyard where a woman was breastfeeding an infant. It took her a moment to register this intruder before she shrieked loud enough to wake a drunk three counties away.

Mary Jane clambered onward, stumbled over some trash bins, and crawled through a clothesline back into the alleyway. The woman was still yelling, and now the voices of men had joined the ruckus. Flash-lights. Rain. A chorus of affronted neighbors. He shuffled, onward, to find some other neighborhood where perhaps he might catch his breath and his bearings.

"I love you," Quinn said.

Evelyn felt herself blush, and she rested her head on his shoulder. They lay on a bed of pinestraw beneath a canopy of trees. The late afternoon sun speckled through the leaves. This had become their spot along the river, the water rushing by and everything good in the world. These past two weeks a dream for her, life coming together in a way nothing ever had before. She pictured her life like one of her childhood jigsaw puzzles: a slow study at first, a patch here, a patch there. Eventually the whole came into focus and the last pieces were easy to fill, and came to a quick finish. That was where she was now, a few quick pieces to fill in before her puzzle was complete and she left childhood behind for whatever came next. Boys—and girls—had avoided her all her life, because of her father in part but also because the Tulls existed in this in-between state, above the mill workers but not of Castle either. They lived on York Street, a quiet avenue of Colonial houses and shaded lawns and families that had lived in Castle since the town's founding in the 1790s. Her father's few years in town had nothing on those generations of history, and although he had said before that his money was good here, same as anyone else's, she knew there were things you couldn't buy, even in America. In many ways, Quinn was like her father in that he was a dreamer. He thought big and believed that with hard work and a little luck the world was his for the taking. When she was alone she had a sick feeling about the future, about making it on her own, away from the father who had sheltered her from the gossiping women and the backbreaking labor of the world. But when she was with Quinn, as now, an afternoon along the river, she relaxed and wanted to believe he was right.

"We shouldn't be doing this," she said.

"Why not?"

"My father doesn't approve. He knows we've been sneaking off together, and he's said as much."

Quinn sat up on his elbow and rested his hand on her hip. He was warm beside her and his body was dark and muscular. Taut. She laid her hand on his and closed her eyes. She was comfortable with him. They belonged together despite the odds.

"What does he say?"

"That I shouldn't be here with you. That he knows your family, and that I should stay away."

"What does he know about my family? My uncle keeps your father in business all by himself."

"That's the point. Daddy doesn't approve of drinking."

"That don't make sense."

"He says whiskey's made for selling, not drinking."

Quinn sat up and crossed his legs. Wind shuddered through the trees above them, and at his back the river wandered lazily southward.

"I've seen him take a drink."

"But he doesn't get drunk," she said. "He stays in control all the time."

"I don't believe that."

"It's true," she said, although only part of that was true. Her father stayed in control on the outside, but at home he needed her. He didn't have anyone to take care of him. They hired help to clean the house, and when she was young they had a woman to look after her, but her father was a private man. He didn't even want a nursemaid around his affairs, much less a real companion. Some of it was the whiskey, because, yes, he was breaking the law and selling moonshine he brewed at his factory, the details of which he had never shared outright with Evelyn, but his privacy was about more than keeping his lawlessness behind closed doors. That was no secret, not to anyone in town. What she believed he wanted kept private was a softness, which only she knew about. She'd seen him cry, something she didn't believe anyone else had ever witnessed, not even her mother. On occasion he would drink himself into a stupor and then, alone in the dark, he wept. Although it had been several years, she could still see him hunched over the dining room table, a jar of whiskey and a glass before him. The last time, she'd come downstairs when she'd heard him rustling around, and she'd found him with his head aloll as though the muscles in his neck had snapped.

"Take a seat, honey," he said. "Talk to your old man."

She sat across from him, startled to see tears in his eyes. The room was dark and cold, but in the moonlight she could see his eyes were wet.

"Don't mind me," he said. "I'll be all right in the morning."

"What is it?"

"I don't rightly know. I've just been thinking about our lives. About time passing. Your mother. Are you happy here?"

"Yes," she said coolly.

"Good. That's good. You need to be happy, because that's all there is."

He drank another shot of whiskey, and his shoulders began to shake. She rose and walked over to him and put a hand on his back, but he shrugged her off.

"I'll be all right in the morning. Go on back to bed."

These were painful memories, so tonight she pushed them away. She reached up and grabbed Quinn's shirt, pulled him back down.

As he rested his head against her and closed his eyes, she thought perhaps they could get out of here, away from her father, and start their own life. It didn't have to be the way it was, the Hopewells in the village and the Tulls in town, and no contact between the two.

Quinn said, "Forget about him. He can't love you like I can. What do you have to say about us?"

She ran her fingers up his shirt, her hand warm and tickling the flesh of his abdomen. "I love you too," she said.

She held him close and felt tight in the throat at the sight of him, a stirring of need with him beside her, warm and earthy. A happiness that made her want to cry, her father be damned. Everyone here be damned. He pressed his lips to her ears and told her again he loved her, whispered that he wanted to take her away, to start a new life together in the mountains. Maybe Asheville, where the air was cooler and you could see ice and snow in the winter. She clung to him as he whispered this story. He would take up farming, grow squash and tomatoes, hew a crib out of a felled poplar, raise a family together. "Let's do it," he said. "Let's get married."

After she left she hurried out of the woods because the choiring of the crickets was beginning to unnerve her, the sunken sun casting long shadows in the grass and burnt husks of harvest leaves. Although the air still simmered around her, her skin was cool to the touch, goosebumped, inanimate. She thought about their plan. Quinn had been squirreling away money for months, most of which he'd spent on the car. But he had enough left over, he said, to make a move. "We could leave this weekend," he said. "Head up to Asheville on a morning train, and on Monday I could find me a new job." Her heart had fluttered at the thought, the two of them making a home for themselves. There at the river, his warm and rough hand on her midriff, his fingers rubbing softly against her ribs and the dry grass tickling her neck, she was ready to follow him anywhere. She did love him. She'd never been in love before, had always stayed too close to home to fall in love. Girls went out—to the pharmacy for sodas, to the river to swim, to a town dance—and that's where they met boys, out on Saturday nights.

Yes, it would be trouble leaving her father and this town. She'd grown up in Castle, in a comfortable house with white columns and spreading branches of elms and magnolias in the lawn. Houses in her neighborhood were like private shrines to this or that minor god, protector and savior, and although she didn't fully know her ancestry, she had the upbringing of an aristocrat. While her father bottled sodas and brewed whiskey, she learned the finer points of Chopin, the history of political philosophy. And now she was fifteen, grown beyond the insular world of York Street. She was playing a dangerous game with Quinn Hopewell, a boy she'd known most of her life—in school, in church—but for some reason she'd never looked twice at him until two weeks ago, when he'd seemed to emerge a man, a sturdy, stable man. Now his face was all she saw when she closed her eyes. She felt ready to give herself up to him, to follow him out of her house, off York Street and away from Castle, to wherever the world might take them.

When she got home, her father sat rocking on the porch. The wood of the runner beat against the wood of the porch. His eyes were closed until she came up, and then without raising his head, he opened his eyes and watched her, a movement almost imperceptible had she not been waiting for it. A man whose intensity lay in his eyes, curious, intelligent, unforgiving. The rest of his face still. The evening light burnished and sad. Slats of shadow from the eaves grated his face, but she could still see that he was drunk. Unlike when she'd found him alone with the whiskey bottle, his eyes were mean today, watchful.

"Where you been?" he asked. He slurred when he spoke, but his voice still commanded the same high power of which he was capable.

"Down at the river," she said. The air around them was still. Bugs flittered around them—mosquitoes, moths, flies—and even though a chill had settled on the evening, she felt hot in her spine.

"With that Hopewell boy?"

Her heart beat in her chest and her mind was blank. Now was the time to speak, but she had nothing to say. Her father had never turned on her, in all her years and despite all the meanness of which she knew he was capable. He'd never turned on her, but now something had broken. The crack had been there for weeks, a hairline fracture in which she'd wedged a chisel that she slowly tapped against with each night at the river. Now, the crack had splintered open, and she had no choice but to carry through and pray.

As Tull rocked, the runners continued grinding against the planks of wood on the porch.

Vrrruppptt. Vrrruppptt. Vrrruppptt. Vrrruppptt.

He said, "I told you already not to be seeing him."

"Well I am." She took a breath. "We're in love and we're leaving together."

He quit rocking. His hands clenched the arms of the chair, and then, like a rattler trapped in a corner, he rose up and struck, slapped her across the face.

Something seemed to have taken possession of him, some darkness that clouded his eyes and made her afraid for the first time. So this was what it was like to be on the other end, in a bad business with Larthan Tull. He grabbed her shoulder and she lurched forward, stumbled, and he shoved her into the wall by the front door. He called her a slut.

"You don't even know it, do you?" he asked, towering over her like some obelisk commemorating the lives of the dead. His eyes boiled with hate and hurt. "You're a slut and you're never going to be anything. You're ruined now."

And he struck her again, this time hard enough to knock her to the ground.

She woke in a dark room, her head bruised and aching. No, the room wasn't dark. She wore a blindfold and was tied to a wooden beam, a bedpost. The thick rope dug into her wrists, and she lay hunched over her legs, her arms pinned above her head and holding her in a half-sitting position. A fire ran up her back when she got up, and she fell back against a wall. The room was hot and dank, and she sweated through her cotton dress, could feel the dampness on her back and behind her knees like morning dew.

Something thudded nearby, below her. She could tell she was upstairs and could hear someone—her father—stomping around downstairs. The rattle of dishes in the kitchen. The slam of a door, followed a few moments later by the cough of a car engine, the crunch of wheels against gravel. Then silence.

The rope was starting to cut off the circulation in her wrists, and she tried to spin her hands around to find an angle of slack. She kicked around with her foot, found the bed, and realized she was in her room. She shifted and leaned her head against her arms, and though the rope tugged against her wrists, she felt tired and eventually drifted into an uneasy slumber.

She dozed. She woke. She dozed. All in darkness.

Tull left her there and drove to the plant to meet Depot for the weekly load. His body quivered as though he hadn't eaten, and he told himself to snap out of it. She was dead to him, he thought. Why even bother tying her up? Why not let her go to the Hopewell boy, or to the dogs for what he cared? He banged his hands against the steering wheel and swerved in the road. "Straighten up," he said aloud. Business, he thought. Deal with Depot and the whiskey now, and the business with Evelyn would be there when he returned.

He had the money from Mary Jane and had been planning to leave the man to Aunt Lou—she would tell him that without money, they had no business, and that would be that, nothing left for him but to pack up with that widow whore and move somewhere he might be wanted—but now Tull wanted blood. Why should a man presume to take advantage of another and get away with it? It would make Tull look stupid, not to follow through and take care of Mary Jane thoroughly. Maybe send a message to the youngblood Hopewell while he was at it.

Still, a second voice told him to leave it to the law or let it be damned. Now might be a good time to retire. To hell with Evelyn and the factory and Aunt Lou. Sell off what stock he had, catch a train somewhere else. He'd overstayed his welcome in Castle and forgotten the law he'd learned in his youth: You can't depend on people, so hold your cards close, hedge your bets, and cut loose when the moment presented itself. Now was that moment, said the voice. You're on your own. Time to run.

Instead he walked into the plant with a .38 caliber, a satchel with five thousand dollars, and some extra instructions for Depot. He sat in the cool of twilight, rolled a cigarette, smoked. The factory's smokestacks rose up like twin pillars of Babylon, steam coughing and circling the lot, machines that ran all night, the smell of burnt potatoes from the cooked sugar. A train rolled through town, the wheels kicking up the occasional spark. The clatter of the rails, the hum of the machines.

Depot drove up in a gray Packard.

"Howdy," Tull said. "You got springs supporting that trunk?"

Depot grunted.

"I got about two hundred gallons already set out for you, if you think you can carry that many."

"I can carry as many as you got."

Tull spat and said, "Come on, then."

He led Depot through the gates of the factory, and the smell of burning sugar—home fries on a griddle—blasted them. He hit a switch and lights flickered on, revealing rows of machines, vats of liquid connected through tubing, boxes of supplies stacked neatly against one wall. Glass bottles along a chute and boxes for them to go in. This was the main floor, and in the back rooms he had barrels of fermenting beer, copper kettles, a closet full of shine. The same recipe his daddy had used, and his daddy before him. Straight from the mountains of East Tennessee, a family farm back when the government left you alone.

"It's back here on the loading dock."

On a pallet were scores of gallon tin cans filled with whiskey, all ready to be sent to Aunt Lou. Without Ernest and Lee, Tull had been backed up for the past two weeks and needed someone reliable to get something done. He'd have to hire better when it was all over. Depot knew the business of brewing whiskey and running a bar, but he'd never run a load before. Tull wanted him for this run in particular. Apparently, he had no qualms about killing a man. Whatever the reason he'd shot Ernest and Lee—whether they were plotting against Tull via Aunt Lou, or whether they'd just insulted Depot's mother—he'd shown a lack of judgment, a good lesson for Tull that no matter how long you'd known a man, and however competent he seemed, if you wanted something done properly, you had to reinforce your expectations constantly. Maybe thirty years ago you could get away with any kind of operation, but the laws had closed in on everything in the twentieth century. You had to comply to do business anymore. Mass production, mass consumption, mass regulation— these were the products of the Industrial Revolution.

Tull said, "While you're in Charlotte, I've got a little janitorial work for you." When Depot made no reply, he went on, "I've done some asking around, and it doesn't figure, Mary Jane shooting Ernest and Lee that night. In fact, Widow Coleman tells me they weren't even planning to hit up Aunt Lou."

"That's a lie there," Depot said. "They were plotting the whole thing out in the back booth."

"They may have been drunk, knowing them. Men plot all manner of things when they've imbibed. You know that."

"And I told you they'd already approached me about buying some of their liquor." The barkeep hung his head. "You told me to handle it."

"You tried, for sure," Tull went on. "That shows some loyalty. You know who butters your bread and you were trying to do the right thing. Taking some initiative. I respect that, but the most important thing, when you go down that road, is don't miss."

Tull pulled out the .38.

"Hopewell is going to meet with Aunt Lou tonight. She's a loose cannon, but she knows you're coming and she knows why. Hopewell doesn't. If the man's body ends up in the river, well, I don't want him found alive."

In the darkness, Depot squinted, but otherwise held still. Then he took the pistol.

"Why don't you pull your car around the alley? It looks rough, covered in grass and all, but you can slide back to this loading dock here, and we'll load her up."

After Depot walked out, Tull raised the gate on the loading dock, and a few moments later the Packard eased behind the factory, its wheels crunching against the loose gravel. After they loaded gallon after gallon in his trunk, the shocks sank, and the tail end sagged. Then Depot got in without a word, started the car, and pulled out the way he'd come in.

Tull watched him drive off with his whiskey, into the cooling twilight, leaving behind a lonesome, broken man. Tull heard Bessie Smith's blue moan on evenings such as this. Time was speeding up on him, and he seemed to care less and less. It wasn't that he was mellowing in his middle age like a good scotch, but rather growing flat like stale beer. No one knows you when you're down and out, Bessie sang, truer word never spoken. You take out your friends for a mighty good time. You buy them bootleg and spot them for a game of cards, but once the bottle runs dry and the money's gone and the cards are filed away, those friends drive off with a piece of your soul, leave you in your castle to contemplate living and dying. You could build a business, but businesses die as fast as a person does in this world, and once death comes for you, you don't have anyone—not your mother who, if things have gone according to their natural order, has been long gone herself, nor your wife nor your children. You could tie your daughter to the bedpost to keep her there, but what would happen when you let her go? She would abandon you, as daughters should. Maybe there were some lucky folks out there who had someone to hold their hands into old age, but even then the reaper would come and pry you away from all you love. The Technicolor world of your childhood fades to black and white or the monochrome sepia hue as forty or fifty years slip by and transform you from a cocksure young buck to an old man alone, until perhaps in those last moments, as the curtain falls and the screen fades, you get a glimpse once again of the bright colors from long ago.

As darkness settled on this weary September night, it found Tull on his loading dock with a bottle of his own brew, and then he was gone, the factory shuttered for the night. Depot cruising through the streets of Charlotte, Tull God knows where, his daughter tied to the post in her upstairs bedroom, and somewhere Quinn Hopewell waited for his ladylove. And somewhere, perhaps, his younger brother was falling into a fitful slumber, sweat streaking down his face. The end is coming for all those here, this town, this world, this life one leaf in time's great history, and the autumn would soon arrive. The leaf would flare in one bright and beautiful last gasp before withering to its dry remains and falling to the earth. Despite new buds, new leaves in the years to come, this world would decompose into a roux of old matter long forgotten, waiting for a new beginning.

Friday. Nearly two weeks on the run and a permanent shift in his soul like water bubbling over the lip of a pot, Mary Jane lay in bed at the boardinghouse and watched a shelf cloud float across the sky. The anvil of a thunderhead in the distance. Heat lightning. A storm that would gather mass but perhaps only bring the promise of rain, a few drops as if to tease the dry earth. Mary Jane knew those worries well, the son of a farmer, and he worried still because you needed corn for liquor. No matter your business, you couldn't escape the tyranny of nature. Many years it seemed as though the blaze of summer had through its own will a determination to ruin a year of crops through drought.

At midday church bells tolled and in the early afternoon a herd of shoats passed under his window. Fatigued yet sober, finally, he swung his legs out of bed and got dressed. He gingerly fastened his suspenders, even though his shoulder was no longer raw meat. The wound had scabbed over and a blue bruise had spread across his shoulder and into his chest, which made him look like he'd come down with the plague.

The boardinghouse's proprietor, a war widow who never could seem to slow down and have a decent conversation, surprised him when he came downstairs, for she sat alone in the dining room with a jar of what Mary Jane suspected was Larthan Tull's whiskey. Her eyes lolled a bit as he came in, but she made no move to hide her drink, nor did she flinch when he sat across from her.

"You're welcome to some of this."

"Much obliged," he said, already bringing the jar to his lips.

"There's no occasion, in case you was wondering. I just sometimes need a break from being responsible."

"Don't we all." He raised the glass and took another long drink.

"Oh, you're a wild one all right. I can see it now. You never did quit carousing around like a young buck, did you?"

"No, ma'am, I guess I didn't."

"Plenty of men like you out there."

"None of them quite like me."

"That's what you can tell yourself, but you're old enough to know there are only so many kinds of people out there."

"Most of them decent, God-fearing folks."

"Maybe, though you might be surprised," she said. "Lot of folk pass through here, and what comes out ain't always fit to tell. Maybe because they're on the road—or out of work or out of luck, one—but a side comes out that I'm sure they wouldn't show their mommas. You can learn a lot about a man by the way he travels."

She hardly paused as she spoke these words, and when she finished she upended the jar of whiskey and licked her lips like a predator before a wounded prey.

He said, "And what does that tell you about me?"

"You believe you're carrying some burden, and that by behaving yourself, staying up in your room when you're sick with the drink, that you're making up for whatever it is you think you've done."

"And have I?"

"Have you what? Made up for it? I can't tell you without knowing the how and why, but I can tell you it's nothing more than any other man that comes through here. Take me, for instance. I got a brother on a chain gang, out in Gastonia. Thought I'd take a day off and bring him and the guys some sandwiches, have a right nice break with them, but instead I've drunk too much to drive myself anywhere, so maybe it'll be next Friday when I can get out there to see him."

"It's only another week."

"How many weeks are there? Not that many."

"I appreciate the drink," he said.

"You take care of yourself."

When he left his head was woozy. He wasn't due to meet Aunt Lou for a few hours, but he would need to be careful to sharpen up before nightfall. Shouldn't be too difficult. He'd spent half his money and was robbed of the rest of it, so he couldn't scare up a wild time even if he had a notion. Which he didn't.

He wandered the rough streets in a daze. The air seemed electric, ionized before the coming night's storm. He moved generally south-west, away from the city and into the countryside, toward nothing until he was free from the bustle. Any direction would take him somewhere eventually. Asheville or Columbia or on up to Richmond. But not on foot. It had taken more than a week to evade the dragnet spoken of by the blind man on the mountain, to wend his way from Castle to Charlotte. No, he was where he needed to be now. It was time, this last effort to get a payoff and stabilize his life.

Along about twilight he tired and stopped on the side of a dusty one-lane and stared at the sky as the stars began to awaken. In the west a bundle of clouds mopped up the last of the day's light so that the stars in the east shined unnaturally bright. Orion, the Archer, a bright speckling lot of them up there, twinkling away like the eyes of the gods man had created. He lay down next to a cornfield and listened to the tall stalks clack and the bugs ratchet like a plague of locusts. He'd never before thought of corn that way, as an eerie unknown void. Growing up on the farm, corn was just corn, one more crop with nothing more mysterious about it than a field of grass.

Autumn meant the harvest was coming, and he could feel it now, in the air, the early chill in the night and the musky, ripe scent of decaying leaves in the air. He planted his feet in the hard red clay of the piedmont. Rocks and mica and roots underneath him, held together by this iron-rich soil, red like the surface of Mars. Mars, a planet out there twinkling, if he knew how to look for it. He sat up on his haunches, ever the country boy, and felt the earth below him, the clay baked and lined with cracks like a roadmap, or broken glass. All variations of gray in the gloaming, the stars, the white half of the hovering moon.

He thought of No Man's Land, the night out of the trenches, wandering among the dead. Tonight, as out on the French plain, as the night he'd come in from the Hillside with a bleeding shoulder and his friends lying dead in the street, he felt no faith in God. For so long he'd been a believer, a Baptist, a good man trying to serve the Lord, but out here in the vastness of it all he thought he might never have truly believed a word of it. What was happening to him? Why was he out here, and how would he ever come back from it?

He lay on the ground, on his stomach, and rested his head on his arm. The ground was still warm from the day's heat, even as cool air passed over his back and ruffled his thinning hair. Goose bumps rose on his flesh, and he began to pray. The twenty-third Psalm came to him, the Lord's Prayer, but he could get neither one right so he quit. The liquor inside him had caught up and slowed him down, and the world no longer seemed to matter the way it had even a few moments ago. All of it vanity, all of it pointless. He closed his eyes, and all he wanted to do was sleep. To lie here and sleep and figure everything out in the morning. But what he really wanted was to feel well again, to have one more day in his life where he had no obligations and felt no guilt.

On the mountain, Ephraim had told him, *For God so loved the world that he gave his only begotten son, that whosoever believeth in him should not perish but have everlasting life.* But it took more than belief, Mary Jane believed, for belief was a meaningless gesture of the mind. Guilt lay in the heart and stemmed from action, or inaction, on which belief had no bearing. He had a task before him, but his hazy thoughts kept him rooted where he was for a long while. He grew drowsy and even dozed for a time.

He woke in darkness with a throbbing head and the inclination to remain where he was for the night. Aunt Lou had told him to meet her Friday evening, which meant this was his moment to sell her on his and the widow's whiskey, to live up to all that big talk with Ernest and Lee, and to have at last a steady flow of income that would allow him to settle down with the widow and perhaps attain a normal life. He knew that even if Aunt Lou signed up for his product this evening, he would still have to deal with Larthan Tull, and that thought nauseated him.

Still, an hour later he stood in Aunt Lou's foyer, ready and waiting to make his pitch. The house was dark and he could hear thumping from upstairs. The sentry who'd let him in had disappeared. Mary Jane crossed his arms and leaned against the wall to wait. He was hungry. It had been a long time since he'd had a full meal, his only sustenance this past week the boiled gruel from the boardinghouse. Despite his hunger, he grew calm as he waited, more sure of himself now that he was back in the city, away from God's dark and the chattering corn.

When Aunt Lou shuffled down the stairs, she rasped, "Evening, Mary Jane. Wasn't sure I'd see you today."

"We had an appointment," he said.

"Come, come."

She ushered him into the dining room and turned on the light.

At the table sat Depot Murphy, with his bullet head and his lazy eye. He looked out of place in the lights of Aunt Lou's dining room, but when Mary Jane saw he held a Colt .38 against the oak tabletop, his appearance no longer seemed to matter.

Willie lay on the bed with his head turned to the wall and listened to the sound of his brother packing. Their mother slept in the other room, and sometime earlier this evening their father had left, no one yet acknowledging that he'd taken to drinking worse than Mary Jane ever did. Joe had merely come in from work and paced around the house a few minutes before slinking off. Willie's grandfather, still weak from his stroke and unable to get out of bed, had said to Willie, "Boy, you're going to have a long road in this life."

Willie hadn't had to ask what Abel meant. "I know," he'd said.

The old man had closed his eyes and gone back to sleep. He slept all the time now, as though in preparation for that final rest.

Later in the day, Quinn, too, had gone out on foot and returned at twilight. Willie was still awake in the darkened room, listening to his grandfather's wheeze and expecting each breath could be the old man's last. Nothing but silence in the rest of the house. Everyone was leaving, and he couldn't understand why. They'd made a home for themselves here, and although it wasn't perfect it was their home and they were here together.

That was important because there were genuine dangers out in the world that you needed numbers to combat. The Bell might be a small community, where everyone knew everyone's business like a big family, but the village also had a family's good sense to leave certain stones unturned, certain things unsaid. No one had ever talked about Mary Jane and Widow Coleman, and the rumors of the Hillside murder had quieted now with the feds in town. Sheriff Chambers still shuffling every which way to investigate. The Hopewells hadn't started locking their doors, but more than once he'd seen his mother fingering the lock as she came in for the last time at night. A pause, her hand on the knob. Should she do it? Were they safe? Was anyone?

The Bible spoke of sin couching at the door. Jesus wouldn't lock his door. He'd wait calmly for someone to break in and he'd offer him a glass of wine and his wallet. But that Old Testament God sure would lock His doors, were He on earth as man. Willie felt certain tonight that God would soon whip up a flood or send in a plague and wipe everyone away. An eye for an eye, bone for bone, blood for blood. Rumor had it people still lived that way in Mexico, where outlaws robbed for the pure pleasure of robbing, even gave away their loot because they had so much of it. Sport, was all, just sport. Sin hurts. His family had fractured, always one step away from another casualty: their sister, their grandmother. Mary Jane on the run and their father off with his whiskey and Quinn packing a bag.

Quinn clicked shut the clasps of his suitcase and Willie stirred and asked, "What are you doing?"

"Nothing. Go on back to sleep." Quinn put his finger to his lips, grabbed his bag, and tiptoed to the back door, where the sound of the hinge would be muffled. The hinges creaked and then he slunk into the backyard. Willie followed him.

"What are you doing?" he asked again.

"Nothing. Go on back to bed." When Willie didn't move, Quinn said, "I'm leaving with Evelyn tonight. We're catching a train first thing in the morning."

"Are you coming back?"

"Not for a while. Maybe never."

Willie hung his head and kicked at the dirt. It must be past midnight now, and the whippoorwills and tree frogs sang their night's refrain, their atonal chorus. Wind cascaded through the tops of shade trees that guarded their lawn, and the treetops tossed, a scatter of black and gray, like the beginning of a picture show when the speakers hiss and pop and the projectionist puts the film into focus.

"You'll be all right," Quinn said. "A few more years, maybe you can move up north with me. We'll start us a business or something. Until then, you got to learn to keep things close if you want to survive in this world. You can't go telling every secret you have."

Quinn slugged his shoulder, and Willie looked up. A pinecone thumped against the grass after falling from a tree. Limbs clapped above them, and the brothers stared at each other in the night. Willie couldn't think of a thing to say to keep his brother here, even for another minute longer. His brother had a girl waiting on him, so what more was there to say?

"I'll see you," Quinn finally said, and walked away from the house. Willie watched his brother creep through the front yard in the moonlit night. Down the ashy road, under the silhouette of the water oaks, his shadow merging into the night. Whippoorwills chirred far off. A frog croaked. Without thinking about it, Willie followed his brother's path to the road and kept going. In front of the house on Harvey Lane, he could still see Quinn's figure, walking like a dandy, a merry jaunt.

Willie crept after him, along the ill-lit highway, a skulking figure like a bobcat on the prowl. Quinn fired up a cigarette, and ashes flecked off the ember in the breeze. A train pulled through, slowed for the curves of town, but did not stop. Late-night boxcars rattled on their way to somewhere else. Soon Quinn and Evelyn would be on the way to somewhere else, too, and for the first time Willie tried to picture leaving the Bell. He'd never considered his future, just assumed he would grow up to work in the mill, which is what boys did—that or the military—but he liked living here. Not as much as he liked his grandfather's farm, but work in the mill was fun. Sure, there were bullies like Peach Skin, but they were a part of life, and Willie had never before considered running away as a means of dealing with conflict. He'd never considered leaving, but as sparks kicked up along the train tracks, as he listened to the pulse and hum of the cars skimming along, he wondered what the future held. Would he too run off to somewhere else? He felt deeply alone as he trailed his brother, cut off from something essential, though what it was he could not say.

It neared two o'clock when they reached the corner of Main and York, and Willie hung back at the corner as Quinn sauntered past the palatial homes until he reached the one marked Tull. Willie crept into a neighbor's yard, everything dark like the mouth of some demon waiting to swallow him. He sneaked under magnolias, through the thick grasses—fescue, rye—and cowered in some hydrangea bushes at the side of the neighbor's house. Quinn stood in Tull's side yard, staring up at a second-floor window at the front of the house. He picked up a stone and tossed it at the black glass, and the glass cracked like a gunshot.

Willie held his breath, half expecting Tull to barge out of the house in a rage, ready to throttle Quinn. But no one came to the window, so Quinn threw another rock and waited. Then he crept onto the porch, and Willie cringed when a board groaned under his brother's weight. Don't, Willie thought, but he remained in the bushes, watched as Quinn found the door unlocked and glided into the house like a rat burrowing through a crack between two boards. He watched the upstairs window for a light, for motion, but nothing came. No one on York Street stirred, and he began to feel tired, his eyes sore. The bushes smelled bitter, and bugs crawled over his skin, but he ignored them. He stood from his haunches and eased to the side of Tull's house, leaned up against the wall and strained to hear noise from above.

Lights flashed from Main and a car turned onto York Street. Willie dropped to the ground just as the long black car pulled into Tull's drive. Tull himself got out and stumbled up to the porch, stomped his boots, opened the door. This was it, Willie knew, the moment where Quinn would meet his comeuppance. All the nights of carousing around, the sins of the flesh, the dangers of Larthan Tull. And here Willie was, on the train ride to Hell right alongside his brother. He fumbled around the ground and found a pinecone, which he hurled up to the second-floor window. The cone scratched against the glass and fell softly to the ground. Willie picked it up and threw it again. Nothing.

He ran to the porch and saw Tull had left the door open. He peered through the screen, but the house was dark. He opened the screen and slid inside. The house smelled like dust and old wood. He paused to listen for movement and waited for his eyes to adjust to the darkness.

Somewhere downstairs, a hinge squeaked, and boots stomped in an uneven shuffle, toward Willie and up the stairs. Willie eased into the house, saw the shape of the stairs and the legs of a man disappear into the second floor, what looked like a rifle at the figure's side.

"Well, well," Tull said. "Why don't we take us a walk?"

Willie looked around him for a weapon. In the kitchen he found a steak knife and a skillet on the counter. He grabbed them both.

Quinn and Evelyn came downstairs first, followed by Tull with a rifle aimed at their backs. Even in the dark Willie could see Tull's eyes were wild and crazed, and that no matter what happened this would not end well. They marched toward the front door, and Willie crept behind them, the knife in one hand and the skillet in the other. To stab the man in the back or wallop him in the head with the pan. He clenched the knife, imagined the blade sinking into Tull's flesh, but he decided the skillet would be more effective, knock him out cold. He tucked the knife into his shorts and took hold of the skillet with both hands.

But he must have made a noise—a scuff on the floor with his shoe, or maybe his shadow flickered into Tull's sight—because right as he raised the pan, Tull veered and struck him with the butt of the rifle. His head banged against the wall, and a hand gripped his throat.

Chambers owed Alma some time together, but until things settled with Tull and the federal agents, he could be found working long past dark. The station cleared out, and he worked into the night, alone with nothing more than a sandwich, his bottle of whiskey, and a new novel by a Georgia writer named Caldwell. The novel was about the antics of a dirt-poor family and Chambers laughed at the familiarity of the characters. The story could take place on the north side of Castle as easily as South Georgia—the same red clay, the same folks hammered by the Depression, the same choices between struggling on the farm or moving to the mill. When he reached the end he quit laughing and set the book aside and felt disgusted with the author for showing him his world in this light. Life was rough all across the country, no doubt about it. Banks closing, fortunes dissolved. Folks said electing Roosevelt in a couple of months would be the country's way out, but Chambers mistrusted the sentiment.

Hoover was supposedly a genius—his whole campaign in 1928 had been one of solutions, direct action to solve our nation's woes—yet he'd been unable to make headway. Roosevelt's New Deal sounded like just another pipedream to Chambers.

In many ways, Castle had been lucky. Business was good, there was work in the mills, and the cotton company took care of its people. Gave people a place of their own. Folks were poor here, but they'd always been poor. They never had the money in the bank to lose, so while some people up north had lost their entire life's savings, it was business as usual for people here. Assuming nothing got worse—another war like the last, another flu outbreak, or something Chambers couldn't imagine. This past summer the stock market had hit its lowest point yet, and no one seemed to know when it would end. Banks were out of money and across the nation people were being thrown into the street. It was like dark waves of doom traversed the country with currents of bad news, and it was only a matter of time before the waves crashed over Castle and hit home. Or maybe it was like a wound that wouldn't clot, bleeding that couldn't be stanched no matter what bandages you pressed against it. That was how Jimmy Boy Coleman had died when Chambers had shot him, and that was how his own boy had died, in the war. Shot in the hip, and the bullet sliced through an artery, and he wouldn't quit bleeding. Chambers'd had to make a dozen phone calls to get that much out of the army, facts he'd never told Alma. Why had he needed to know so badly? His boy was dead, so wasn't that enough? No, he thirsted for the grisly details as if in knowledge he could take on his dead son's pain.

On Friday night he went on home to Alma earlier than usual, drove with the flask of whiskey between his legs. He could feel something in his blood, a sensation he got on occasion when a tough puzzle was challenging him. That same sense of longing for the gristle. Gnawing at him. He swigged the whiskey, and his head buzzed. He never used to drink so much, in the office, on the job. He wasn't sure how much people in town knew—the office girls surely knew about the whiskey he kept in his drawer—but as soon as folks became displeased with him, maybe because he wasn't solving the Hillside murders fast enough, or maybe if the whiskey trade dried up here, when something happened the newspaper would run a story about Chambers. The headline would be lurid—Corruption in the Sheriff's Office, maybe—and all of Chambers's faults would come out on display. They wouldn't throw him in jail for drinking, but they would take his badge. No matter. He was finished after this term anyway. Maybe he would take Alma down to the coast after all, or maybe he'd move out west, get lost on a ranch somewhere in Texas or New Mexico, and spend his last days driving cattle.

At the house, he left his boots and his gun at the door and trudged upstairs where he found his wife asleep on her side, the sheet covering her wide hips, her mouth open. Sound asleep. She'd always been a solid sleeper, never troubled by what ailed the world. Two minutes of stillness and she was out for the night. He envied her that, himself one to lie awake into the clockless hours, a lifetime of unsettled rest. He slipped out of his clothes, slid under the covers. The whiskey had numbed his mind near to the point of making the room spin. A febrile sweat broke out and made his skin clammy. The sheets were cool and luxurious, and nothing had ever felt so good. When he sidled up against Alma, she shifted to allow for his arm to slide beneath her. Her mouth closed, and he even thought he saw her smiling.

Then he all but blacked out in the bed next to her, but he didn't sleep long before the phone rang to wake him up. He lay in bed a moment, his mind cloudy with the vestige of some dream, a mood, a memory. The sound refused to go away, so he rose to answer it.

"Hello?" He struggled to clear his throat.

"Sheriff, this is Wilma Meacham. You up?"

"Nearly."

"God bless you," she said. "Something's going on at the Tull place up the street. I heard some banging around. The lights are all out, but I definitely heard noises. Woke me up."

"I'll be up there directly."

When he'd hung up he scratched his head and went to splash water on his face. Alma didn't stir or ask him what the story was this time. She continued sleeping like the dead while he got dressed. He was still drunk, knew he wasn't in any condition to go out. Sweat clung to his neck like dew. The room was no longer spinning, but he felt woozy and off kilter. He'd slept on his bad arm, and now the arm wouldn't respond to signals from his brain. His fingers limp, his wrist and forearm tingled, the arm from the elbow down mere body with no life with which to grasp. Electrical pulses misfiring in his feverish brain, an accumulation of energy that perhaps he harnessed and used to careen into the night. He sped through town until he reached Tull's place, and along the way his left arm ached as blood started to flow back to his hand.

When he arrived, the white house was gloomy and silent, blocked partly from the street by spindly limbs of water oaks, the banana leaves of magnolias, the white columns and upstairs windows seeming to make a face, the front doorway a maw, the gateway to Hell itself.

Chambers held his hand to his revolver, crept up to the porch, and peered through the windows only to see nothing but blackness. He knocked, drew his gun. No one answered, so he eased the screen open, tested the door. Unlocked.

The floor in the entryway creaked as he stepped inside. He shut the door behind him and allowed his eyes to adjust to the dark. This was the first time he'd ever been in here. Tull's home looked like his own—a couch, a coffee table, bookshelves with dusty classics. A grand piano, a portrait of Tull over the fireplace. In it, Tull's face was stoic, his eyes boring out of the canvas like bullet holes.

Near the kitchen, a dark sticky spot on the floor gave him pause. Blood, not fully dried. No other signs of a scuffle. Everything in its place.

He continued to sweep the downstairs, and then, finding nothing, he moved upstairs. No one was there, but in one of the bedrooms a rope dangled from the wood of the bed frame and a crumpled blanket was on the ground. Definitely not a good sign.

Finding no one, Chambers drove out along Highway 9 to the river, where he turned onto Woodridge Road and circled Coleman's farm. Off toward the Bell, the shadow of the mill's smokestack loomed over the treeline, always a beacon. He saw a light shining on the riverbank, but he let it pass. Some kids out sparking or drinking or carrying on somehow. No reason to bust them tonight. What was left of the night. He needed to find Tull.

He drove on, and in front of the Hillside the tires crunched on the roadside gravel. Lights were on inside the inn, a few cars parked in front. He knocked. A moment later, someone asked, "Who's there?"

"The law," he said, in no mood to play along. "You don't let me in, I'm going to fetch the revenuers."

The door opened. Young Tommy Cope took a few steps back when he saw Chambers had his pistol drawn. He must look a sight, woken half-drunk to scour the town for Larthan Tull, his body braised by the liquor and the heat and the fatigue of it all. He didn't even want to know why this teenager was running the bar tonight.

"Larthan here?" he asked.

"No, Sheriff, he ain't. Hasn't been here since twilight."

"Where'd he go?"

"I don't know. He was here when I got in. Said he had some business to take care of. Had a few drinks and left."

Chambers scanned the room. The usual drunks, Lester playing pool, Shorty in a booth in the back, and across from him Joe Hopewell. Chambers hadn't spoken with Shorty all week, not since he'd let him out, and although he didn't think the man had had time to get messed up in whatever Tull was planning, he decided he ought to ask anyway.

He stumbled across the room and stopped in front of the booth. "Evening, gentlemen. Mind if I join you?"

"Go right ahead, Sheriff," Shorty said, and Joe slid over to make room for him.

Both men drunk, he could see that from here. It felt good to sit down, the wood of the booth cool against his back. He said, "Either of you seen Larthan today?"

"No, but you ort to talk to his boy," Shorty said, nodding at Joe.

"Why's that?"

"Seeing that Evelyn."

Chambers looked at Joe. Joe shrugged.

"Larthan know that?"

Joe shrugged again. "I told my boy to stay away from her, but what can you do? He's near seventeen. He's his own man now."

"Ain't that the truth," Chambers said. "I remember when my youngest was seventeen. That was when he decided to follow his brother off to Europe. Broke his momma's heart. Mine too, you want to know the truth of it."

"Least he had a cause. You should be proud, Sheriff."

"I am, I am. How you doing, Shorty?"

"I'm fine as ever. Have you know I been walking straight as an arrow ever since you let me out."

"Have you now?" Chambers eyed the tumbler of bourbon in front of him.

"I'm just here to support my buddy Joe. He's having a time of it."

"I was sorry to hear about Susannah's father," Chambers said. "How's he doing?"

"Still hasn't got out of bed," Joe said. "Likely never will."

"Jesus, fellas, the things they don't tell you about the world."

"Amen," Shorty said, and he slugged the bourbon.

"Sheriff?" Joe offered him a sip.

"Thank ye." Chambers took a swig, the liquor warm and rough to swallow, but it made his head feel better. He hadn't realized how bad he was hurting until the smoky liquid hit his lips and relieved him.

"Hell's bells," Shorty said. "Don't go hitting any flowerbeds. They'll lock you up for that."

Chambers took another gulp. "Behave yourself, gentlemen. And if you see Larthan, you call the precinct. I got a feeling something bad's about to happen."

Depot sat at Aunt Lou's table and watched Mary Jane's hopes drain from his face. The man had come in planning to make a king's ransom off his upstart liquor business, and here was Depot Murphy. Depot had missed him once with the shotgun, let the boss down, but he wouldn't miss him again. You could count on that. The man seemed to know it too, for he'd gone pale and squeamish like at heart he was still that boy wearing mary-jane dresses. Poor man, poor man.

"Now, Mary Jane," Aunt Lou said. "I understand you had some capital you were prepared to invest. That what you're here to discuss?"

Mary Jane told her it was.

She nodded toward Depot as she said, "This man here says that capital don't belong to you."

"I earned it, and I have it, so I'd say it does."

"And I'd agree with you, as possession is ninety percent of the law. If you'd kindly lay it on the table, this whole matter'll be straightened out right now."

In the darkened hallway, another man beaded a rifle straight at Depot. Tull was right about Aunt Lou. She was a loose cannon.

Mary Jane said, "The money's hid. I came here to discuss the business before bringing anything with me."

"Well, that changes things, doesn't it?" Aunt Lou gripped the back of the chair beside Depot. "This man says Tull has your money, and that it's his now, and he's got a new business proposition for me."

She waited for Mary Jane to speak, but at first he had nothing to say. Depot knew exactly what the man was thinking: They couldn't have the money. How could they have found the money? What he wasn't letting himself acknowledge, Depot saw, was that Tull knew everything. He knew when someone was trying to cheat him, and he knew when a barkeep flubbed a cleanup job. He could find some money, don't you worry about that.

Still, Mary Jane was a stubborn one. He said, "I kindly doubt they've found money, and if they have, you're doing business with some damned depraved individuals."

"Tsk, tsk, tsk. That's not a polite way to do business," she said. She looked at Depot, who upturned his hands.

"All I know is what Larthan told me," he said. "He says we've got the money, and you can count on that."

"All I needed to know," Aunt Lou said.

"I can't believe this," Mary Jane said, his head flicking back and forth between the two. "You're going to accept blood money. You call that good business?"

It was shameful, Depot thought, a man going out begging this way. Cringing before the firing squad.

"I haven't said anything about blood money," she said. "All I'm doing is pointing out that Mr. Murphy has made an offer on behalf of Mr. Tull. Maybe it doesn't matter whose money is where. Since I've had good and longstanding relations with Mr. Tull, I'm inclined to accept his bid over yours."

"Now wait a second."

"Especially since I know Tull has the money he's offering, and you haven't brought anything that I can see other than a promise."

She turned and nodded at her man in the hall, headed out of the dining room.

"Hold on—"

But Mary Jane never finished. Depot raised the .38, leveled the sights, and shot him in the chest. A clean shot through Mary Jane's heart, and black blood seeped onto Aunt Lou's floor. She hadn't paused when the shot had gone off, and she now stood in the kitchen doorway, lit a cigarette, and waited. Men from the hall were already dragging the body away. Depot tucked the pistol in the back of his pants.

She said, "Did Mr. Tull really have his money, or is it still hid away somewhere like he said?"

"He had it hid away, but Larthan said he found it."

"He say where?"

"No, and I don't think we want to know."

She nodded. "Your boss sure does have a way with folks."

"I wouldn't want to wind up on his bad side," Depot said, thinking about his meeting with Tull earlier tonight. When Tull had pulled out the .38, Depot had felt sure he was about to be shot. He went on: "Tull's a cold man, but lots of men are. There's something else about him I've never been able to put my finger on."

"Didn't you know, Mr. Murphy? He's the Devil, and he's going to take us all back to Hell with him when his work here is done."

He stared at her, and she grinned and began to laugh. She laughed so hard she choked, and then she quit laughing and put the cigarette back in her mouth. He left her there and drove the two hours south to Castle, haunted by her words and contemplating that she herself might be the Devil. Heat lightning flared through the cloudbanks and lit up the sky like the northern lights. He passed through the piedmont, where the corn was at its tallest, waves of it like a sea of dark by the side of the road, the rural pavement gray and gravelly, the night some vortex in which he saw strange reckonings. Wind and shadows and leaves upturned. Insects smacked into the windshield.

By the river, Tull eyed the Hopewell brothers and tried to figure out his next move. He and Evelyn couldn't just leave now. These boys were involved. But if he killed them, he wouldn't be able to take her with him. Too many dead, and on the run she would be a liability. Even without them dead she might be trouble. Shouldn't have tied her to the bedpost. That left her and Quinn Hopewell against him, when what he'd intended was to separate her from Quinn and garner some space. Now that all of them were out here together, he couldn't very well shoot the boys in front of her, and he couldn't shoot her too. That would go too far, even in the manic state in which he now found himself. But what would be better, her dead or her abandoned to the Hopewells? If he simply left now? If he turned and walked away, free again in a way he hadn't been since he was young and shacking up with Esmerelda in a whorehouse? Twenty years and he hadn't gotten anywhere. Richer, yes, and his bloodline passed along, yes, out of his control now, but his soul was in the same place. Stagnant. Or maybe he'd made a wide loop—childish dependence to adolescent rebellion to freedom as a young man, and now back again, with a dependent child in his middle years, rebellion as his daughter grew, freedom as an old man. Time one wide loop of turn and return, only this return like a half-life, his body and soul bruised from the pressure of all the years.

And where was his family? Gone, long since he'd left them, just as now he was about to leave his daughter. His parents long dead, his brother old if still alive, some other Tull lineage. Larthan's soul was an orphan, abandoned to an indifferent universe by an uncaring God, the mystery of life in the grave, his father dead in a field, his mother dead from fever. And maybe once the loop reached an end, and Tull himself became one again with the earth, all the mystery would be revealed. Until then, he had to keep moving forward like an engine along its track, the last switch long past, the next somewhere in the hazy curves ahead.

He stopped in a clearing, where the moon and the starlight shone against their ashen faces. He said, "All right, everybody. Let's stop here."

The brothers halted. Evelyn clung to the elder, and her eyes cut into Tull from the darkness. Late, almost morning, but still no sign of dawn in the east. Soon Depot was supposed to meet him at the train station and get his payoff before going home. He didn't know Tull was planning to catch a train, but then, Tull hadn't known it either at the time. Depot's business in Charlotte should be over now, and with any luck he'd be across town right now, taking care of Mary Jane.

"I'm not going to kill you boys, but if you'll kindly set down, I'll cuff you for the night. Evelyn and I are getting on a train in a few hours and we'll be off. I'll make sure someone comes along to get you in the morning. Shouldn't be but a few hours."

"I'm not going," Evelyn said.

"What?" he said. "Yes, we're going."

Wind rattled the trees around them and sucked the air toward an unseen thunderhead that marred the stars. She said, "You can go, but handcuff me here, too."

He'd half expected her to resist, so he reached over and took her by the arm, yanked her to him. What he didn't expect was for the younger Hopewell to have a knife, and for the knife to be jammed into his side like a snakebite. He didn't feel much at first, just the pressure against his rib, and then the knife glanced beyond the bone and into the heart of him. The damage registered before he felt any pain, the knife two inches deep into his right side, Willie Hopewell backing away with spooked wide eyes and Evelyn pulling away as well and then the pain struck.

Tull jerked and reached for his daughter, caught hold of her dress and yanked her to her knees. Quinn leaped in and wrenched her from his grasp, and Tull stumbled, felt the handle of the knife. The pressure sent an electric current along his nerves so that everything hurt and the tips of his fingers throbbed until his hands were numb. He howled and sank to his knees, reached for his gun in the dark grass, the boys wrestling with him and Evelyn somewhere in the melee. He opened fire with the rifle—pow!—and his ears rang after the shot. Nothing stirred in the woods around him. Then he was running. He tumbled through the forest, the knife still in his side, and with each step he felt as though he were being sawed in half. Each step cut away at more flesh. He grew woozy. He fell in the darkest grove between the river and town, reached around and pulled the shank from his side. Blood puddled onto his shirt, a sopping mess, and he took off his undershirt, folded it, pressed it against his side. He paused a moment, nearly lost consciousness, but something stirred and drove him onward. He woke and took his belt and wrapped it around his torso, pulled it tight with the shirt against the wound, fastened it. He put his jacket back on as he continued through the underbrush. Finally a quiver of dawn on the horizon, another day to contend with. He moved on.

Willie lay in a heap of pinestraw and groundcover, ferns and ivy and baby oaks around him. He'd been shot in the leg and had lost consciousness when it was still dark outside. Now the sun flamed across the sky and lemon light glared at him through the forest, created a patchwork of tawny shadows around him, ochre and olive green. Quinn lay beside him, knocked unconscious by the butt of Tull's gun, but no bullet had entered his body, no tears in his flesh. Just a swollen knob on his temple, already strawberry colored and growing darker, which would cause the vision of his left eye to blur on occasion for the remainder of his days.

Neither Evelyn nor her father was anywhere in sight. Willie rose and looked at his leg. The bullet had grazed his calf and the blood had already clotted and crusted over the wound. Leaves stuck to his legs as he stood and limped to a small rise by the riverbank to scan the forest and the water. He saw her there, prone on her back in a pool by the river's edge, half submerged in the water. A bullet had gone straight through her heart. Her white dress clung to her skin and was translucent in the water and stained red on her chest. Above the wound, though, her skin was pale and had a bluish sheen that made her look so peaceful, so calm. Her hair a tangled mess in the water, the skin on her throat white and smooth and soft. There was something profound and mysterious about her body there, bobbing as the dark water seemed to carry off her soul like some provision of grace left to the world.

Willie scrambled away from the river and into the forest. When he ran out of energy he stopped and shouldered against a birch tree and threw up on a spot of mossy earth. Later, when the sheriff found him there, he would ask the old man if there was any way to escape this feeling. Chambers would tell him, "If there was, I wish I knew it. You just do what you can to endure it." For now, though, Willie breathed in the scent of fecund soil, gasped for breath, and began to weep. He would be thirteen in less than a month.

A pounding woke him up, and Chambers saw that he slept in his car in front of the station. Pink light clouded through the windows, and glue stuck to his eyes and blurred his vision. Once again, someone beat against the window. He opened the door and saw Jeffreys and O'Connor standing there.

"Mary Jane Hopewell was shot in Charlotte," O'Connor said.

"His body was found near a dumpster by a paperboy," Jeffreys said. "Rolled up in a sheet and left sitting up against a wall."

Neither agent seemed particularly interested in why Chambers had been asleep in his car, nor did they seem surprised. He stretched his back out and looked up the street. Dawn light bled over the south end of Main, a purple stain like wine on white fabric. Chambers still had cracked glass in his mind from the night before. A hangover, his first in a while, and he knew from experience that it would only get worse in the next few hours.

"We know Aunt Lou is involved, and we already have agents at her house now to question her. We think we might catch Tull and Depot Murphy at the train station directly."

"The train station."

"Tull purchased a ticket for St. Louis last night. Leaves at eight o'clock."

"Murphy made a midnight run to Charlotte last night," O'Connor added. "One of em's planning to get on a train."

Chambers sniffed, rubbed his eyes. "You fellas want a cup of coffee?"

"We've had some," O'Connor said.

"But if you're making a pot, we'll gladly take a cup," Jeffreys added.

"Come on in."

They went into the precinct, and he turned on the lights, put on coffee. Today was Saturday, so no one would be coming into the office unless he called them in. How bad things always seemed to happen when he had no backup, Chambers didn't know. The law of the land, he supposed. He went to the bathroom and splashed water on his face, stared at himself in the mirror. A scruffy gray beard coming in, loose flesh under his jaw, his neck thin. He didn't look old so much as frail. Where had the tough man from years ago gone? How did the transition happen so quickly?

He stepped into his office and called Alma.

"Where are you?" she asked.

"Down at the station. Some federal agents are here to arrest Larthan today."

"What happened to you last night?"

"I got called away. Everything's going down at once. How are you?"

She didn't answer him.

"I'm hoping this business today won't take too long, and that I should be done by noon. Once it's over, I can take a few days off."

"OK," she said, though he could tell she didn't believe him. He wondered why he'd even called her at all, because now that he had her on the line, only a weak dam held back a flood of everything they'd not said to each other in the past two weeks. Now was not the time for the dam to burst.

"I'll see you," he said, and hung up before she could answer. "Let's go fellas," he said to the agents. "I'll follow you."

He put his car in gear and spun the steering wheel with the palm of one hand, a thermos of coffee sloshing around between his legs.

The train station was a few blocks away. The tracks threaded through town from the west, and the depot was north of the town square, halfway between the Bell in the west and the Eureka village over to the east. They parked on a ridge beyond the station and Chambers got into the back of the Ford, where the three of them watched through a line of trees the action at the station. Not much at first, a quiet country stop, ordinary, uninteresting. It all seemed too easy to Chambers, that after weeks of drifting around, wondering about Mary Jane Hopewell and Larthan Tull, the liquor business and the federal agents and what folks in town thought of him, here it was, a quiet Saturday morning and everything was about to be resolved. Mary Jane was dead, and the federal agents were going to walk down and arrest Larthan, shut down the soda factory, so that by Monday morning it would all be over. They could get back to business as usual in town. He would have to go out and see Widow Coleman and then Evelyn Tull, tie up paperwork at the precinct, but then he was free to relax with Alma, try to straighten out what was left of their lives. He believed he'd somehow managed to make it through these last weeks unscathed. He waited.

As dawn exploded on the morning, the three of them watched Larthan Tull came up, looking like a wild man with his hair in knots and his eyes sunken in his face, like he hadn't slept since the beginning of Prohibition and had offered himself up for the long rest, had risen to the pearly gates only to be struck back to earth by the sword of Saint Peter. Perhaps God Himself had given the order: no more forgiveness for the likes of such men. Prepare for last days, end times.

Through binoculars Chambers saw Tull walked with a limp, and then he saw the bloodstains on the platform, each step a new smear. Tull was hurt, and hurt bad. He leaned against a pillar and drooped his head as if in supplication. The sun fired over the horizon, full circle now, risen from dawn to day. Dew clung to the grass and mist still hovered in the shade, but the day's heat would burn all that away soon.

The three men got out of the Ford and walked toward the station, but Tull didn't seem to notice their approach. Chambers checked his revolver, cleaned and oiled and unused. He thought of Jimmy Boy Coleman and the card game, how one bullet in the boy's leg had killed him, the only time Chambers had ever killed a man.

A passenger train rumbled toward the station from the south. On either side the engineers leaned from the cab and peered out at the rolling countryside. The whistle wailed as the train snaked along, slowed as it clattered closer to the station.

Just then a gray coupe pulled up. Depot Murphy got out, his hair slicked back like he was some buck, and Tull stood and waited for him.

The train ground to a halt with a low rumble and the chug of black soot and steam from its engine. The squeal of rails, steel against steel, a moan like some wounded animal.

The four closed in on Tull—the two agents and Chambers from the hillside, Depot from the car—and they crowded in on the whiskey baron at once. Their boots clopping against the wood planks of the platform, the lawmen walked with purpose.

Depot slowed, but before he could turn and run off, Jeffreys called out, "Whoa there." The barkeep watched them like a chess pawn stuck on the wrong square. No hand to guide him to safety now.

A look of panic flickered into Tull's eyes, but he blinked it away so fast it might never have been there. Even still, when Chambers saw the bloodsoaked side of Tull's shirt and jacket, the drain of it along his leg, he stopped. This man was beyond the edge, his skin pale and damp with sweat. He would be lucky to live past noon. No need for some dramatic confrontation.

But the agents never slowed with their approach, as if to say let's get this over with. Jeffreys pulled Depot aside to cuff him, and O'Connor moved in on Tull, who for his part seemed not to care that whatever plan he'd made had been disrupted, that somewhere he'd crossed a bridge with no return ticket.

When O'Connor reached for his arm, Tull snatched himself away and pulled a revolver from his coat and shot O'Connor in the head.

Blood and brain matter sprayed onto the platform, and everyone else stared in shock as O'Connor's lifeless body dropped to its knees and fell onto its back.

As Chambers reached for his own gun, Tull turned to Jeffreys and Depot and shot each in rapid succession, two guncracks with only enough time for Tull's arm to realign itself after the pulse of the previous.

He whipped around and turned the gun on Chambers, but the sheriff opened fire first, and with four bullets he laid Larthan Benjamin Tull out dead on the platform.

When it was over, the gun he held was hot in his hand. Smoke curled from the barrel like a smoldering cigar. Four men lay dead on the platform. The engineers and passengers on the train all gaped out the windows at the massacre. If anyone spoke or screamed, Chambers couldn't hear them over the ring of his ears.

He leaned against the same pillar Tull had rested against moments ago. One man for another, two images that side by side were a perfect replica for future Americana: the first a lone bootlegger, hurt and waiting for a train, the second a sheriff holding his revolver, four dead bodies at his feet and a trainload of passengers staring in shock. Chambers had killed another man, and there was no one left but him to clean up the mess. He breathed in the crisp morning air and waited, as if someone would come along and tell him what to do next.

Later he would receive the news of Evelyn's death at the river. He would ride in the ambulance with Walt Pearson to recover her body and begin a reconstruction of the night's events. There he would find the Hopewell brothers, Quinn on his haunches with his head in his arms and Willie propped against a tree a ways off, both of them irreparably wounded, Quinn with the loss of the only woman he would ever open his heart to, Willie with something much harder to define, some abstract understanding that the world was not on your side.

Later still Chambers would get word of a botched raid against Aunt Lou, how revenuers stormed her house to find a petite old woman sipping tea, no sign of legal wrongdoing. She was out one supplier, and other revenuers would double down to snare her in the web of justice, a word that no longer held any meaning for Sheriff

Chambers. He was nearing the end of his allotted three score and ten, and he was tired.

For now, as he leaned against the pillar at the train depot, his next job was to calm the gathering crowd, round up some deputies, and begin the long process of moving on. He called down to Columbia to report the deaths of agents Jeffreys and O'Connor, left a message with a receptionist for someone there to call his office, where he would not be. He was in no mood to shuffle around like his role still mattered, so, when the passengers had been escorted away from the station and younger men had arrived to record the scene and clear the bodies, Chambers took the long walk home.

Along the road into the town of Castle, the grasses swayed in the wind. Sweat dampened his shirt, and when he reached up to wipe his brow, his arm twinged, that old familiar ache he'd been lugging around for half a century. He was a relic, here in the twentieth century, a busted-up old man who would be buried soon enough. Just a name on a stone, some etching for future generations to discover, to ponder over, to write about. New nations and new lives, a steady march forward until the end of all time.

Alma was waiting for him on the porch, shelling peanuts, a glass of tea on the railing. She quit at his approach, said, "I wondered if you were ever coming home." Then her expression changed and she stood up, wiped the dustings from the peanut shells from her hands, and asked, "What happened?"

He shook his head. "It doesn't matter."

He took her hand and guided her into the house, to the bedroom, where they lay down in a splash of sunlight. Rather than ask for details, she squeezed his hand and lay quietly beside him, which was all he needed. After a time he dozed, and he dreamt of strange horses in a field, their coats shimmering in a golden light.

Acknowledgments

Thank you: Chris Arnold, Brian Beglin, Megan DeMoss, Benjamin Kolp, Bret Lott, Mark Powell, Brian and June Sealy, Emily Sealy, Emily Smith, Betsy Teter, and the wonderful people at Hub City.

For readers interested in the history of the South Carolina textile industry, the University of North Carolina Press's *Like a Family: The Making of a Southern Cotton Mill World* and Hub City Press's *Textile Town* are excellent resources.

An excerpt of *The Whiskey Baron* originally appeared, in somewhat different form, in *The Sun*.